HARPER'S JUSTICE PREQUEL

BLOOD JUSTICE

R.J. SLOANE

desert life
media

Blood Justice: Harper's Justice Prequel
By R.J. Sloane

Publisher:
Desert Life Media, LLC
Gilbert, AZ 85295

www.rjsloanewesterns.com

Printed in the United States of America

ISBN: 978-1-960217-56-1

When justice is executed,
it is a joy to the righteous
but a terror to evildoers.

— Proverbs 21:15 CSB

Prologue

———

Grady

THE MUSTANG FOUGHT like the devil himself.

I gripped the corral fence, watching Pa work the wild-eyed horse with gentle hands and quiet words. At fifteen, I was all elbows and knees, but I had my father's gift with animals. The morning air carried the rich scent of leather oil from Pa's work gloves, mixed with the dusty smell of hay and the sharp tang of horse sweat.

"See how he's favoring that left front hoof?" Pa said, never taking his eyes off the bucking bronco. "That's not defiance, son. That's pain talking."

Lee Thatcher had a way of reading horses that bordered on the mystical. He could spot lameness that other men missed, sense fear where others saw only stubbornness. The mustang snorted and shied, his hooves raising small clouds of red dust that caught the morning light. Pa held firm to the lead rope with hands that had gentled a thousand horses before this one, the rough hemp texture familiar as his own skin.

"Easy now," Pa murmured, voice soft as velvet. "Nobody's gonna hurt you, boy. We're just gonna help you remember what it feels like to trust."

I watched, fascinated, as the horse's ears swiveled forward despite its fear. The animal's nostrils flared wide, testing Pa's scent for any hint of danger. Pa had that calming effect on animals. And people, for that matter. There wasn't a neighbor within fifty miles who wouldn't drop everything to help Lee Thatcher, because they knew he'd do the same for them.

"Now watch his eyes," Pa continued, still working the rope with practiced ease. The leather creaked softly in his weathered hands. "See how they're starting to soften? That's when you know you're getting through."

The morning sun climbed higher, painting the corral fence with golden light. Dust motes danced in the air between us like tiny spirits, and somewhere in the pasture beyond, a meadowlark called its liquid song. The familiar sounds of our ranch filled the air—the distant lowing of cattle, the creak of the windmill turning in the gentle breeze, the soft whicker of horses in the far paddock. It was shaping up to be a perfect day. The kind that made a man grateful to be alive and working the land his father had claimed.

"Your turn," Pa said, offering me the lead rope. The hemp was still warm from his grip. "Remember what I taught you. Firm but gentle. Show him you're the leader, but not the enemy."

My hands trembled slightly as I took the rope, feeling the mustang's energy transmitted through the braided fibers like electricity. The horse's dark eyes fixed on me, measuring, calculating. For a moment, I felt the weight of his fear and my own inexperience. The rope felt foreign in my palms, too thick, too important.

"I don't know, Pa. What if I spook him?"

"Then you'll learn something valuable," Pa said with a smile that made the corners of his eyes crinkle like old leather. "Fear's a teacher, son, but it shouldn't be a master. Trust yourself."

I stepped forward, keeping my movements slow and

deliberate. The hard-packed earth felt solid beneath my boots, grounding me. The horse tensed, muscles coiling beneath his dusty coat like steel springs, but he didn't bolt. I could feel Pa watching, ready to step in if needed, but giving me the space to succeed or fail on my own.

"That's it," Pa whispered. "You're doing fine."

The rope felt alive in my hands, vibrating with the horse's tension and energy. Every twitch of his muscles traveled up through the hemp to my palms. I tried to channel Pa's calm confidence, to project the same steady presence that made animals trust him instinctively. The scent of sage and wild grass drifted on the breeze, mixing with the earthy smell of the corral and the sweet fragrance of Ma's morning glories blooming by the house.

"Grady! Lee!"

Ma's voice carried across the yard from the house, warm and musical as a church bell. Amy Thatcher stood on the porch, wiping her flour-dusted hands on her apron, her brown hair catching the morning light like spun copper. Even from a distance, I could see her smile. The one that had captured Pa's heart twenty years ago and never let it go.

"Come wash up!" she called. "Lunch is ready, and I won't have you eating my good stew with dirty hands!"

Pa chuckled, the sound rumbling deep in his chest like distant thunder. "Your mother's got more sense than both of us put together. Horse training can wait. A man should never keep a good woman and a hot meal waiting."

I handed him back the lead rope, reluctant to leave but knowing better than to argue with Ma when she had that tone in her voice. She'd birthed two children in a cabin, buried one in the winter of '85, and could outwork most men when it came to running a household. But she ruled with love instead of fear, and that made all the difference.

"We'll finish with him after we eat," Pa promised, securing the rope to the fence post with practiced efficiency.

"Maybe by then he'll have decided we're not so bad after all."

As we walked toward the house, our boots crunching on the hard-packed earth, Pa placed a hand on my shoulder. It was a simple gesture, but it carried the weight of approval and pride that made my chest swell. The familiar scent of leather and honest sweat clung to his work clothes, mixed with the faint aroma of the horse liniment he'd used that morning.

"You did good work today, son. That horse was watching you like he was seeing something he could respect."

"Really?"

"Really. Another few sessions and you'll have him eating out of your hand." Pa squeezed my shoulder. "Your grandfather would be proud. He always said the Thatchers had a way with horses."

The house smelled like heaven when we stepped inside. Beef stew simmering on the stove filled the air with rich, savory aromas—tender meat, carrots, potatoes, and Ma's secret blend of herbs. Fresh bread cooled on the sideboard, its golden crust still crackling softly from the heat. Coffee percolated in the blue enamel pot, the familiar burbling sound as comforting as Ma's lullabies. She had outdone herself, as usual.

"Wash," she commanded, pointing toward the basin she'd set out with clean towels. The soap smelled of lavender from her garden. "Both of you. I can smell horse and dust from here."

Pa winked at me as he rolled up his sleeves, the cotton fabric soft from countless washings. "Yes, ma'am. Wouldn't want to offend the cook."

"You'd better not be mocking me, Lee Thatcher," Ma said, but her eyes sparkled with mischief. "I've got a wooden spoon, and I'm not afraid to use it."

The wooden kitchen table was scarred from years of use, its surface worn smooth by countless meals and conversations. As we sat down to eat, I marveled at how perfect everything seemed. The food was delicious, the conversation easy, and the love between my parents was as solid and comfortable as the surrounding house. This was what a man worked for. Not just the land or the cattle, but the family that made it all worthwhile.

"Oh, I nearly forgot," Ma said, reaching into her apron pocket. "Got a letter from Ellie Mae yesterday. She's settling in well at the newspaper in Prescott. Says the work is challenging, but she loves writing about territorial history." Ma smiled as she unfolded the letter. "She's found herself a little boarding house room near the courthouse and made friends with some of the other working ladies in town."

Pa grinned. "Always knew that girl would make her mark on the world. Takes after her mother—stubborn as a mule when she sets her mind to something."

"She's hoping to visit for Christmas if the weather holds," Ma continued, tucking the letter back in her pocket. "Though she admits the newspaper work keeps her busier than she expected."

"Mrs. Henderson stopped by this morning," Ma said, passing Pa a second helping of stew. The ceramic bowl was warm against her hands. "She said she saw some strangers riding through yesterday. Four men, all armed, heading south toward the road."

Pa's fork paused halfway to his mouth. Something flickered across his face—a shadow that darkened his usually calm expression. Too quick for me to read completely, but Ma caught it like she always did.

"Probably just drifters looking for work," Pa said carefully, but his voice carried a note of forced casualness. "Lots of men on the move this time of year."

"Maybe." Ma didn't sound convinced. Her intuition was sharp as her kitchen knives. "But Mrs. Henderson said they looked... rough. The kind of men who don't ask permission for what they want. She mentioned seeing unusual brands on their horses—burn marks that looked fresh, like they'd been changed recently."

A chill ran down my spine despite the warm kitchen. There had been talk lately of rustlers operating in the territory, men who took what they wanted and left blood in their wake. Stories of altered brands, stolen cattle, and ranch families found dead in their burned-out homes. But surely they wouldn't bother with a small spread like ours.

"Don't worry yourself, Amy," Pa said, reaching across the table to squeeze her hand. His calloused fingers were gentle against her smooth skin. "We're too small for that kind of trouble. They want the big ranches, the ones with hundreds of head."

Ma nodded, but I could see the worry lingering in her eyes like storm clouds on the horizon. She had the intuition that came with frontier living, the ability to sense danger before it showed itself. The same instinct that made her scan the tree line every evening before calling us in for supper, or keep the shotgun loaded by the kitchen door.

That's when the earth started trembling.

Hoofbeats. Thunder rolling across the valley floor like the drums of war, growing louder with each heartbeat. The coffee cup rattled against its saucer on the table.

Pa went rigid, his hand moving instinctively toward the gun belt hanging on the kitchen chair. The leather holster was worn smooth from years of use, the grip of his Colt polished by his palm. Ma's face went white as fresh snow, her worst fears materializing in the sound of approaching riders.

My blood turned to slush. Something about those riders, the way they moved, deliberate as wolves stalking prey, made every nerve in my body scream *run*. The rhythmic pounding grew closer, accompanied by the jingle of spurs and the creak of leather saddles.

"Grady." Pa's voice cut through the thunder of hooves like a blade, sharp with urgency. "Barn. Now. Hide in the loft and don't come out, no matter what you hear."

"Pa, I can help—"

"Now, boy!" The steel in his voice brooked no argument. His hand was already on his gun, thumb testing the action of the hammer.

I stumbled from my chair, my legs suddenly unsteady. Through the kitchen window, I could see dust rising in the distance like smoke from a grass fire. Four riders, just as Mrs. Henderson had said. Moving fast and hard toward our little piece of paradise, their horses' hooves striking the ground like hammers on an anvil.

"Amy, get inside and stay down," Pa commanded, strapping on his gun belt with practiced efficiency. The leather felt familiar against his hip, a weight he'd carried for protection more than violence. "Keep away from the windows."

But Ma was already moving toward the door, her jaw set with the stubborn courage that had seen her through twenty years of frontier life. "This is my home too, Lee Thatcher. I won't hide while strangers threaten what we've built."

Four riders exploded over the ridge in a storm of dust and death, fanning out like wolves cutting off escape routes. They moved with the precision of men who'd done this before, who knew exactly how to corner their prey. Their horses were lathered with sweat, foam flecking their muzzles from hard riding. The acrid smell of fear-sweat and dust filled the air.

The leader rode a black stallion that seemed to have emerged from a nightmare itself. Death's own mount, his massive frame wrapped in midnight from hat to boots. Behind him came two younger killers with wolf-lean faces that shared the same cruel jaw, their eyes cold as winter ice. And an older man whose silver hair gleamed above ivory-handled Colts that caught the sunlight like promises of violence. Even from a distance, I could see the distinctive engravings on those gun grips—serpents wrapped around skulls.

These weren't drifters looking for work.

These were executioners.

I ran for the barn, my heart hammering against my ribs like a caged bird. The familiar smells of hay and leather couldn't comfort me now. Sweet alfalfa, saddle oil, and the warm scent of horses felt foreign, tainted by the approaching violence. I scrambled up the wooden ladder to the loft, my boots slipping on the smooth rungs. Splinters caught at my palms as I pressed myself against a stack of feed sacks where I could see through the gaps in the barn siding.

The riders reined up twenty yards from the house. Close enough for killing. Far enough to run if things went sideways. Dust swirled around their horses' hooves in choking clouds, and I could smell the acrid scent of fear—mine, and maybe theirs too. Their horses danced nervously, sensing the tension that crackled in the air like lightning before a storm.

Pa stepped out onto the porch, his hand resting on his gun butt. Thirty feet of open ground separated him from the riders, but it might as well have been thirty miles. There was no cover, no advantage except the moral authority of a man defending his home. The porch boards creaked under his weight, a sound I'd heard a thousand times before but which now seemed ominous as a death knell.

"Afternoon," the man in black said, his voice smooth as snake oil but carrying an undertone of violence that made my skin crawl. No name. No courtesy. Just death on horseback making conversation. His black hat was pulled low, shadowing eyes that seemed to absorb light without reflecting any back.

"State your business," Pa replied, his voice steady as bedrock despite the odds stacked against him. I could see the slight shift in his stance, weight balanced on the balls of his feet, ready to move.

"Heard you got fine cattle, Thatcher."

My stomach dropped like a stone in a well. They knew Pa's name. This wasn't random. They'd planned this, scouted us, chosen us for reasons I couldn't fathom. The way the man said our name, casual as discussing the weather, made it clear we'd been marked for death long before they rode into our yard.

"They're not for sale," Pa said, and I heard the first note of real tension creep into his voice. His thumb hooked near his gun belt, a gesture so subtle I almost missed it.

The man in black smiled. A razor slash across granite that promised terrible things. "Who said anything about buying?"

The words fell like stones into a still pond, sending ripples of dread through my entire body. This was it. This was how people died out here. Alone under the Arizona sky, forgotten before their blood dried in the dust. The casual cruelty in his voice was worse than shouting, worse than threats. It was the sound of a man who killed for pleasure.

Ma appeared in the doorway behind Pa, her chin raised in defiance despite the terror I could see in her white-knuckled grip on the door frame. She'd heard enough to understand what was happening, but she wouldn't abandon her husband to face it alone. The flour on her apron seemed stark as snow against the dark wood of the doorway.

"You got ten seconds to ride on," Pa said, his thumb finding the hammer of his Colt. The metal clicked softly as he eased it back, the sound carrying clearly in the sudden stillness. "After that, we got problems."

"Already got problems," the killer replied. His hand moved toward his gun with the slow deliberation of a man who knew he held all the cards.

Time slowed to a crawl. I saw the man in black's hand move like it was underwater. Saw death itself reaching for iron with practiced ease. Saw Pa's fingers close around his gun grip, the muscles in his forearm tensing as he started his draw. The leather of his holster whispered against the metal barrel.

Too slow.

"No!" The scream ripped from my throat before I could stop it, echoing across the yard like the cry of a dying animal.

Thunder cracked across the yard like the world splitting apart. Pa's chest exploded in a fountain of crimson, the impact lifting him off his feet and slamming him backward against the porch rail. The sharp crack of breaking wood mixed with the echo of the gunshot. His unfired gun spun away into the dust, useless as his shattered dreams, the metal catching the sunlight as it tumbled.

"Lee!" Ma's shriek could have raised the dead from their graves, raw with anguish that seemed to tear the very air.

She ran toward him, her skirts billowing around her legs, but the man in black was already moving. Uncoiling from his saddle like some massive serpent, spurs ringing against the porch steps. He caught her arm in one meaty fist, spinning her around to face him with the casual cruelty of a man who'd done this before. His fingers left dark bruises on her pale skin.

"Shoulda minded your business, woman."

He pressed the barrel of his smoking Colt against her temple, the metal still hot from killing my father. I could see the burn mark it left on her skin, a small circle of seared flesh that would never heal. The smell of burned gunpowder drifted across the yard, acrid and final.

"Please," Ma whispered, and I heard a lifetime of love and sacrifice compressed into that single word. Her voice shook, but her eyes held a dignity that even death couldn't steal. "I have children."

"Had children."

The second shot was different. Closer, more intimate, final as a coffin lid slamming shut. Ma folded like a broken doll, her blood mixing with Pa's in the dust where she'd planted morning glories just that spring. Their life together ended in gunpowder and screams and the laughter of devils. The white flowers she'd tended so carefully were already being stained with crimson.

I bit through my tongue to keep from crying out, tasting copper while my parents' blood soaked the ground below. My vision blurred, my breath came in ragged gasps, but I held myself motionless through sheer terror. If they found me, I was dead. If I moved, I was dead. If I breathed too loud, I was dead. The taste of my own blood filled my mouth as I struggled not to sob.

"Search the house," the killer ordered, like he was discussing the weather, already holstering his gun with practiced ease. "Take what we need. Burn the rest."

The others dismounted, spurs ringing against the porch steps like funeral bells. Their boots left muddy prints on the clean boards Ma had scrubbed just that morning. Glass exploded as they kicked in windows, the sound sharp as breaking bones. Wood splintered as they tore apart furniture my parents had saved months to buy. They laughed as they destroyed fifteen years of dreams, taking pleasure in the casual desecration of a life built on love and hard work.

The crash of Ma's good china echoed from the kitchen. The thud of axes biting into Pa's handmade table. The rip of fabric as they shredded the quilt Ma had stitched by lamplight through three winters. Each sound was another wound in my heart, another piece of my life reduced to rubble.

I squeezed my eyes shut, but I couldn't block out the sounds. Couldn't stop seeing Ma's face in that last second. Not afraid, just heartbroken for the boy hiding in the barn who'd have to carry this weight forever. The smell of her lavender soap still clung to the air, mixing with the gunpowder and blood in a combination that would haunt my nightmares.

The acrid smell of smoke began to fill the air. They were burning everything, just like the man in black had promised. Our home, our memories, our future. All of it going up in flames while I cowered like a rabbit in a hole. Orange light flickered through the gaps in the barn siding as fire consumed the kitchen where Ma had made countless meals with love.

When the destruction finally ended and the riders mounted up to leave, one of the younger killers called out, "What about the boy? Mrs. Henderson said she saw a kid."

My heart stopped beating. The words hung in the air like a death sentence, and I could feel my blood turning to ice water in my veins.

"If there was a boy, the fire'll take care of him," the man in black replied, his voice carrying easily across the yard. "Let's ride. We got what we came for."

I listened to their hoofbeats fade into the distance, but I didn't move for what felt like hours. Couldn't move. The paralysis that had kept me frozen during the murders now held me captive in my grief and terror. My muscles had locked up, leaving me shaking like a leaf in a windstorm.

When I finally climbed down from the loft, the house was a smoking ruin and my parents lay still in the yard. The sun was setting, painting the sky red as the blood that stained the earth beneath them. Smoke drifted across the scene like funeral shrouds, and the smell of burned dreams filled my nostrils.

I crawled to them on hands and knees, afraid my legs wouldn't support me. They lay tangled together in death, Pa's arm thrown protectively over Ma even at the end. Their faces were peaceful now, the terror and pain replaced by the stillness that comes when all struggles cease. Blood had pooled beneath them, already attracting flies that buzzed with obscene life.

"I'm sorry," I whispered through tears that burned like acid. "I'm sorry I didn't help. I'm sorry I was a coward."

But the dead don't forgive. They just stare at heaven with empty eyes while the living drown in guilt and rage and the terrible weight of what might have been. The evening breeze stirred Ma's hair, and for a moment I thought she might wake up, might smile and tell me it was all a nightmare.

Mrs. Henderson found me there three hours later, still kneeling between their bodies. She wrapped me in a quilt and took me to her house, where she cleaned the blood from my hands and tried to make me eat soup I couldn't taste. Her own hands shook as she held the spoon, and I could see the horror in her eyes as she looked at me—a boy transformed into something else by violence.

The next morning, Sheriff Rawlings rode out from town. He was a decent man, but overworked and under-equipped for the kind of violence that had visited our farm. The badge on his vest was tarnished, and his gun belt showed the wear of a man who'd rather use words than bullets.

"I need you to look at them, son," he whispered, his weathered face creased with sympathy. "For the official record. Can you tell me these are your parents?"

I stood between two pine boxes in the back room of the funeral parlor, staring down at faces that looked like wax figures of the people who'd raised me. Ma's hair was combed neat, Pa's hands folded peacefully across his chest. They looked smaller somehow, diminished by death in a way that made my chest ache with emptiness.

"Yes sir," I said, my voice cracking like a boy's instead of the man I'd become in the space of a single afternoon. "That's Lee and Amy Thatcher. That's my parents."

Sheriff Rawlings made notes in a leather-bound book, his pencil scratching across the paper with official finality. The sound seemed too ordinary for what it represented—the end of two lives, the destruction of everything I'd known.

"Can you describe the men who did this?"

I closed my eyes and saw them again. Four riders bringing death to our peaceful valley. "The leader wore all black. Big man, maybe six and a half feet tall. Rode a black horse with white stockings on the front legs. Had dead eyes and yellow teeth, with a gold tooth in front."

"What about the others?"

"Two younger men who looked like brothers. Same jaw, same cold eyes. And an old man with silver hair and ivory-handled guns. The grips had serpents carved around skulls."

"You get a good look at their faces?"

"Yes sir. I'll remember them till the day I die."

And I would. Every line, every scar, every detail was burned into my memory like a brand on a steer's hide. The man in black's cruel smile. The casual way he'd pressed his gun to Ma's head. The laughter as they destroyed everything good in my world. Even the way their horses moved, the distinctive gait of the black stallion, the nervous head-tossing of the roan.

Three days later, I stood at their graves while the preacher spoke pretty words about the Almighty's plan and eternal rest. The neighbors had come to pay their respects. Good people who brought food and offers of help that couldn't fill the hole in my chest. Mrs. Henderson stood beside me, her hand on my shoulder, but even her kindness felt distant through the fog of grief.

When the last mourner left and the gravediggers finished their work, I kneeled between the fresh mounds of earth and pressed my palms to the soil that covered my parents' bodies. The dirt was still soft, still carrying the scent of deeper earth and endings.

"I swear on your graves," I said, my voice steady as iron despite the tears on my cheeks. "I'll find them. Every last one. And I'll send them to perdition where they belong."

The wind scattered my words like smoke, but the

promise burned in my chest. A coal that would never go cold, never be extinguished until the debt was paid in full. Somewhere in the territory, those four killers were laughing over their easy victory, spending whatever they'd gained from murdering my parents. But their laughter wouldn't last.

The man in black. That face was branded on my soul, along with his voice, his laugh, his casual cruelty. I didn't know his name yet, but I'd find it. I'd find him. And when I did, there would be a reckoning six years in the making.

I walked down from that hill a different boy than the one who'd climbed it. The laughter was gone from my eyes, replaced by something harder. Something that would burn cold and steady until the day I looked into those dead eyes again and made him pay for what he'd stolen from me.

Justice was coming for the man in black.

He just didn't know it yet.

1 - Burned Brands

Grady

THE MAN IN black always came at dawn.

I jerked awake, sweat soaking through my nightshirt despite the cool April morning. The dream was always the same. Ma's voice calling my name. Pa's blood spreading across the dirt. And those dead eyes staring down at me from beneath a black hat, yellow teeth gleaming in a killer's smile.

"You can run, boy," the voice whispered in my memory. "But I'll find you when I'm ready."

Six years. Six years since that nightmare became real, and still the man in black haunted my sleep. I sat up in bed, running shaky hands through my sandy hair. Sunlight streamed through the window of the small house I shared with Deacon Colter at the edge of Colter Ranch. The sounds of morning drifted in—cattle lowing in the distance, roosters crowing, hoofbeats fading into the distance as the day ranch hands rode out to work the herd.

Normal sounds. Safe sounds. But they couldn't chase away the echo of gunshots or the smell of smoke that seemed to cling to my nostrils every time I closed my eyes.

A knock on my door interrupted the dark thoughts.

"Grady? You up?" Deacon's voice carried concern. He'd probably heard me thrashing around again.

"Yeah, I'm up." I swung my legs over the side of the bed, bare feet hitting the cold wooden floor. "Give me five minutes."

"Coffee's ready when you are."

That was Deacon. Always thinking ahead, always taking care of things. If I was the restless energy in our friendship, he was the steady hand that kept everything from flying apart.

By the time I made it to the kitchen, he'd already set out two steaming cups and a plate of biscuits left over from last night's supper. The rich aroma of coffee mixed with the lingering scent of butter and honey from the biscuits. Deacon sat at the small table, brown hair still tousled from sleep, reading yesterday's newspaper by the morning light.

"Bad one?" he asked without looking up.

"Same as always." I poured myself coffee, the bitter brew helping to wash away the taste of fear. The ceramic cup was warm against my palms, grounding me in the present. "The man in black. Ma and Pa. You know."

Deacon folded the paper and studied my face with those thoughtful brown eyes. "Maybe it's time to talk to someone about it. Pastor Williams, or—"

"Talking won't bring them back." I took a long sip of coffee, feeling the heat burn down my throat. "Won't put that killer in the ground where he belongs."

"Justice isn't always about putting men in the ground, Grady."

"Sometimes it is."

We'd had this conversation before. Deacon believed in law and order, in doing things the right way. I believed in results. It's what made us good partners and kept us from being great friends. That thin line between justice and vengeance that I walked every day.

"We better get moving," I said, changing the subject

before Deacon could start one of his lectures about talking to Pastor Williams. "Derek's expecting us at the stockyards by eight."

"You know, avoiding the subject doesn't make it go away," Deacon said as he cleared our breakfast dishes with his usual precision—plates stacked just so, cups nested perfectly.

"Neither does talking it to death." But there was no real heat in my words. This was our morning ritual: Deacon worried, I deflected. We both pretended it wasn't the same conversation we'd been having for six years.

An hour later, we were riding toward Prescott in the cool morning air. Sunbeam picked his way carefully down the rocky trail, his golden coat gleaming in the slanted sunlight. The familiar creak of saddle leather and the rhythmic clip-clop of hooves on stone provided a steady rhythm to our journey. Beside me, Deacon rode Sergeant with the easy grace of a man born to the saddle, the blood bay's coat dark with the sheen of good health.

"You hear anything more about those cattle that came in yesterday?" I asked as we crested the hill overlooking town.

"Just that they're sick as dogs, and Derek's worried about contamination." Deacon adjusted his hat against the glare. The brown felt worn soft from years of use. "Ray Sawyer's supposed to meet us there. Says he's got something important to discuss."

"Probably wants to lecture us about proper veterinary procedure again," I said with a grin.

"Hey, his procedures kept us both employed for three years." Deacon's tone was mock-defensive. "And they'll keep us alive if we ever have to treat something that bites back."

It was an old joke between us—Deacon's need for careful methodology versus my tendency to jump in first and ask questions later. Usually it worked in our favor, balancing caution with action.

Ray had been our mentor when we both worked as veterinarians. First together under his guidance, then separately when Deacon took a job at the stockyards and I stayed with the clinic. He was a good man, fair and honest, but he didn't talk unless he had something worth saying.

"Think it's about the promotion he mentioned last month?" I asked.

"Could be. Territory's been looking for qualified Livestock Inspectors. Men who know cattle and can spot trouble."

The idea sent a thrill through me that I tried to keep off my face. Livestock Inspectors had authority across the territory. They could track rustlers, investigate theft, follow leads wherever they went. If there was a man in black out there killing farmers and stealing cattle, a Livestock Inspector would be the one to find him.

"Might be interesting work," I said carefully.

Deacon shot me a sideways look that said he'd caught the excitement I'd tried to hide. "Might be dangerous work. Rustlers don't take kindly to being hunted."

"Some things are worth the risk."

"And some risks aren't worth the consequences." His voice carried a note of warning that I recognized. Deacon had a way of seeing around corners that I didn't, anticipating problems before they became disasters. "Just remember, not everything that needs fixing can be fixed with a fast draw and good intentions."

The rebuke stung because it was fair. I had a tendency to act first and think later, especially when something stirred up memories of that night six years ago.

We rode in companionable silence after that, each lost in our own thoughts. The town of Prescott spread out below us—a growing community of ranchers, miners, and merchants trying to carve a civilization out of the Arizona Territory. The stockyards sat on the eastern edge, a maze of corrals and loading chutes that handled cattle from across two counties.

The smell hit us before we saw the problem. Sweet rot and sickness, the kind of stench that made horses shy and men breathe through their mouths. The acrid odor of diseased animals mixed with the normal scents of cattle and manure, creating something that made my stomach churn. Sunbeam snorted and tossed his head as we approached the isolated corral where thirty head of cattle stood clustered in misery.

"What a mess" Deacon muttered, pulling on his leather gloves. The supple cowhide was stained from years of veterinary work. "What happened to these animals?"

The cattle looked like walking skeletons. Ribs showing through dull coats, heads hanging low, white sores visible around their mouths and hooves. The smell of infection hung heavy in the air, mixed with the sharp scent of animal distress. Polled Shorthorns, good stock when healthy, but these looked ready for the boneyard.

Derek Gardner, the stockyard manager, met us at the gate, his weathered face creased with worry. Dust coated his work clothes, and the lines around his eyes spoke of sleepless nights. "Glad you're here. This is the worst I've seen since that outbreak five years back."

"Foot-and-mouth?" I asked, though I already knew the answer from the distinctive lesions.

"That's what Ray thinks. He's been here since dawn, taking samples and checking the paperwork." Derek pointed toward the barn where we could see Ray Sawyer's familiar figure bent over a table covered with documents.

We made our way through the maze of corrals, our boots crunching on the mixture of dried manure and scattered straw. The sick cattle barely glanced at us. Never a good sign. Healthy stock would've scattered or at least shown some curiosity about strangers. These animals just stood with their heads down, occasionally letting out pitiful lowing sounds that spoke of misery beyond words.

"Morning, boys," Ray called as we approached. His gray hair was disheveled, sleeves rolled up despite the morning chill. The familiar scent of carbolic acid clung to his clothes from the disinfectant he used. "Glad you could make it. We've got ourselves a real puzzle here."

"Foot-and-mouth?" Deacon asked, his medical instincts kicking in.

"Among other things." Ray gestured to the papers spread across an improvised desk made from two sawhorses and a plank. The documents rustled slightly in the morning breeze. "Take a look at this paperwork and tell me what you see."

I studied the documents while Deacon examined the nearest animals. Bills of sale, shipping manifests, health certificates. Everything looked official at first glance. Clean handwriting, proper stamps, all the signatures in the right places. The paper felt expensive beneath my fingers, the kind used for legitimate business transactions.

But something nagged at me. Call it instinct honed by six years of looking for patterns, but the details didn't add up.

"These papers say the cattle came from B. Irving up near Ash Fork," I said. "But I've never heard that name before."

"Neither have I," Ray said. "And I know most of the ranchers in the northern part of the territory."

"What about the brands?" Deacon asked, straightening from his examination of a sick steer. His hands were already stained with the reddish dust that clung to everything in the stockyards.

That's when I saw it. Walking along the fence line, I stopped beside a red Polled Shorthorn heifer and pointed to the mark on her left hip.

"Deacon, come look at this."

He joined me, studying the brand with the careful attention to detail that made him such a good veterinarian. The mark read "I Bar 8," but even from a distance, you could see something was wrong. The scar tissue was raised and irregular, not the clean lines of a properly applied brand.

"Feel along the edges," I said.

Deacon ran his fingers over the brand, his touch light and precise. The hair around the mark was coarse and grew in different directions, telling its own story. "Hair growth's different here. And here. This was burned over another brand."

My gut twisted like someone had driven a knife into it. I'd never seen it in person, but I'd imagined it a thousand times in my nightmares. The same sloppy, hurried work. The same arrogance of men who thought they were too smart to get caught.

"Check the others," I said, my voice tight.

We moved through the herd systematically, examining each animal with the thoroughness of trained investigators. I watched Deacon work—the careful way he ran his hands over each brand, the methodical notes he took, the systematic approach that never missed a detail. It was one thing that made us good partners. Where I saw the big picture, he caught the specifics that could make or break a case.

"This is organized," Deacon said as we finished our examination, wiping his hands clean with deliberate precision. "Calculated. Someone planned this carefully."

"Too carefully," I agreed, though part of me felt a familiar stirring of excitement. This wasn't amateur work. These outlaws might know others running similar schemes. Like the gang that had destroyed my family.

Deacon must have caught something in my expression, because he paused in cleaning his hands. "Grady. Whatever you're thinking, think it through first."

"I'm not thinking anything except that we need to follow the evidence."

"The evidence. Not your hunches about men in black."

The words hit harder than he'd probably intended. I turned away, pretending to study the cattle, but I could feel him watching me with that careful attention he used to diagnose problems.

Ray nodded grimly. "That's what I was afraid of. Which brings me to why I asked you boys here this morning."

He gestured for us to follow him away from the corrals, toward a spot where we could talk without being overheard. The morning sun climbed higher, and sweat began to soak through my shirt despite the cool air. The familiar weight of my gun belt felt reassuring against my hip.

"The territorial government is establishing a new position," Ray said. "Livestock Inspectors with authority to investigate theft, track rustlers, and coordinate with local law enforcement across county lines."

My heart started beating faster. This was it. The opportunity I'd been waiting for without even knowing it.

"They need men with veterinary training," Ray continued. "Men who can spot altered brands, forged papers, disease used to cover up theft. Men who know cattle and aren't afraid of hard work or danger."

"What exactly would the job involve?" Deacon asked, ever practical.

"Travel throughout the territory. Investigate complaints from ranchers. Work with local sheriffs to track down rustlers and recover stolen stock. Build cases that will hold up in court."

I could feel the excitement building in my chest like steam in a boiler. This was more than just a job. It was a chance to hunt the kind of men who'd destroyed my family. To use the law as a cover for a personal mission six years in the making.

"The pay is good," Ray added. "Better than what you're making now. And you'd be working for Perry Quinn, the new Supervisor of Livestock Inspection. Good man, fair boss, knows the territory like the back of his hand."

"When would we start?" I asked, trying to keep the eagerness out of my voice.

"If you're interested, you can meet Quinn this afternoon. He's setting up his office on Gurley Street, next to the bank."

Deacon looked uncertain. "I don't know, Ray. I've got a good thing going at the stockyards. Derek's been fair to me, and the work is steady."

"The work would be steady with the territory too," Ray said. "And you'd be doing something important. Protecting honest ranchers from thieves and killers."

The word "killers" sent a chill down my spine. Somewhere out there, the man in black was still breathing, still riding, still destroying families like he'd destroyed mine. If I took this job, I might finally get the chance to look him in the eye again.

"I'm interested," I said.

Deacon studied my face, those perceptive brown eyes seeing more than I wanted them to. "What's got you so fired up about this, Grady?"

How could I explain that every altered brand, every stolen cow, every piece of forged paper was another link in a chain that led back to a barn where a fifteen-year-old boy watched his parents die? How could I tell him I wasn't looking for justice—I was looking for revenge?

"Just a feeling," I said finally. "This kind of operation takes planning. Organization. The kind of men who do this don't stop with cattle and horses."

Ray nodded. "That's exactly why we need good men on the job. Men who can see the bigger picture."

Deacon's gaze sharpened, reading the tension in my jaw like words on a page. "The bigger picture," he repeated slowly. "That's what this is about for you, isn't it? Not just these cattle. Something bigger."

I felt heat creep up my neck. Deacon knew me too well for comfort sometimes. "Does it matter? A job's a job."

"It matters if my partner's keeping secrets that could get us both killed."

The accusation hung between us like a challenge. Part of me wanted to tell him everything—about the nightmares, about the faces I still saw in every shadow, about the cold rage that had been burning in my chest for six years. But how could I tell my best friend that I wasn't looking for justice—I was looking for revenge?

"No secrets," I said, which wasn't exactly a lie. "Just experience. I've seen what men like this can do."

Deacon held my gaze for a long moment, then nodded. But I could see he wasn't entirely convinced.

"I'll think about it," Deacon said, but I could tell he was already leaning toward yes. That was Deacon. Once he saw a need, he couldn't walk away from it. It was one thing I both admired and worried about in him.

"Fair enough," Ray said. "Why don't you boys finish up here, then ride over to Quinn's office around two o'clock? You can meet him, see what you think of the set-up."

After Ray left, Deacon and I spent another hour examining the cattle and reviewing the paperwork. But I could feel the tension between us, the weight of things unsaid.

"Grady," Deacon said finally, as we prepared to leave. "I meant what I said about secrets. If we're going to be partners in this, really partners, I need to know what I'm getting into."

I looked at him—really looked at him—and saw six years of friendship, of trust, of having someone watch my back without question. He deserved better than half-truths and careful omissions.

"The men who killed my parents," I hissed. "They were organized outlaws. Just like this." I gestured toward the cattle. "I don't know if there's a connection, but..."

"But you're hoping there is."

"Yeah. I'm hoping there is."

Deacon was quiet for a moment, processing this confession. "That's what I thought. And Grady? That's exactly why we need to do this right. By the book. With evidence and procedure and careful investigation." He gripped my shoulder. "Your parents deserve justice, not revenge. There's a difference."

"I know the difference."

"Do you? Because sometimes when you get that look in your eyes—the one you had when you were talking about outlaws—I'm not so sure."

The words stung because they carried truth. "Are you saying you don't want to be partners?"

"I'm saying I want to be partners with the man who became a veterinarian to help people, not the man who's hunting ghosts." His grip on my shoulder tightened. "But I'll be partners with both, if that's what it takes to keep you alive and sane."

"The original brand," I said, tracing the outline under the altered mark with my finger. The scar tissue felt rough and raised. "That's a 'T Bar 9.'"

Derek Gardner, who'd been watching us work, straightened with recognition. "Jack Thompson's brand. He's got a spread about twenty miles north of here. Good man, honest as the day is long."

"We need to ride out there tomorrow," I said. "See if he's missing any stock."

"That'd be Livestock Inspector work," Deacon pointed out.

"Then maybe we better take that job."

By noon, we'd finished our examination and written up our report. The cattle would have to be destroyed to prevent the spread of disease, but that was the least of our problems. Whoever was behind this operation had resources, connections, and organizational skills that spoke of serious money.

"Come on," I said as we prepared to leave. "Let's go meet this Perry Quinn."

The livestock inspection office sat on Gurley Street between the bank and Miller's Dry Goods, a narrow building with large windows and a sign that still smelled of fresh paint. The scent of new wood and varnish mixed with the dusty street smells of horses and wagons. Inside, maps covered one wall, showing every ranch and range in the territory. Another wall held sketches of registered brands, arranged in neat rows.

A young woman with strawberry hair and blue eyes looked up from her desk as we entered. She was organizing brand sketches by registration date, each one carefully numbered and filed. The scratch of her pen on paper filled the quiet office, along with the rustle of documents as she worked.

"Can I help you?" she asked, her voice pleasant and proper.

"We're here to see Perry Quinn," Deacon said. "Ray Sawyer sent us."

"Of course. I'm Lilian Harper, Mr. Quinn's secretary. He's expecting you."

As she stood to announce us, Deacon stopped and studied the brand wall with the intense focus he usually reserved for sick animals. I felt the familiar tightening in my chest. I knew that look. Deacon had spotted something that needed fixing, and nothing would stop him from fixing it.

"Excuse me, Miss Harper," he said. "Mind if I ask how you've organized these?"

"By registration date," she said, a note of pride in her voice. "Oldest to newest, left to right."

I watched Lilian's face as Deacon nodded slowly, then began moving the sketches around. Her mouth dropped open, her cheeks flushing with indignation as he rearranged her carefully organized system. The papers rustled as he worked, each movement deliberate and methodical.

"What are you doing?" she asked, her voice rising

with barely controlled frustration.

"Fixing it," Deacon said matter-of-factly, continuing to move papers. His fingers were gentle but sure as he repositioned each sketch.

I winced. That was about the worst thing he could have said. Miss Harper had obviously spent considerable time organizing those brands, and now Deacon was telling her it was wrong. I could see the storm building in her blue eyes.

"There's nothing to fix," she said, her voice sharp enough to cut glass. "I organized them by date for a reason."

Deacon, oblivious to her growing anger, kept working. "I know. But this way groups similar brands together. See? All the 'A' brands here, variations next to each other. Much easier to spot alterations and forgeries."

Time to step in before my partner dug himself into a hole he couldn't climb out of. Deacon had many gifts, but reading social situations wasn't always one of them.

"What my friend is trying to say," I said, moving closer to the wall, "is that your system works perfectly for record-keeping. This is just a different approach for a different purpose."

Lilian's eyes flicked to me, some of the fire dimming as she recognized I was trying to help rather than criticize. Her posture softened slightly, though wariness remained in her expression.

"You see," I continued, "when we're investigating brand theft, we need to compare similar marks quickly. A rustler who alters a 'T Bar 9' into something else is likely to pick another brand that starts with 'T' or uses similar elements."

Deacon finished his rearrangement and stepped back, wiping his hands on his vest. "Ask me to name any brand starting with 'T.'"

He turned his back to the wall and immediately rattled off, "T Bar 9, T Bar A, Rocking T C."

"How did you—" Lilian stopped, understanding dawning in her blue eyes. "You memorized them just from arranging them."

"Pattern recognition," Deacon said with a slight smile that transformed his usually serious face. "Occupational hazard."

I caught his eye and gave him a subtle nod—our signal that he'd done well, that the crisis was averted. He returned it with the barely visible shoulder shrug that meant "thanks for the rescue."

"Your filing system is excellent for official records," I added. "But this arrangement helps us spot forgeries and alterations. Both have their place."

Some of the tension left Lilian's shoulders. She studied the rearranged wall with a thoughtful expression, her anger giving way to fascination. I caught a hint of lavender perfume as she moved closer to examine Deacon's work.

"I can see how that would be useful," she admitted. "For investigation work."

Before the situation could get more awkward, an older man with graying hair and keen eyes emerged from the inner office. His boots made solid sounds on the wooden floor as he approached.

"You must be Colter and Thatcher," he said, extending his hand. "Perry Quinn. Ray Sawyer has told me good things about both of you."

The next hour flew by as Quinn explained the scope of the livestock inspection program, the authority we'd have, and the problems we'd be expected to solve. The more he talked, the more convinced I became that this was exactly what I'd been waiting for.

"The rustling problem is getting worse," Quinn said, spreading a map across his desk. The paper crackled as he unfolded it, revealing detailed markings of ranches and territorial boundaries. "Organized gangs with inside information, forged papers, and connections to corrupt buyers. We need men who can track them down and build cases that will stick in court."

"What about this case?" I asked, pointing to the papers from the diseased cattle. "These animals were stolen from Jack Thompson, weren't they?"

Quinn nodded. "That's exactly the kind of investigation you'd be handling tomorrow. Ride out to Thompson's place, confirm the theft, gather evidence, and track down the perpetrators."

"When do we start?" I asked.

Deacon looked at me with surprise, then at Quinn. "I haven't said yes yet."

"But you will," I said with confidence. "Because you can't walk away from a job that needs doing." That was Deacon's strength and weakness both. He couldn't see suffering without trying to fix it.

"You can start tomorrow morning," Quinn said. "Would be great if you could ride out to Thompson's place first thing."

As we prepared to leave, Lilian handed us each a copy of the brand registry, neatly bound and organized according to Deacon's new system. The leather covers were warm from her touch, and the pages smelled of fresh ink.

"You were right," she said quietly to Deacon. "This way is better. For investigation work."

"Your way was right too," I said. "For record-keeping. Maybe you could maintain both systems. Official records by date, investigation copies by pattern."

She smiled at that, the first genuine smile she'd given either of us. "That's actually an excellent idea, Mr. Thatcher."

The warmth in her voice when she looked at Deacon didn't escape my notice. Neither did the way he suddenly found excuses to linger near her desk.

Outside, as we untied our horses, Deacon shook his head. "Well, partner, looks like we're Livestock Inspectors."

"Looks like." I checked Sunbeam's cinch, then

glanced at my friend. "And Deacon? Thanks for what you said back there. About justice versus revenge."

"You needed to hear it."

"Yeah, I did." I swung up into the saddle. "But that doesn't make it easier to swallow."

"The best medicine never does." He mounted Sergeant with practiced ease. "That's what makes it medicine instead of candy."

I laughed despite myself. "You're a philosopher now?"

"I'm a veterinarian. Same thing, just with more manure involved." His grin took the sting out of his earlier lecture. "But seriously, Grady. We do this right, or we don't do it at all. Agreed?"

"Agreed. But if we find a connection to my parents' case..."

"Then we follow it by the book. All the way to the end, whatever that looks like." He reined Sergeant toward the street. "But we follow it together."

"Together," I agreed, and meant it. Even if the path ahead led to places I wasn't sure either of us was ready to go.

As we rode back toward the ranch, I couldn't shake the feeling that this was it. My first real chance in six years. Somewhere out there, the man in black was still breathing, still killing, still laughing about the night he destroyed my world.

But now I wore a badge. Now I had the law on my side. Now I had a partner who'd stand with me no matter what danger we rode into.

Now I could hunt him properly.

The thought should have brought me comfort. Instead, it just made me hungry for justice.

And maybe, if I was honest with myself, a little hungry for blood.

2 - Crooked Paper

―――――――

Deacon

THE THOMPSON SPREAD looked exactly like what it was: an honest man's ranch. Clean fences that ran straight as a surveyor's line, well-maintained buildings with fresh paint on the barn doors, cattle that hadn't been run half to death by night riders. A place that spoke of hard work and pride, where a man's word was his bond and his handshake was better than any contract.

Jack Thompson himself met us at the gate, his long blond mustache twitching as he squinted against the midday sun. Heat waves shimmered above the hard-packed earth, distorting the view of the distant mountains, and the wind whispered through the dry grass of the pasture.

"Livestock Inspectors?" He looked us over with the careful eye of a man who'd dealt with his share of trouble. Weathered hands rested on the gate latch, calloused from years of honest work. The smell of sun-warmed leather and horse sweat hung in the air between us. "What brings you out this way?"

"Missing cattle," I said, dismounting Sergeant with the hesitant movements of a man who'd spent four hours in the saddle. My boots hit the hard-packed earth with a solid thud, and I felt the familiar ache in my lower back that came from long rides. The reins felt slick with sweat in my palm as I tied them to the hitching post. "Wondering if you might be short any stock."

Thompson's face darkened like storm clouds rolling in over the mountains. Lines deepened around his eyes, aging him ten years in as many seconds. "Matter of fact, I am. About forty head went missing three weeks back. Figured it was rustlers, but the sheriff said there wasn't much he could do without proof."

Grady swung down from Sunbeam, his movements tight with barely controlled energy. I'd noticed it getting worse as we rode closer to Thompson's place during our long morning journey. Whatever was eating at my partner ran deeper than our work with this new job.

"You alright?" I asked quietly as we approached the gate. "You've been wound tighter than a watch spring since we left the ranch."

"I'm fine," he said, but the way his hand kept drifting toward his gun belt said otherwise.

"Grady." I caught his arm. "If this is about what we discussed yesterday—about your parents—maybe I should take the lead here."

"I said I'm fine." The snap in his voice drew Thompson's attention from across the yard.

I held up my hands in surrender. "Alright. But we do this following the evidence. Carefully. No jumping to conclusions."

"Mind if we take a look at your herd?" Grady asked, his voice controlled but with an undercurrent of tension I recognized. "Compare some brands?"

"Be my guest." Thompson gestured toward the main corral, where a dozen head of prime beef stood in the shade of a cottonwood. The cattle shifted restlessly in the heat, their tails switching at persistent flies. "Though I got to warn you, what's left ain't much to look at. They took my best stock."

As we walked toward the cattle, I caught Grady's arm again. "Remember what we talked about," I murmured. "Professional. Methodical."

"I know how to do my job, Deacon."

"I know you do. But sometimes knowing and doing are different things when it's personal."

He pulled away from my grip, but I saw him take a deliberate breath, centering himself the way I'd taught him to do with difficult animals.

As we walked toward the cattle, our boots crunching on gravel mixed with scattered hay, Thompson's wife appeared on the porch. She was a sturdy woman with graying brown hair pinned back sensibly, brushing flour from her apron. Her movements spoke of efficiency and care, a woman who ran a household with quiet competence. The rich aroma of chicken stew drifted from the kitchen window, making my empty stomach clench with hunger.

"Will you boys be staying for the noon meal?" she called, her voice carrying the warmth of genuine hospitality.

My stomach rumbled in response, loud enough that Grady smirked. We'd been riding since before dawn with nothing but coffee and hardtack, a trail breakfast that stuck to your ribs but did little for taste. After four hours in the saddle, the prospect of a home-cooked meal was more welcome than gold.

"That's mighty kind of you, ma'am," I called back, touching the brim of my hat. The felt was damp with sweat from our long ride.

Thompson led us to his branding iron, hanging neat and clean in the barn that smelled of leather, hay, and honest sweat. Shafts of sunlight slanted through gaps in the board siding, illuminating floating particles of dust and chaff that caught the light like tiny stars. Somewhere in the loft above, a barn cat meowed softly, and the familiar sounds of horses shifting in their stalls provided a comforting background rhythm.

"T Bar 9," he said, running his thumb along the metal with the reverence of a man who understood that a brand was more than just a mark. It was a legacy. "Been using this mark for years. My daddy used it before me."

I studied the iron, noting the clean lines and precise angles. The metal felt smooth under my fingers, polished by years of careful maintenance. Good workmanship by a skilled blacksmith, a brand that was hard to alter convincingly. The metal showed honest wear, darkened by years of use but maintained with care.

"What we found at the stockyards," Grady said, his voice tight as a fiddle string, "was cattle with 'I Bar 8' burned over what looked like your mark."

Thompson spat in the dust, the sound sharp in the quiet barn. "Figures. Take a good brand and make it crooked. That's rustlers for you. No respect for a man's life work."

We spent the next hour examining Thompson's remaining cattle. The sun climbing higher and sweat soaking through our shirts despite the morning chill having long since burned away. I watched Grady work—noted how his hands shook slightly when he touched the legitimate brands, how his jaw clenched when he compared them to the altered marks we'd seen at the stockyards.

I checked brands against the iron, studying the paperwork Thompson kept in meticulous order in a wooden filing box that smelled of cedar and old ink. Everything was clean, legitimate, exactly what you'd expect from a man who ran his business honestly. But I kept one eye on my partner, watching for signs that his emotions might override his judgment.

"Grady," I hissed as he kneeled beside a heifer, running his fingers over her flank with unnecessary intensity. "Easy. You're making the cattle nervous."

He looked up at me, and for a moment I saw something wild in his eyes—a hunger that had nothing to do with justice and everything to do with revenge.

"The brands are identical," he said, his voice tight. "Same style, same depth, same iron temperature. Whoever altered those cattle at the stockyard knew exactly what they were doing."

"That's good to know," I said carefully. "This level of planning means experienced rustlers."

"Experienced murderers," Grady corrected, and the certainty in his voice sent a chill through me.

"We don't know that yet."

Each document told the story of careful management. Bills of sale with legitimate signatures, breeding records that went back two generations, correspondence with buyers who paid fair prices and on time. The paper felt substantial beneath my fingers, quality stock that suggested serious business dealings. The meticulous record-keeping showed pride and attention to detail, the complete opposite of the sloppy forgeries we'd been seeing.

"You ever hear of someone called B. Irving?" I asked as we finished up, wiping sweat from my forehead with my sleeve. The cotton was damp and gritty with dust from our long ride.

Thompson shook his head, squinting into the distance where the heat shimmer made the horizon dance. "Can't say I have. And I know most of the ranchers between here and Flagstaff. Been in this business thirty years, and there ain't many names I don't recognize."

That confirmed what I'd suspected. B. Irving was as fictional as a dime novel hero, a name pulled from thin air to legitimize stolen cattle.

As we walked toward the house, something caught my eye. Movement near the barn that didn't belong. A figure ducking back into shadow, quick as a spooked deer. The hair on the back of my neck prickled with warning. I stopped, my hand instinctively moving toward my gun, the leather of my holster familiar and reassuring under my palm.

"What is it?" Grady asked, following my gaze with

the alertness of a man who'd learned to read danger.

"Thought I saw someone." I studied the barn's shadowed interior, but whoever had been there was gone. Could've been a ranch hand, or maybe just my imagination. But the prickling between my shoulder blades said otherwise.

"Probably just one of the boys," Thompson said, but his voice carried a note of uncertainty. "Though most of them are out with the herd."

Over Mrs. Thompson's excellent chicken stew, served in a simple but well-kept dining room with mismatched chairs and a wooden table worn from years of family meals, we got the full story. The theft had happened during a thunderstorm three weeks past, taken by riders who clearly knew what they were doing. The rich broth warmed me from the inside out, chasing away the anxiety that had settled in my bones during our investigation.

"They knew which pasture held my best stock," Thompson said, mopping up broth with a chunk of bread that his wife had baked fresh that morning. The bread was still warm, with a golden crust that broke apart in flaky layers. "Knew exactly where to hit and how to get out clean. They even knew where I kept my best breeding bull."

The thefts these good people had suffered was evident in every word. The knowledge that strangers had watched them, learned their routines, planned their destruction while sitting at this very table, accepting their hospitality.

"Any strangers been around lately?" Grady asked, setting down his spoon with a soft clink against the wooden table. "Asking questions, maybe looking for work?"

Mrs. Thompson and her husband exchanged glances, the kind of wordless communication that comes from years of marriage.

"Now that you mention it," Thompson said slowly, "there was a fellow came by last month. Said he was looking to buy cattle, but something about him didn't sit right. Nervous type. Kept looking over his shoulder like he expected trouble to come calling."

I pulled out my notebook and pencil, the leather cover worn smooth from years of use. The familiar weight of it in my hand was comforting, a tool of order in a chaotic world. "Remember what he looked like?"

"Young fella, maybe twenty-five. Dark hair, thin as a rail post. Had a scar across his left cheek, like someone had taken a knife to him." Thompson touched his own cheek unconsciously. "Eyes like a snake. Cold and calculating. Looked right through me like I wasn't even there."

I made careful notes, arranging the details in neat columns, but I was watching Grady out of the corner of my eye. His face had gone pale, and his hands were clenched into fists at his sides.

"This man," Grady said, his voice barely controlled, "did he say where he was from? Who he worked for?"

The intensity in his voice made Thompson take a step back. I set down my pencil and touched Grady's shoulder in warning.

"Easy, partner," I murmured. "Just gathering information."

Grady shook off my hand, his attention fixed entirely on Thompson. "Did he give a name?"

"Said he represented some buyers down south. Never gave a name, though. Called himself Mason, if I remember right." Thompson's voice carried distaste, like the name itself left a bad taste in his mouth. "Paid cash for information about the local herds, asking all sorts of questions about our schedules, where we kept our stock. Should've known he was up to no good."

The reaction was immediate. Grady shot to his feet so fast his chair scraped against the floor, his face flushed and his breathing rapid. I saw his hand move instinctively toward his gun before he caught himself.

"Mason," he repeated, the name coming out like a

curse. "You're sure that's what he called himself?"

"Grady," I said sharply, standing as well. "Sit down."

"I'm fine."

"No, you're not. You're about thirty seconds from either shooting something or falling over." I gripped his shoulder firmly. "Sit down and breathe."

Thompson was looking between us with growing alarm. "Is there a problem with that name? Do you boys know this Mason fellow?"

"We might," I said carefully, never taking my eyes off Grady. "But we'll need to verify that through official channels."

Grady was staring at me like I'd grown a second head. "Official channels? Deacon, this could be—"

"Could be a lot of things," I cut him off. "Could be coincidence. Could be someone using a false name. Could be information we need to investigate properly." I tightened my grip on his shoulder. "Properly. Not by jumping to conclusions."

The tension between us was thick enough to cut with a knife. I could see the war playing out on Grady's face—his need for immediate action warring with six years of trust in my judgment.

"Paid cash and rode out the same day," Thompson continued. "Haven't seen hide nor hair of him since, but now I wish I'd run him off the place soon as I laid eyes on him. Man had a way of making your skin crawl just by looking at you."

"What kind of horse was he riding?" I asked, adding another line to my notes. "Any distinctive markings or tack?"

"Black gelding, good quality. Saddle was fancy too, with silver conchos that caught the light. More expensive than what most drifters carry." Thompson frowned in concentration. "Come to think of it, that should've been another warning sign. Man dressed like a cowpoke, but riding gear worth more than most folks make in a year."

After thanking Mrs. Thompson for the meal that had restored our strength after the morning's hard ride, and for her husband for his cooperation, we headed back toward Prescott with more questions than answers. The long ride would give me time to think, to piece together what we'd learned—and to deal with whatever was eating at Grady.

The sun was already past its zenith as we set out, and I knew we'd be riding into Prescott just as the businesses were closing for the day. My horse moved easily beneath me, refreshed by the rest and the good hay Thompson had provided. But the tension between Grady and me made the leather reins feel slippery in my hands.

"You know something about that Mason fellow," I said as we crested the first hill. It wasn't a question. The way Grady had reacted to the name was too specific, too intense for casual recognition.

Grady was quiet for so long I thought he wouldn't answer. When he finally spoke, his voice was barely above a whisper, almost lost in the sound of hoofbeats and creaking leather.

"Maybe. Description sounds familiar."

"From where?"

"Long story." He adjusted his hat, pulling the brim low to shade his eyes from the afternoon sun. "Tell you later."

"No." I reined Sergeant to a halt again. "Tell me now. We're partners, remember? That means I get the whole truth, not just the convenient parts."

Grady kept riding for a few more paces before stopping and turning back to me. The look on his face was one I'd never seen before—part desperation, part shame, part wild hope.

"The night my parents died," he said slowly, "there was a neighbor woman who saw the killers ride away. She heard one of them call another by name." He met my eyes. "Mason."

I felt like I'd been punched in the gut. "And you

think—"

"I think it's too much of a coincidence. Young man, scar on his face, cold eyes, calling himself Mason, asking detailed questions about ranching operations." His voice grew stronger, more certain. "It's him, Deacon. It has to be."

"It has to be because you need it to be," I said gently. "But need and fact are different things."

"So we just ignore it? Pretend we never heard the name?"

"We investigate it. Properly. We talk to Perry, maybe send word to the sheriff in Chino Valley, see if they have any records about Mason or men fitting this description." I urged Sergeant forward until we were riding side by side again. "But we don't go off half-cocked chasing shadows."

"And what if he disappears while we're filling out paperwork?"

"Then we'll track him down the right way. With badges and warrants and the full authority of the law." I caught his eye. "The way your parents would have wanted it done."

The words hit home. I could see it in the way his shoulders sagged, the way his grip on the reins loosened.

"I've been waiting six years, Deacon."

"I know. And maybe—maybe—your wait is almost over. But if it is, we do this right. We build a case that will stick in court. We make sure justice is served, not just revenge."

He nodded slowly, but I could see the war still raging in his eyes—patience versus desperation, procedure versus passion.

"Partners?" I asked.

"Partners," he agreed. But I made a mental note to keep a close eye on him in the days ahead. Because I knew my friend, and I knew if push came to shove, years of grief might override years of friendship.

Grady kicked his horse into a trot away from me.

Then I sent a quick prayer heavenward for him. To keep his wits about him. For me to keep him safe. When I finished, I nudged Sergeant to catch up, letting the gentle whisper of the breeze do the only talking as we rode back to Prescott.

The sun was setting by the time we reached the outskirts, painting the sky red and casting long shadows across the dusty streets. Most businesses were closing up for the day, shopkeepers sweeping their front steps and turning their signs around. But as we rode past the Livestock Commission office, I noticed a warm glow still emanating from the windows, the yellow lamplight a welcoming beacon in the gathering dusk.

"Lilian's still there," Grady observed, reining in Sunbeam. His voice carried a knowing tone that made me glance at him suspiciously.

I looked toward the office, seeing her silhouette moving past the window. She was probably finishing up the day's paperwork, making sure everything was properly filed and organized. That dedication to order and completeness was something I admired about her. The lamplight caught the copper highlights in her hair as she moved.

"Why don't you walk her home?" Grady suggested, dismounting and tying his horse to the hitching post with practiced efficiency. "I want to jot down some notes about what we learned while it's still fresh in my mind."

I caught the look he gave me—part encouragement, part gentle pushing. "You sure?" I asked, though my pulse quickened at the thought of spending time alone with her. The prospect both thrilled and terrified me in equal measure.

"Go on," he said with a knowing look that made heat creep up my neck. "Can't have a lady walking home alone after dark. Besides, you've been wound tighter than a clock spring all day. Maybe some pleasant company will help you relax."

It was a peace offering, I realized. His way of showing

that despite our disagreement about Mason, our friendship remained solid. Grady might be driven by demons I couldn't fully understand, but he still cared about my happiness.

"Thanks," I said, meaning more than just permission to walk Lilian home.

I dismounted and tied Sergeant beside Sunbeam, my hands fumbling slightly with the reins. The leather felt slippery in my suddenly nervous fingers. The bell above the door chimed as I entered the office, the familiar sound somehow more musical than usual. Lilian looked up from the stack of papers she was organizing, her face lighting up with surprise and something warmer.

"Deacon! I didn't expect to see you back so late. How did your visit with Mr. Thompson go?"

"Productive," I said, hanging my hat on the peg by the door with care. The office smelled of ink and paper, with a faint hint of lavender that I was beginning to associate with her presence. My voice came out rougher than intended, and I cleared my throat. "What has you working so late?"

"Just trying to get caught up on the filing." She gestured at the neat stacks covering her desk, each pile perfectly aligned and sorted. The papers rustled softly as she moved them. "I like to start each day with everything in its proper place."

Order and organization made the world make sense. Seemed we shared that trait. I noticed the way she'd arranged the papers in perfect rows, corners aligned just so. There was something deeply satisfying about seeing systems work the way they should.

"That's admirable," I said, stepping closer to her desk. "Most people don't appreciate the importance of proper organization."

"Most people haven't had to manage a household and keep track of everything while dealing with..." she paused, then shook her head. "Well, let's just say I learned early that chaos can be dangerous."

There was something in her tone, a shadow that crossed her face, that made me want to know more. But before I could ask, she was already reaching into her desk drawer.

"Grady," she said, turning to where he sat scribbling in his notebook at the small table by the window, "here's a key for you." She pulled a brass key from her drawer, the metal catching the lamplight. "Since it's your first official day, you'll need this to lock up when you're working late."

He looked up from his notes and accepted the key with a nod of thanks before returning to his writing, the pencil scratching steadily across the paper.

"Let me walk you home," I offered, my hands fidgeting with my hat brim. The felt was soft and familiar, worn smooth by years of handling. "It's getting dark out there."

A pleased smile curved her lips, transforming her whole face, and a faint blush colored her cheeks like roses in the morning light. Her hand moved nervously to her gorgeous strawberry blond hair, tucking a loose strand behind her ear in a gesture that made my chest tighten with unexpected emotion.

"That's very kind of you." She began gathering her things with efficient grace, her movements precise and economical. "Just let me get my things together."

I watched her organize her papers one final time, straightening edges and checking that everything was properly sorted. There was something mesmerizing about the careful way she worked, each movement deliberate and purposeful.

The evening air was cool and pleasant as we walked down the boardwalk toward the residential part of town. Our footsteps echoed in the relative quiet, most folks having retreated indoors for supper. The wooden planks creaked softly under our weight, and somewhere in the distance, a piano played a melancholy tune. I found myself stealing glances at her profile, the way the lamplight caught the copper highlights in her hair.

"How long have you been in Prescott?" I asked, genuinely curious about this woman from work.

"Just a few weeks," she said, pulling her shawl tighter around her shoulders. The evening breeze carried the scent of wood smoke and cooking food from the houses we passed. "I needed to get away from my father's ranch."

Something in her tone made me look at her more closely. There was a tightness around her eyes, a careful control in her voice barely concealing hidden pain. "Needed to?"

She was quiet for a moment, as if weighing how much to share. When she spoke, her voice was steady, but I could hear the effort it took. "Let's just say it wasn't the safest place for a young woman. My father... he associates with questionable men. Men who don't respect boundaries."

I felt a flash of anger on her behalf, hot and protective. "I'm sorry. That must have been difficult."

"It was. But I'm making a fresh start here. I've got younger siblings back at the ranch. I'm hoping to bring them to Prescott once I get established." Her voice grew warmer when she spoke of her family. "They're good kids. They deserve better than what they're getting."

"How much younger?" I asked, thinking of my own sister Violet and how protective I felt toward her.

"I have five siblings back at the ranch. My oldest brother Shane is twenty-six—he's fiercely protective of all of us, but he's also trapped there. He can't leave because he knows what our father might do to the rest of us if he's not there to... to keep things from getting worse." Her voice grew quieter, more worried. "He wrote to me last month, told me to get settled here quickly, that he's sensing something dangerous coming. He wants me to be ready to bring the others to safety—Justine, who's nineteen, Hayley who's seventeen, and my two youngest brothers, Flynn and Ike."

The bitterness in her voice suggested she'd seen more than her share of the ugly side of living in the West. It also explained why she'd been so eager to take a job with the Livestock Commission, and why she worked with such focused determination.

"Well, you're safe here," I said, meaning it with every fiber of my being. "And if you need help bringing your siblings to town, I'd be happy to lend a hand."

She stopped walking and turned to face me, her blue eyes bright with gratitude in the lamplight. Standing there with the warm glow illuminating her face, she looked beautiful and vulnerable and stronger than anyone should have to be.

"That's very kind of you, Deacon. I haven't had many people I could count on."

In that moment, with her looking at me like I'd just offered her the world, I felt something shift in my chest. This wasn't just good manners anymore. The feeling was deeper, more complex than simple attraction. I swallowed hard, my mouth suddenly dry.

"Here we are," she whispered, gesturing toward a small house with a neat front porch. Even in the dim light, I could see that she'd already made improvements—swept steps, tidy window boxes, everything in its proper place. "Thank you for walking me home."

"Any time," I managed, my voice coming out quieter than intended. The words carried more weight than simple politeness, and we both knew it. "I'll see you in the morning."

I watched until she was safely inside, her silhouette visible briefly in the window as she lit a lamp. Only then did I turn back toward the office, but as I walked through the quiet streets, I couldn't shake the feeling that someone was watching me. The hair on the back of my neck stood up, and I glanced over my shoulder more than once, searching the shadows for movement.

When I reached the office, Grady was standing outside beside the horses, but his posture was tense, alert. His hand rested near his gun, and his eyes continuously scanned the street. His notebook was nowhere to be seen.

"You feel it too?" he asked quietly, his voice barely above a whisper.

"Someone's watching us."

"Been getting that feeling since we left Thompson's place. Spotted a man in black about a block back. Soon as I looked his direction, he melted into the shadows."

My blood chilled. A man in black. Just like Thompson had described Mason. "Think it's the same Mason fellow?"

"Could be. Or could be my imagination running wild." But his voice suggested he didn't think it was imagination at all. "Either way, we need to be careful. If someone's tracking our investigation, they're probably not planning anything friendly."

We mounted up and headed out of town toward the ranch, both of us staying alert. The feeling of being watched persisted the entire ride home, like an itch between my shoulder blades that I couldn't scratch. Every shadow could hide a gunman, every sound could signal danger.

It wasn't until we were well onto Colter land that the sensation finally faded. But even then, as we settled the horses for the night, I couldn't quite shake the certainty that our investigation had attracted some very dangerous attention.

And somewhere in the darkness, I had the distinct feeling that a man in black was planning his next move.

3 - Chasing Ghosts

Grady

IN THE DAYS since we'd chatted with old man Thompson, I couldn't get what he'd said out of my mind. A scar-faced man calling himself Mason, asking detailed questions about cattle operations, paying cash for information about local herds. The description matched too closely with the witnesses' accounts from my parents' murder for it to be coincidence.

I'd spent three restless nights going over every detail, every word Thompson had shared with us. During the days, I tried to focus on the paperwork Perry Quinn had assigned us, cataloging stolen cattle reports and cross-referencing brands. But my mind kept wandering back to that name: Mason.

Deacon noticed my distraction, of course. He had a way of reading people that came from years of observing animals, looking for subtle signs of illness or injury. This morning, as we worked side by side in the office, he'd given me several concerned glances over the stack of files between us.

"You're wearing a hole in that paper," he said finally, nodding toward the report I'd been staring at for the past ten minutes without really seeing.

I set down my pencil and rubbed my eyes, feeling the grit of sleepless nights. "Just thinking."

"About Thompson's scar-faced visitor?" There was a note of warning in his voice—the same tone he used when he thought I was about to do something reckless.

I nodded. There was no point in denying it. Deacon knew me too well for me to hide what was eating at me.

"And about doing something stupid regarding said visitor," he added, straightening some papers with the clipped movements that meant he was trying to stay calm.

"I haven't decided anything yet."

"That you're considering options worries me." Deacon leaned back in his chair, scrutinizing me. "We agreed to investigate this properly, remember? Through official channels."

"Official channels take time. What if Mason disappears while we're filing reports?"

"Then we track him down the right way. With evidence and warrants." His voice got that edge like when he was trying not to lecture me. "Not by charging into saloons asking questions that'll get you killed."

I nodded. There was no point in denying it. Deacon knew me too well for me to hide what was eating at me. The scent of ink and paper filled the air, mixing with the faint aroma of coffee from the pot Lilian kept brewing throughout the day.

"I think I need to do some digging," I said quietly, mindful of Lilian's presence. "Ask around town, see if anyone else has seen this Mason character."

Deacon's hands stilled on the paper he'd been reading. "What kind of asking around?"

"Saloons, mostly. Places where men talk when they've had too much to drink."

"Absolutely not." The words came out flat and final. "That's exactly the kind of reckless—"

"It's investigation," I cut him off. "The kind that gets

results."

"The kind that gets you killed." Deacon was counting something under his breath—probably the files on his desk. He always counted when he was trying not to lose his temper. "Grady, we talked about this yesterday. We do this by the book."

"The book doesn't always work, Deacon. Sometimes you need to—"

"Sometimes you need to use your head instead of your heart." He met my eyes across the desk. "And right now, your heart is screaming for revenge while your head knows better."

The accusation stung because it carried truth. But sitting here shuffling papers while Mason roamed free felt like swallowing glass.

"That could be dangerous. If this Mason is connected to the rustling operation, word might get back to him that someone's asking questions."

"So what? Let him know we're coming. Maybe it'll scare him into making a mistake."

Deacon stood up abruptly, sending his chair scraping backward. "Listen to yourself. You're talking like this is some kind of dime novel where the hero always wins." He began straightening each item on his desk in his usual annoying, repetitive way. "This is real life, Grady. Real bullets. Real consequences."

"I know that better than anyone."

"Do you? Because the man sitting across from me right now sounds like he's forgotten the difference between justice and suicide."

The words hit like a slap. I pushed back from the desk, my own chair scraping against the floor. "I'm not suicidal. I'm determined."

"Same thing, in this case." Deacon's voice was getting louder, drawing a concerned look from Lilian. He noticed and forced himself to lower it. "You want to honor your parents' memory? Then stay alive long enough to see their killers face a judge and jury."

"And what if they never face a judge? What if Mason slips away while we're playing by rules that don't apply to men like him?"

"Then we live with that. Because the alternative—you getting yourself killed on some half-planned revenge mission—is worse."

The office fell silent except for the sound of our heavy breathing and the continued scratch of Lilian's pen. She was trying to pretend she wasn't listening, but I could see the tension in her shoulders.

"Maybe I should come with you," Deacon said finally, his voice resigned.

I shook my head. "Two men asking questions draws more attention than one. Besides, someone needs to keep working other angles. See if Perry has any more files on cattle theft in the area."

"I don't like the idea of you going alone."

"I'll be careful. Just listening mostly, maybe buying drinks for men with loose tongues."

Deacon sat back down heavily, his hands automatically straightening the papers he'd disorganized in his anger. "This is a mistake, Grady. A big one."

"Maybe. But it's my mistake to make."

"No, it's not." His voice was quiet, but intense. "We're partners. Your mistakes become my mistakes. Your risks become my risks." He looked up at me with something like pain in his eyes. "If you get yourself killed chasing ghosts, where does that leave me? How do I explain to your sister that I let you throw your life away?"

The personal appeal hit harder than any argument about procedure. Ellie Mae had lost enough family. She didn't need to lose me, too.

"It won't come to that," I said, but even I could hear how hollow the promise sounded.

"You don't know that. And neither do I." Deacon leaned forward, his hands flat on the desk. "But I know this—if you're determined to go anyway, then we figure out how to do it smart. Together."

Lilian looked up from her work, her blue eyes moving between Deacon and me. The scratch of her pen had stopped, and I could sense her attention even though she tried to appear focused on her documents.

"Is everything alright?" she asked, her voice carrying genuine concern.

"Just discussing our next move in the investigation," Deacon said smoothly. "Nothing to worry about."

She smiled and returned to her papers, but I caught the way her eyes lingered on Deacon for just a moment longer than necessary. The woman was sharp, and she was tactful enough not to press for details when we clearly needed privacy to discuss our work.

I waited until she was consumed in her work again, the scratching of her pen resuming its steady rhythm, before continuing. "I was thinking I'd start tonight. Hit a few of the places on Whiskey Row, see what I can learn."

"The Palace?" Deacon asked, his voice dropping to match mine. He was organizing his pencils now, lining them up in perfect rows. Again. It wore on my last nerve.

"Among others. It's a place where information flows as freely as the liquor."

Deacon was quiet for a moment, his brown eyes thoughtful. I could see him weighing the risks against the potential benefits, his methodical mind working through all the outcomes. The afternoon sun filtered through the windows, casting his face in alternating light and shadow.

"If you're determined to do this—" he started.

"I am."

"Then we do it right. You go in looking for work, not information. Let them bring up rustling. Don't ask about it directly. And you set up signals—times to check in, ways to call for help if things go wrong."

Relief flooded through me. "You're not going to try to stop me?"

"Would it work if I tried?"

"No."

"Then I'm going to try to keep you alive instead." He straightened the last pencil, then looked up at me. "But Grady—this is your one chance. If it goes sideways, if you get hurt or nearly killed, we do this my way from then on. Agreed?"

It wasn't ideal, but it was better than going alone with no backup plan. "Agreed."

"And if we find a connection to your parents' case, we follow it legally. With warrants and evidence and proper procedure."

That was harder to promise, but I nodded anyway. "I understand."

"Understanding and agreeing are different things," Deacon said, watching my face carefully. "I need your word, Grady. Your actual word you won't go off on some revenge mission if we find these men."

The promise stuck in my throat like a bone. How could I swear to show restraint if I came face to face with my parents' killers? But looking at Deacon's concerned face, seeing the worry and friendship there, I forced the words out.

"You have my word."

"Good." But I could see he wasn't entirely convinced. "Because the last thing I want is to lose my friend to his own demons."

The truth was, I needed to do this alone. The hunt for my parents' killers was personal, and while I appreciated Deacon's partnership, there were some things a man had to face by himself. Some demons that couldn't be shared, no matter how deep the friendship ran.

But his concern meant more to me than I could say. In six years, he'd never once questioned my right to seek justice for my parents. He'd just tried to keep me sane and legal while I did it.

We worked in comfortable silence for the rest of the

afternoon, sorting through reports and building a clearer picture of the rustling operation's scope. The shuffling of papers and the occasional scratch of pencils provided a backdrop to our thoughts. It was bigger than we'd initially thought, with cattle disappearing from ranches across three counties. The pattern was always the same—deliberate thieves who knew exactly what they were looking for, altered brands that fooled casual inspection, and forged papers that legitimized the sales.

As the sun sank toward the western mountains, painting the office walls with golden light, I gathered my things and prepared to leave. Deacon caught my arm as I headed for the door, his grip firm but gentle.

"Be smart about this," he whispered, his voice carrying weight. "If something feels wrong, get out. Don't be a hero."

"I will."

"And if you're not back by morning, I'm coming looking for you. With a posse, if necessary."

I smiled, touched by his concern. The warmth in his eyes reminded me why I valued him so much. "Fair enough."

"Grady." His grip on my arm tightened. "I meant what I said earlier. We're in this together, for better or worse. Don't make me regret trusting you tonight."

The weight of his trust settled on my shoulders like a mantle. "I won't let you down."

"You better not. Because if you get yourself killed playing the lone wolf, I'll never forgive you." Despite the serious words, there was affection in his voice. "And neither will Ellie Mae."

"I'll be careful," I promised. "And Deacon? Thanks for not trying to lock me in a jail cell to keep me safe."

"Don't think I didn't consider it," he said with a wry smile. "But I figure if you're determined to walk into the lion's den, better you do it with a plan than without one."

4 - First Blood

Grady

THE WALK TO Whiskey Row gave me time to think about my approach, my boots echoing on the wooden boardwalk as evening shadows lengthened around me. The smell of wood smoke and cooking food drifted from the houses I passed, mixing with the dusty scent of the street and the faint aroma of horses from the livery stable. I couldn't just walk into the Palace Saloon and start asking direct questions about the Mason brothers. That would mark me as law enforcement or someone with a personal grudge, either of which would shut down conversation faster than a church bell on Sunday morning.

No, I needed to be subtle. Play the part of a drifting cowboy looking for work. Maybe someone who'd heard rumors about easy money to be made by men who weren't too particular about the law. Let other people bring up the subject of cattle theft, then listen carefully to what they had to say.

Prescott's Whiskey Row came alive after dark, its collection of saloons, gambling halls, and brothels drawing men from across the territory who had money to spend and consciences to drown. The Palace Saloon anchored the north end of Montezuma Street, its false front and painted sign promising entertainment for those brave enough to venture inside. Piano music drifted through the batwing doors, mixing with the sound of laughter and raised voices.

I took a moment to check my appearance before entering, adjusting my hat and loosening my gun in its holster. I'd deliberately chosen older clothes—pants and a shirt that had seen better days, an outfit a down-on-his-luck cowboy might wear. My gun hung loose on my hip, positioned for a quick draw, but not ostentatiously displayed.

The batwing doors swung open to reveal exactly what I'd expected. A crowded, smoky room filled with men who worked hard and played harder. The stench of tobacco smoke hung heavy in the air, mixing with the scents of whiskey, sweat, and something else I couldn't quite identify—something that spoke of violence barely held in check. The piano player in the corner was pounding out a lively tune that competed with the noise of conversation, laughter, and the occasional argument over cards.

I pushed through the crowd to the bar, noting faces and listening to the fragments of conversation that floated through the smoky air. Ranch hands discussing their bosses, with voices roughened by dust and hard liquor. Miners complaining about working conditions, their clothes still stained with the earth they'd spent their days digging through. Gamblers arguing over the odds on everything from horse races to territorial politics, their fingers stained with ink and their eyes sharp with calculation.

The bartender was a thick-set man with graying hair and scars that suggested he'd settled more than his share of disputes with his fists. His knuckles were swollen and scarred, and a thin white line ran from his left ear to the corner of his mouth. He looked me over with a professional assessment as I approached, his eyes taking in everything from my worn boots to the way I carried myself.

"What'll it be?" he asked, his voice carrying the rasp of a man who'd spent too many years breathing smoke and dust.

"Beer," I said, sliding a coin across the scarred wooden surface. The bar was sticky with spilled liquor and marked with countless rings from glasses and bottles.

He drew the drink and set it in front of me, the foam thick and yellow in the dim lamplight. Already turning his attention to the next customer, he moved with the efficient grace of a man who'd served thousands of drinks to thousands of men, most of whom he'd rather forget.

I took a sip and grimaced slightly. The beer was warm and bitter, with an aftertaste that suggested the barrels hadn't been cleaned in recent memory. But it would serve its purpose—giving me a reason to linger and listen.

I found a spot at the end of the bar where I could observe the room without being obvious about it, positioning myself so that my back was to the wall and I had clear sight lines to both the front and back exits. The crowd was the usual mix of working men and questionable characters, a place where a man's past was his own business as long as he paid for his drinks and didn't start trouble.

For the first hour, I just listened. Conversations flowed around me like water, carrying fragments of information about ranches, cattle prices, and the general state of law enforcement in the territory. I caught references to missing stock, complaints about rustlers, and speculation about which ranchers might be next to get hit. Nothing specific about the Mason brothers or their operation, but I was patient. These things took time.

"You look like a man between jobs," the bartender observed during a lull in business, wiping down glasses with a stained rag.

I turned to face him, keeping my expression neutral. "Might be. Depends on what's available."

"What kind of work you looking for?"

"The kind that pays well and doesn't ask too many

questions."

His eyes sharpened slightly, and I could see him reassessing me. The cloth stilled in his hands as he studied my face more carefully. In a place like the Palace, that kind of statement could mean anything from simple ranch work to something considerably less legal.

"There's always ranch work," he said carefully, his voice dropping to a level that wouldn't carry beyond our immediate conversation. "If a man's not particular about the brand on the cattle he's handling."

It was a delicate opening, the hint that could lead to bigger revelations if handled correctly. I took another sip of beer, feeling the bitter liquid burn slightly as it went down, and nodded thoughtfully.

"A man's got to eat," I said. "Can't always be choosy about where the money comes from."

"True enough." The bartender leaned closer, lowering his voice even further. The smell of whiskey and stale tobacco clung to his clothes. "Word is there's good money to be made for men with the right skills. Cattle work, but not the usual kind."

"What kind of skills we talking about?"

"The kind that involves moving stock without too much paperwork. If you catch my meaning."

I caught it perfectly. He was talking about rustling, feeling me out to see if I might be interested in joining the operation. It was exactly the opening I'd been hoping for. My pulse quickened, but I kept my voice steady.

"Sounds interesting," I said. "Who would a man talk to about that kind of opportunity?"

The bartender's expression became guarded, his eyes flicking around the room to make sure no one else was listening. "Depends on whether the man can keep his mouth shut and follow orders."

"I can do both."

He studied my face for a long moment, weighing risk against potential profit. The sounds of the saloon continued around us—the clink of glasses, the shuffle of cards, the occasional burst of laughter—but it felt like we were isolated in our own bubble of conspiracy.

Finally, he seemed to reach a decision.

"There're some boys come in here regular. The Mason brothers. They're always looking for good men, if you know what I mean."

My pulse quickened, but I kept my expression casual. The name hit me like a physical blow, but I kept my face neutral. "When might I expect to see them?"

"Could be tonight, could be next week. They keep their own schedule." He went back to wiping glasses, but his movements were more deliberate now, as if he was thinking through the implications of what he'd just told me.

I nodded and took another drink, letting the conversation lapse naturally. The beer tasted even more bitter now, but I forced myself to sip it. I'd gotten more information than I'd dared hope for on my first night. The Mason brothers were known quantities in the Palace, regular customers who recruited for their operation from among the saloon's clientele.

Now I just had to wait and see if they showed up.

I didn't have to wait long. About an hour later, the temperature in the room seemed to drop as three men walked through the batwing doors. The piano music didn't stop, but conversation became more subdued, and several men found reasons to look elsewhere or suddenly develop an intense interest in their drinks.

I didn't need an introduction to know I was looking at trouble. The leader was maybe thirty, with the lean build of a man who lived by violence. A jagged scar ran from his left temple to his jaw, giving his face a lopsided, menacing appearance that matched Thompson's description perfectly. Behind him came a younger man who shared the same sharp features, probably a brother, and a third man built like a bull with hands that looked like they could crush bones.

"The Mason brothers," the bartender murmured, his voice barely audible over the saloon noise. "Caleb's the one with the scar, Bart's the younger one. The big fellow is Snake Morrison, works with them regular."

I watched as the three men claimed a table near the back of the room, noting how other patrons gave them a wide berth. These weren't just tough men; they were dangerous ones, the kind who settled disputes with violence and didn't much care about the consequences. The way they moved, the way they positioned themselves at the table with clear views of all exits, spoke of men who lived expecting trouble.

Caleb's voice carried over the din as he called for whiskey, his tone holding the easy arrogance of a man accustomed to getting what he wanted. I caught fragments of conversation, references to "the next job" and "easy pickings," but nothing specific enough to be useful. The three men spoke in low tones, their heads bent together in consultation.

I was considering my next move when Caleb's eyes found mine across the smoky room. For a moment, we stared at each other, and I felt the weight of his assessment. He was sizing me up, trying to determine if I was a threat, an opportunity, or just another face in the crowd. His pale blue eyes were cold as winter ice, and there was something predatory in his gaze that made my skin crawl.

I raised my beer in a casual salute and turned back to the bar, not wanting to appear too interested. But I could feel his gaze on the back of my neck like a physical weight, and I knew I'd attracted his attention.

"Friend of yours?" the bartender asked quietly, his voice tight with concern.

"Never met the man. Just being polite."

"Might want to be careful about that. Caleb Mason don't much like strangers taking an interest in him."

I nodded and finished my beer, the warm liquid leaving a bitter aftertaste that had nothing to do with its quality. I was debating whether to stay or leave when I heard boot steps approaching behind me. I'd accomplished what I'd come for—confirming that the Mason brothers operated out of the Palace and learning something about their recruitment methods. Pushing for more information tonight might be too risky.

But as I prepared to leave, Caleb Mason stood up from his table and walked toward the bar. He moved with the confident stride of a mountain lion, his spurs ringing softly against the wooden floor, and I could see other men shifting uncomfortably as he passed. The scent of leather and gunpowder clung to him, mixed with something that spoke of violence and blood.

"Bartender," he called, his voice cutting through the saloon noise like a knife. "Set up my usual. And give our new friend here another beer."

The bartender's face went carefully neutral as he poured whiskey for Caleb and drew another beer for me. His hands moved with practiced efficiency, but I could see the tension in his shoulders. I accepted the drink with a nod of thanks, though every instinct screamed that this was a dangerous moment.

"Much obliged," I said, keeping my voice steady.

Caleb studied my face with those icy pale blue eyes. Up close, the scar was even more prominent, a jagged line that spoke of violence survived and lessons learned. "Don't believe I've seen you around before."

"Just passing through. Heard this was a good place to drink and mind your own business."

"It surely is. Long as a man knows how to do both." There was an edge to his words, a subtle threat that wasn't quite overt enough to challenge directly. The whiskey glass looked small in his scarred hands.

I took a sip of beer and nodded. "I'm a man who appreciates his privacy."

"Good to hear. Privacy's important in our line of

work."

"What line of work would that be?"

Caleb's smile was sharp as a knife blade, revealing teeth that were surprisingly white and straight. "The kind that requires discretion and a strong stomach. Not everyone's cut out for it."

"I've done my share of jobs that others might find... distasteful."

"Have you now?" His eyes glittered with interest, and he leaned closer. The smell of whiskey on his breath mixed with something foul and dangerous. "What kind of jobs?"

I was walking a tightrope now, trying to sound experienced enough to be useful while not claiming specific knowledge that could be verified. "Moving things from where they were to where they needed to be. No questions asked."

"Interesting." Caleb leaned against the bar, his posture casual, but his attention focused entirely on me. "What's your name, friend?"

"Jake," I said, using the first name that came to mind. "Jake Wilson."

"Well, Jake Wilson, you might be just the man we're looking for. Assuming you can prove you're as good as you claim."

My heart hammered against my ribs, but I kept my expression neutral. This was it—the chance to get inside their operation, to learn who they worked for and how their network functioned. "What kind of proof you looking for?"

"The kind that shows you can follow orders and keep your mouth shut. We got a job coming up that might suit a man with your particular talents."

Before I could respond, a commotion at one of the card tables drew everyone's attention. Two miners were arguing over a hand of poker, their voices rising as accusations of cheating flew back and forth. The sharp crack of a chair hitting the floor echoed through the saloon as one man lunged to his feet. Within seconds, chairs were scraping against the floor as other patrons backed away from the impending violence.

When I turned back to continue my conversation with Caleb, he was gone. I spotted him near the back exit, murmuring with his brother and Snake Morrison. As I watched, all three men slipped out into the night like shadows, leaving me with nothing but questions and the bitter taste of missed opportunity.

"Probably for the best," the bartender said quietly, his relief evident in his voice. "Getting mixed up with those boys is a good way to end up dead."

I finished my beer and dropped another coin on the bar, the metal ringing against the scarred wood. "Reckon you're right."

But as I walked out of the Palace into the cool night air, I couldn't shake the feeling that I'd been closer to answers than I'd been in six years. Caleb Mason was recruiting, and he'd been interested enough in me to consider bringing me into whatever operation he was running.

The question was whether I had the courage to pursue that opportunity, knowing it might lead me straight into the hands of my parents' killers.

I headed back toward the Livestock Inspection office where I'd left Sunbeam tied up, my mind already working on how I might engineer another meeting with the Mason brothers. The night air was cool against my face, carrying the scents of sage and distant wood smoke. If they were planning a job, it would give me a chance to observe their methods, maybe even identify their boss.

It was dangerous—potentially suicidal—but it might be my only chance to get close enough to the truth to make it count.

As I walked through the quiet streets, I didn't notice the three figures who detached themselves from the shadows behind the Palace. I was too focused on planning my next move to pay attention to the sound of soft-soled boots following at a discreet distance.

The ambush came without warning.

One moment I was walking peacefully through the darkness, thinking about Caleb Mason's recruitment offer. The next, a rope sailed out of the night to catch me around the chest, yanking me backward with bone-jarring force. The hemp burned against my ribs as it tightened, cutting off my breath and sending pain shooting through my chest.

I stumbled and nearly fell as whoever held the other end jerked me into a narrow alley between two buildings. The rough brick walls seemed to close in around me as they dragged me deeper into the darkness. Before I could recover my balance, heavy boots were kicking me in the ribs and stomach, each blow accompanied by grunts of effort from my attackers.

"Should have minded your own business," Caleb Mason's voice cut through the darkness like a blade. "Should have kept your nose out of other people's affairs."

I tried to curl up to protect myself, but there were too many of them and they'd done this dance before. They kicked me like a dog in the dirt, each blow meant to teach me a lesson without putting me in the ground permanent-like. Their heavy boots drove the wind from my lungs and set my ribs on fire.

"Who sent you?" Caleb demanded between kicks, his voice cold and sinister. "Who's paying you to ask questions about us?"

"Nobody," I gasped, tasting blood in my mouth. "Just looking for work."

"Wrong answer."

The beating continued. Ribs cracked with sounds like breaking kindling, blood flowed from my nose and mouth, and consciousness wavered like a candle flame in a strong wind. But through it all, I held onto one thought. I was closer to my parents' killers than I'd ever been before.

All I had to do was survive long enough to make

them pay.

5 - Secrets and Scars

Deacon

THE SOUND OF slow hoofbeats in the darkness woke me from a restless sleep. I'd been tossing and turning for hours, worried sick about Grady. He'd left that afternoon to investigate the Mason Gang lead, promising to be back by ten. That was five hours ago.

I pulled on my boots and stepped out onto the porch of our small house, the cool night air raising goosebumps on my arms. Moonlight illuminated Sunbeam's golden coat as the horse plodded slowly toward our hitching post, each hoofbeat heavy and deliberate in the stillness. But it was the sight of my best friend that made my blood run cold.

Grady was barely upright in the saddle, swaying dangerously with each step. His black duster was torn and bloodied, his hat missing. Even from a distance, I could see the dark stains on his shirt, black in the moonlight but unmistakably blood.

I ran toward them, my boots clomping against the hard packed earth, reaching Sunbeam just as Grady started to slide sideways. His legs buckled the moment I helped him down, and I had to catch his full weight to keep him from hitting the ground. The metallic smell of blood mixed with sweat and fear filled my nostrils.

"Heaven help me. Grady, what happened to you?"

His left eye was swollen nearly shut, a deep purple bruise spreading across his cheekbone like spilled ink. Blood had dried in a crusty line from his nose to his chin, and when he tried to speak, I could see his lip was split badly, the flesh torn and swollen.

"Caleb Mason," he managed through gritted teeth, each word clearly painful. "Found him at the Palace."

My stomach dropped like a stone in a well. I'd told him to wait for me if there was trouble. We were supposed to handle the Mason investigation together, but Grady had gotten impatient. The guilt hit me like a physical blow, making my chest tight and my breathing shallow. I should have been there. I should have had his back.

"Can you walk?" I asked, slipping his arm over my shoulders and feeling him lean heavily against me.

He nodded, though I could feel him trembling with the effort. "Don't fuss, Deacon," he muttered, but there was no real heat in it. "I'm not dying."

"Close enough," I said, and felt him squeeze my shoulder in the way he always did when he wanted to say "thank you" without the words. We made it up the porch steps and through the front door before his legs gave out completely. I helped him into one chair at our kitchen table, my hands already organizing themselves into the familiar patterns that helped calm my racing mind.

"Let me get my veterinary bag," I said, already moving toward the corner where I kept my medical supplies.

I opened the leather satchel and immediately began arranging the contents on the table in precise order. Antiseptic bottles lined up by size, left to right. Clean cloths folded into perfect squares and stacked exactly two inches apart. Needle and thread positioned at precise right angles to the bottles. The familiar ritual of organization helped steady my breathing, even as my mind raced with worry about Grady's condition.

I lit the oil lamp on the table, adjusting the wick three times until the flame burned at exactly the right height, then pumped water into a basin and set it precisely in the center of the medical supplies. The warm light flooded the small kitchen, making Grady's injuries look even worse than they had in the moonlight.

"Let me see," I said, pulling up another chair and positioning it exactly parallel to his before sitting down.

He winced as he straightened, and I could see the effort it cost him. The scent of lamp oil mixed with the antiseptic smell created a familiar, comforting aroma that helped focus my mind. Carefully, I began cleaning the blood from his face, checking each cloth after use and arranging the used ones in a neat pile to my left.

"Tell me what happened," I said quietly, dabbing at the cut on his forehead.

Grady was quiet for a long moment, staring at the scarred wooden surface of our table. I counted the visible wood grain lines—seventeen major ones, each running parallel to the table's edge. When he finally spoke, his voice was barely above a whisper.

"I couldn't wait anymore, Deacon. Six years I've been waiting for justice. When I found the lead on Caleb Mason, I just... I had to do something."

"So you went to the Palace and ran into trouble." I tried to keep the accusation out of my voice, but some of it leaked through, anyway. I folded the used cloth into a perfect square and placed it exactly one inch from the last one in my growing pile. "We're a team, Grady. That means we watch each other's backs."

"I know that," he said, wincing as I cleaned another cut. "But this isn't just about the job, and you know it. This is about my parents."

"Your parents, yes. But my investigation too. My career. My reputation." I had to stop cleaning his wounds for a moment, my hands clenching into fists. "If you get yourself killed playing the lone wolf, where does that leave me?

Where does that leave our case?"

"I didn't plan for it to go sideways like this." He touched his swollen lip gingerly, then looked at me with something like apology in his good eye. "You're right. I should have waited for you. Should have trusted you with... with all of it."

"All of what?" I set down the antiseptic bottle, giving him my full attention.

Grady was quiet for a long moment, staring at our table. "There are things about that day... about my parents' murder... that I've never told you. Details that still wake me up screaming."

The confession hung between us like a bridge neither of us was sure we should cross. My hands automatically reached for the salt and pepper shakers on the table, aligning them perfectly with the sugar bowl, needing the familiar motions to process what he was telling me.

"Six years we've been friends," I mumbled. "Six years you've been carrying this alone."

"I didn't want to burden you with my nightmares."

"Burden me?" I stopped arranging and looked at him directly. "Grady, we're not just friends. We're brothers. Your nightmares are my nightmares. Your fights are my fights." I paused, then added more gently, "But I can't help you if you don't trust me with the truth."

"Something felt off about the whole thing, Deacon. The way he looked at me, like he was sizing me up for something specific. Not just as potential recruitment."

I straightened the kitchen utensils in their holder, needing to keep my hands busy. "What did they talk about?"

"That's when things went bad. Before I could hear much of anything useful, a fight broke out at one of the card tables. Two miners arguing over poker. By the time I turned back, Caleb and his men had slipped out the back."

"So you followed them?"

"Tried to. But they were gone by the time I made it

outside." Grady touched his ribs gingerly, wincing at the contact. "That's when they jumped me in the alley. Caleb and two others—his brother Bart and a big man named Snake Morrison."

"What did they want?"

"To send a message. Caleb kept asking who sent me, who was paying me to ask questions about them." Grady's voice turned bitter. "When I stuck to my story about just looking for work, they made it clear that strangers asking questions weren't welcome."

The rage that swept through me was so intense I had to grip the edge of the table to keep from exploding. My knuckles went white as I held on, counting to ten, then twenty, then thirty, until the initial fury passed. They'd beaten my best friend like a dog just for being in the wrong place.

"Did you learn anything useful before it all went sideways?"

"The bartender confirmed what we suspected. The Mason brothers recruit from the Palace regularly. They've got some kind of operation going, something involving cattle that doesn't require much paperwork." He met my eyes. "And Caleb was interested enough in my story to consider bringing me in, at least until that fight interrupted everything."

I stood abruptly, my hands automatically straightening the dish towels hanging by the sink, then moving to align the coffee tin with the flour canister. The familiar motions helped steady my breathing, but they couldn't calm the storm in my chest.

"I thought you wanted this job for altruistic reasons. Not just revenge."

"Deacon—"

"No." I turned to face him, my hands still moving automatically to organize the items on the kitchen counter. "You let me think this was about justice, about protecting ranchers, about doing the right thing. But this whole time, you've only had revenge on your mind."

"It's both," he said quietly. "It can be both."

"Can it?" I challenged. "Because tonight you nearly got yourself killed chasing ghosts instead of building a case. Tonight, you threw away a week of careful investigation because you couldn't wait until it was safer. Or for me." I gestured at his battered face. "How is that justice, Grady? How is that protecting anyone?"

Grady looked away.

"They could have killed you tonight." I gestured at his battered face, then automatically checked that the oil lamp wick was still at the proper height—once, twice, three times.

"I made progress. And I'm still breathing." Despite his injuries, there was steel in Grady's voice. "For six years, I've been chasing ghosts. Now I've seen one man involved. I know he's real, and I know we're getting close."

I puffed my cheeks and expelled a loud breath before settling into my chair again. That cut on his forehead needed stitching. I picked up the needle, threading it with steady hands despite the emotional turmoil in my chest. But first I had to count the stitches I would need—one, two, three, probably four total. Then I arranged the thread in perfect loops, each one exactly the same size. The familiar ritual helped center me after our difficult conversation.

"We need to be more careful from now on," I said, beginning the delicate work. "No more going off alone. No more taking risks like tonight. We do this as partners, or we don't do it at all."

"Agreed. But we don't stop, Deacon. No matter what they do to try to scare us off, we don't stop."

"I wouldn't dream of it." I tied off the first stitch with a perfect square knot, then checked the spacing before starting the second. "But next time, we plan it properly. We follow procedure. We use our heads instead of just our hearts."

"Even when it's personal?"

I paused in my stitching to meet his one eye that wasn't swollen shut. "Especially when it's personal. That's when we need procedure most."

"This isn't your fault."

"Parts of it are mine," I said quietly, continuing my precise stitching. "I knew something was eating at you these past few weeks. I could see it in the way you moved, the way you couldn't sit still during meetings. I should have pushed harder, made you talk to me."

"I wasn't ready to talk."

I tied off another stitch. "I kept telling myself that when you were ready, you'd share. But maybe part of me didn't want to know. Maybe I liked having a partner whose motives I didn't have to question." I glanced up at him. "It's easier than admitting that justice is messy and complicated and personal for all of us."

"You'd probably be sitting in that chair getting stitched up, too." Grady winced as I started the next stitch. "At least this way, one of us is still in fighting shape."

"Next time, we both go in fighting shape. Or we find another way." I focused on the stitching, but added quietly, "I can't lose you, Grady. Not to them, not to your need for revenge, not to anything. You're the only person who really understands me, who accepts all my quirks without question."

"You're not going to lose me," Grady said, his voice rough with pain and emotion. "And Deacon... you're not just my partner. You're my brother. The Colters gave me a family when I lost mine, but you gave me something else. You gave me a friend who sees the world the way I do."

I worked in silence for a few minutes, focusing on the familiar motions of medical care. Each stitch exactly one-quarter inch apart, each knot tied the same way, each thread cut to precisely the same length. It helped calm my racing thoughts, at least temporarily. The scent of antiseptic and lamp oil created a cocoon of familiar order around us.

"What's our next move?" I asked finally, setting the needle and scissors down.

"We keep investigating, but we're smarter about it. The bartender seemed willing to talk more. Maybe I can go back in a few weeks. After this heals up, try a different approach."

"We go back," I corrected, beginning the methodical cleanup. "Together this time."

He nodded slowly. "Together. And we dig deeper into their cattle operation. If they're recruiting at the Palace, they're not just small-time rustlers. This is bigger than we thought."

I fell into the familiar routine of cleaning up. The process helped steady my nerves after everything that had happened. When I finished, I helped him to his feet, careful not to jar his injured ribs.

"You need to see an actual doctor. Some of these cuts are deep, and I think you might have cracked a rib."

"In the morning. Right now, I just want to sleep."

I steadied him when he swayed, helping him toward the narrow stairs that led to his room on the second floor. My mind was already organizing tomorrow's tasks. Doctor visit, checking our investigation notes, planning our next careful move.

"You sure you can make it up there?" I asked.

"I'll manage."

"Grady." I caught his arm before he started up the stairs. "Whatever happens... However this investigation ends... we're still brothers. That doesn't change."

He nodded, gripping the banister. "Get some sleep, Deacon. Tomorrow we begin the hunt in earnest."

I watched him climb the stairs slowly, counting each step—twelve total—and listening for the sound of his door closing. Before I could even think about sleep, I needed to care for Sunbeam. The horse had done his job by bringing Grady home safely, and it wouldn't be right to leave him tied up all night. I led him to the barn, gave him a quick brushing, and made sure he had water and feed.

Then I returned to the house and my room on the first floor. As I settled into bed with my clothes still on, I straightened the blankets, adjusting the pillow until it was perfectly centered, checking that my boots were aligned precisely beside the bed.

The familiar rituals helped calm my mind enough to think clearly about what we'd learned. The Mason brothers were more dangerous than we'd anticipated, willing to beat a man senseless just for asking the wrong questions.

But we also knew more than we had that morning. We confirmed Caleb Mason's whereabouts and that he was looking to hire men for questionable activities. It was a start.

Most importantly, Grady was alive. Battered and broken, but alive.

I checked my gun was positioned exactly six inches from the edge of the nightstand, then ensured my holster hung perfectly straight on the bedpost. Tomorrow, we would be smarter. We would be more careful. And we would start the methodical work of bringing these men to justice, no matter how long it took or how dangerous it became.

I closed my eyes and tried to sleep, but all I could see was Grady's beaten face. The rage in my chest burned steady and cold, and I counted—heartbeats, breaths, the number of boards in the ceiling above me. Anything to create order in the chaos of emotion that threatened to overwhelm me.

Lord, I prayed silently, help me keep my anger righteous. Help me seek justice, not revenge. And please protect Grady tomorrow and in the days ahead. Give us wisdom to do this right.

The prayer helped settle something in my chest, though the anger remained. Someone was going to pay for what they'd done to my best friend. And when we found them, justice would finally be served.

The next morning came too soon. I'd managed maybe two hours of sleep before the sun crept through my window. I went through my morning rituals with more precision than usual—everything had to be exactly right after the chaos of last night.

After checking on the still-sleeping Grady and leaving him a note, I saddled Sergeant with unusual care. The cinch tested three times, both stirrups adjusted to precisely the same length, the bit positioned perfectly. My hands needed the control after feeling so helpless the night before. Despite everything that had happened, I took the familiar route to Lilian's house.

She'd be expecting me, and I didn't want her to worry. More than that, I needed to see her. After the darkness of last night, I craved something good and pure and normal. Something that didn't require organizing or counting or checking to make sense.

She was waiting on her porch when I arrived, looking fresh and lovely in a blue dress that brought out her eyes. The sight of her made something tight in my chest loosen just a fraction. Her hair was arranged in perfect waves, and I appreciated the symmetry of her appearance.

"Good morning," she said, stepping down to meet me. Then she paused, studying my face with those perceptive blue eyes. "Deacon, you look terrible. Did you sleep at all?"

"Rough night," I said, which was certainly true. I helped her up onto Sergeant behind me, taking extra care to ensure she was properly positioned and secure, trying not to think about how natural it felt to have her arms around my waist.

"Is everything alright? You seem..." She paused, searching for the right word. "Distant."

I guided Sergeant toward the main road, maintaining exactly the proper distance from the fence line. Lilian had a way of reading people that sometimes caught me off guard. It was one thing I'd grown to love about her, but right now it made me nervous.

"Just tired," I said. "Grady and I were up late discussing a case."

It wasn't exactly a lie, but it wasn't the whole truth, either. The deception sat heavy in my stomach, creating an imbalance that made me want to organize something, to set things right.

"The Mason investigation?" she asked, and I felt her shift slightly behind me.

"Among other things." I kept my voice carefully neutral, even as my mind raced. How much did she know about what we were working on? How much had I told her in casual conversation? I began mentally cataloging every conversation we'd had, organizing them by topic and level of detail shared.

"I hope you're being careful," she whispered, her breath warm against my shoulder. "These men sound dangerous."

"We're always careful." Another half truth. If we'd been truly careful, Grady wouldn't be lying in bed with stitches in his forehead. I adjusted my grip on the reins repeatedly, needing them positioned exactly right.

We rode in comfortable silence for a few minutes, and I relaxed despite everything. There was something about Lilian's presence that calmed the chaos in my mind, even when my hands wanted to straighten and organize everything within reach. The way she rested her cheek against my shoulder, the soft sound of her breathing, the trust she showed in letting me guide us safely to the office.

"Deacon?" Her voice was quiet, almost hesitant.

"Yes?"

"I know it's not my place to ask, but... if you ever need someone to talk to about your work, about anything that's troubling you... I'm here."

She paused for a moment. I craned my head to look at her.

"My brother Shane always said that keeping secrets

from people you trust only makes the danger worse."

The sincerity in her voice made my throat tight. Here she was, offering comfort and support, and I was keeping secrets from her. But what choice did I have? The uncertainty created an imbalance that made my chest tight, made me want to count something, organize something, create order.

"Thank you," I said, and meant it. "That means more than you know."

When we reached the Livestock Commission office, I helped her down from Sergeant, my hands lingering on her waist perhaps a moment longer than necessary. I noticed her shawl had shifted during the ride and gently straightened it. She looked up at me with those clear blue eyes, and I saw genuine concern there.

"Promise me you'll get some rest today," she said, reaching up to touch my cheek briefly. "You can't help anyone if you collapse from exhaustion."

The gentle touch of her fingers against my skin sent warmth spreading through me, quieting the chaos in my mind. For just a moment, I forgot about dangerous criminals and beaten friends. There was only Lilian, looking at me like I mattered to her.

"I promise," I said, catching her hand and squeezing it gently—once, twice, three times—before releasing it.

She smiled then. A smile that made me believe everything might work out after all, that there was still beauty and order in the world despite the chaos. "Good. I'll see you this evening?"

"Wouldn't miss it."

I watched her walk into the office, noting the way her blue skirts moved in perfect rhythm, before I turned Sergeant toward Doc Armstrong's office. I needed to arrange for him to see Grady at noon.

By the time I reached the clinic, I'd decided. I secured Sergeant at the hitching post with extra care, checking the lead rope twice to ensure it was properly tied, then straightened my own clothes before heading inside.

I would protect our investigation, our pursuit of justice. But I would also protect what I was building with Lilian. Whatever secrets lay between us, whatever dangers lurked ahead, I wouldn't let them destroy the best thing that had ever happened to me.

Not without a fight.

And if that meant being more careful, more deliberate, more precise in everything I did, then that's exactly what I would do. Order and control had always been my weapons against chaos.

Now they would be my weapons against the men who had hurt my best friend.

6 - The Net Closes

Grady

THE RIDE BACK to Colter Ranch was taking longer than usual, but I couldn't complain. A week had passed since my beating at the hands of the Mason Gang, and while my ribs still ached with every step Sunbeam took, the long trip to Phoenix had been worth the discomfort. The swelling around my eye had finally gone down enough that I could see clearly again, and the stitches Deacon had put in were ready to come out. Doc Armstrong had been right. I was tougher than I looked.

Our gear clinked softly as the horses moved, and leather creaked with each step. Sunbeam's ears kept moving, alert but calm, while Sergeant just kept plodding along like he always did.

The weight of what we'd discovered, pressed on my mind. In my saddlebags, wrapped in oiled leather, were copies of documents that showed this was bigger than we'd thought. What had started as simple cattle theft was turning into something much worse.

"Those signatures from Phoenix," I said, breaking the comfortable silence that had settled between us. The scent of pine resin and crisp mountain air drifted on the evening breeze. "Ray's right. They're too similar to be coincidence."

Deacon shifted in his saddle, the leather creaking softly under his weight as his brown eyes grew thoughtful while he considered the evidence we'd spent the afternoon cataloging. "B. Irving appears on bills of sale from Flagstaff to Tucson. Same handwriting, same paper stock, same ink. This isn't some local rustler with a running iron."

"Well-run outfit," I agreed, my jaw tightening as I felt the familiar burn of anger in my chest. "Organized. Well-funded. The kind that doesn't happen without backing from someone with real money and influence."

The implications sat sour in my stomach like a rotten apple. In my years of dreaming about finding my parents' killers, I'd always pictured them as common outlaws. Desperate men who killed for survival, who could be hunted down and brought to justice by a determined lawman with a badge and a gun.

But this was different. This was a network that stretched across the territory, with tentacles reaching into stockyards, railroad offices, and government bureaus. Corruption that could buy judges, silence witnesses, and make inconvenient lawmen disappear in the night.

"The brands Ray sent from Phoenix," Deacon continued, pulling a folded paper from his vest pocket with the careful precision he used for everything. The document rustled softly in the evening air. "Look at this pattern."

I reined Sunbeam closer so I could study the sketches in the fading light. Ray had documented a dozen cases of brand alteration, each one showing the same sophisticated technique. Clean burns that followed the natural grain of the original mark. Meticulous work that would fool casual inspection and even some experienced inspectors.

"Lazy N becomes Lazy M," I observed, tracing the alterations with my finger. Heavy paper. The kind the government uses for important documents. "Flying P becomes Flying R. Someone's teaching these rustlers how to do it right."

As we crested the hill overlooking the ranch, I felt the familiar comfort of approaching home. The sound of cattle lowing drifted up from the corrals, mixed with the distant voices of ranch hands finishing their evening chores. Our small house sat at the edge of the sprawling Colter operation, close enough to be part of the family but far enough to give us independence.

"More than teaching," Deacon whispered as we approached the barn, his voice carrying the weight of realization. "Someone's coordinating the entire operation. Choosing which ranches to hit, which brands to alter, where to sell the stock."

We dismounted and led our horses into the barn, the familiar smells of hay and leather greeting us like old friends. The routine of caring for our mounts gave me time to think as I pulled Sunbeam's saddle and began brushing his golden coat.

"This isn't random cattle theft," Deacon continued from Sergeant's stall, his voice echoing slightly in the barn's interior. "This is deliberate theft on a grand scale."

The word "deliberate" echoed in my mind as I worked the brush through Sunbeam's mane, feeling the coarse hair slip between the bristles. Like the way my parents had been murdered. Not in a fit of rage or desperation, but with cold calculation. The way the killers had searched our house before burning it. The way they'd taken only what they needed and left the rest to burn.

Had their deaths been part of something larger? Had the man in black been following orders from someone higher up the chain?

The thought made my blood run cold. For years, I'd carried the image of that killer's face burned into my memory. I'd dreamed of the moment I'd look him in the eye and make him pay for what he'd stolen from me. But if he was just a hired gun, just another piece in someone else's game...

"You're thinking about them again," Deacon breathed quietly as we finished with the horses and headed toward the house, our boots thudding on the dusty path.

"Hard not to. Every altered brand we find, every forged document, it all leads back to the same question. Were my parents killed by rustlers, or were they killed to cover up something bigger?"

The interior of our house welcomed us with the warmth of home. The familiar scent of lamp oil and coffee lingered in the air, mixed with the faint aroma of the soap we used for washing. Deacon immediately moved to light the oil lamps while I started coffee on the stove, the familiar domestic routine helping to settle my churning thoughts.

"Does it matter?" Deacon asked as he settled into his chair at our small kitchen table, arranging his papers in neat stacks with unconscious precision.

The question caught me off guard. "What do you mean?"

"I mean, does knowing why they died change what you need to do about it?" Deacon's voice carried the gentle wisdom that had helped me through the darkest nights of the past six years. "Dead is dead. Murder is murder. Justice is justice."

"But if they were killed as part of some larger conspiracy—"

"Then we bring down the whole conspiracy. We don't just catch the shooter. We catch everyone who gave the orders, everyone who profited from it, everyone who helped cover it up." His brown eyes met mine with quiet intensity. "We make sure it never happens to another family."

The words stirred something deep in my chest as I poured coffee for both of us, the rich aroma filling our small kitchen. For so long, my quest for justice had been personal. About avenging my parents, about satisfying the burning need for revenge that had driven me through six years of nightmares and rage.

But listening to Deacon, thinking about families like the Thompsons who'd lost their life's work to these organized thieves, I saw it differently. This wasn't just about the past anymore. It was about protecting the innocent people who might be next on the list.

"Sometimes I wonder if I'm chasing justice or still just feeding my need for revenge," I admitted as I sat across from him at the table, wrapping my hands around the warm ceramic cup.

"Maybe there's not as much difference as you think," Deacon murmured, warming his hands around his coffee cup. "The Lord calls us to defend the innocent and punish the wicked. Sometimes that means getting your hands dirty. Sometimes that means doing things that decent folks would rather not think about."

I studied my friend's face in the lamplight. There was steel beneath his gentle exterior, a core of moral certainty that I envied. Deacon never seemed to struggle with the questions that kept me awake at night. He saw suffering and moved to heal it. He saw injustice and worked to correct it. He saw evil and stood against it, without agonizing over the complexities.

"You ever wonder if we're in over our heads?" I asked, taking a sip of the bitter coffee. "Two former veterinarians trying to bring down a territorial conspiracy?"

"Every day," he said with a rueful smile that softened his usually serious features. "But then I think about Mrs. Thompson crying over her stolen cattle. I think about honest ranchers losing everything they've worked for while thieves get rich. I think about your parents..."

His voice trailed off, but I knew what he meant. The alternative to fighting was to let evil triumph unopposed. And neither of us could live with that.

The peaceful quiet of our home settled around us as

we sipped our coffee. After the intensity of the day's discoveries, it felt good to just sit and think, to let the weight of evidence settle in our minds like sediment in still water. The lamp flames flickered slightly in the evening breeze that crept through the gaps around our windows.

"Tomorrow we need to ride out to the Franks' place," I said, setting my cup down with a soft clink against the wooden table. "See if Wendel's missing any cattle that match those altered brands from Phoenix."

"Agreed. And Ray said he'd keep looking for more examples of B. Irving's handiwork." Deacon leaned back in his chair, the wood creaking softly. "The more evidence we can gather—"

The thunder of approaching hoofbeats cut him off mid-sentence. We both looked up sharply. The peaceful moment shattered like glass hitting stone. It was full dark now, and honest folks didn't usually ride hard after sunset unless something was wrong.

"Expecting anyone?" I asked, my hand instinctively moving toward my gun belt, feeling the familiar weight of my Colt.

"No." Deacon stood and moved toward the window, peering out into the darkness. The sound of his boots thunked on our wooden floor. "Could be ranch business, but..."

The hoofbeats grew louder, more urgent. A single rider moving fast, pushing their mount hard. The rhythmic pounding echoed off the surrounding hills. We both moved toward the door as the sound reached our front yard.

I opened the door just as the rider burst into the circle of light cast by our porch lamp. Even in the darkness, I recognized the flowing hair and determined posture. Lilian Harper, riding like the devil himself was on her trail.

She pulled up hard twenty feet from our porch, her horse lathered and blowing from the wild ride. Steam rose from the animal's flanks in the cool night air. In the lamplight, I could see her face was pale with fear and determination.

"Lilian!" Deacon stepped forward, concern evident in every line of his body. "What's wrong? What are you doing here so late?"

She slid from her saddle with practiced ease, but I noticed her hands were shaking as she loosened the reins. Whatever had driven her to make this desperate night ride, it had shaken her badly. The smell of horse sweat and fear hung in the surrounding air.

"I had to warn you," she hissed, her voice tight with controlled fear.

Deacon held the door open for her, and she stepped inside. Without hesitation, she pulled a pistol from her coat and set it on our kitchen table. The metallic click of steel against wood spoke volumes about her preparation for this ride and her determination to protect herself.

"There was a man at the office today," she continued, accepting the chair Deacon offered with trembling hands. "At the end of the day. He... he knew your name, Grady. He said to tell you that you'd be meeting soon."

Ice formed in my veins. A man who knew my name. Who'd taken the trouble to track me down and deliver a personal message through Lilian. That could only mean one thing: the Mason Gang knew we were investigating them.

"What did he look like?" I asked, fighting to keep my voice level.

"Tall. Massive shoulders. All dressed in black, from his hat to his boots." She wrapped her arms around herself as if warding off a chill. "He had the coldest eyes I've ever seen. Like looking into a winter grave."

The description hit me like a physical blow. All in black. Massive build. Cold eyes. It was him. The man from my nightmares. The killer who'd murdered my parents while I hid in the barn like a coward.

After six years of searching, he'd found me first.

"Did he say anything else?" Deacon asked, moving closer to Lilian with protective instincts I recognized.

"He studied the brand wall for a long time. Said he liked how it was organized, that it made things easier to memorize." She shivered despite the warmth of our house. "Then he said he wasn't there for me, but that Thatcher should know they'd be meeting soon."

The casual way he'd studied our evidence, memorizing the brands we'd so carefully arranged. The easy familiarity with which he'd used my name. The confidence that he could walk into a territorial office in broad daylight and deliver threats without consequence.

This wasn't just a message. It was a demonstration of power. A way of showing us we weren't the hunters in this game. We were the prey.

"You did right coming to warn us," I said, though my mind was already racing ahead to the implications. "But it was dangerous riding out here alone in the dark."

Deacon was already moving toward the window again, studying the darkness with his characteristic thoroughness. "If they're watching the office, they might know you came here."

"We need to get you back to town," I said, standing and reaching for my gun belt. The leather felt reassuring under my hands. "It's not safe for you to ride home alone, and it's not safe for you to stay here if they're looking for me."

Lilian nodded, understanding immediately. She retrieved her pistol from the table and tucked it back into her coat with movements that spoke of familiarity with firearms. "I can handle myself, but I'd appreciate the escort."

Within minutes, we had our horses saddled. Lilian's mount had recovered from the hard ride, though I could see the animal was still panting. We'd have to take it easy on the return trip.

As we rode out from the ranch toward the trail to

Prescott, I couldn't shake the feeling that we were walking into a trap. The night air was cool against my face, carrying the scent of pine and distant smoke. The man in black had found me, had delivered his message, and now we were exposed on a dark trail with limited cover.

But we had no choice. We had to escort Lilian safely home. Whatever was waiting for us in the darkness, we'd face it together.

The trail wound through stands of pine and oak, with scattered boulders providing potential cover for ambushers. Every shadow could hide a gunman, every bend in the path could reveal death waiting with patient eyes. Our horses' hooves made soft sounds on the trail, muffled by the pine needles.

We'd ridden perhaps half the distance to town when the first shot cracked through the night like thunder.

Lilian's horse reared and screamed, a sound of pure animal terror cutting through the darkness. I saw the animal stagger as crimson bloomed on its flank, then collapse with a bone-jarring crash that sent Lilian flying from the saddle.

"Ambush!" I shouted, drawing my Colt as muzzle flashes erupted from the boulders on both sides of the trail. Lead whistled past my ear, so close I felt the heat of its passage and smelled the acrid scent of burned gunpowder.

More gunshots exploded around us like a deadly symphony. Deacon's voice cut through the chaos as he returned fire, his revolver barking defiance at the hidden killers. The sound echoed off the rocks and trees, creating a cacophony of violence in the peaceful night.

The man in black had kept his promise. We were meeting at last, and this time there would be no barn loft to hide in. This time, it was kill or be killed.

The ambush had begun.

7 - Blood and Bonds

———————

Deacon

THE CRACK OF rifle fire split the night like the world breaking apart.

I saw the muzzle flash bloom orange in the darkness before I heard the bullet whistle past my ear, so close the heat singed my cheek. The acrid smell of gunpowder filled the air, mixing with the scent of frightened horses and pine needles. Lilian's scream cut through the chaos as her horse reared and crashed sideways, throwing her hard to the rocky ground.

Time slowed to a crawl. She lay motionless in the dirt, her body twisted at an unnatural angle, and my heart stopped beating entirely. The woman I'd been falling in love with was dead, killed because I'd failed to protect her.

No.

The word exploded from my chest with such force it felt like my soul was tearing in half. I spurred Sergeant forward without thought, without plan, with no consideration for the bullets whining through the surrounding air. Nothing mattered except reaching her, protecting her, even if I was too late.

"Deacon!" Grady's voice cut through the gunfire, but

I barely heard it over the roar of blood in my ears.

I threw myself from the saddle before Sergeant had fully stopped, hitting the ground hard enough to drive the air from my lungs. The impact sent a sharp pain through my knees and elbows, but I ignored it. More muzzle flashes erupted from the boulder field on both sides of the trail—they caught us in a crossfire with nowhere to run. But I didn't care about tactics or cover or survival. I crawled toward Lilian's still form on hands and knees, my Colt in one hand, expecting every second to feel a bullet tear through my back.

She had to be alive. She had to be.

Another shot kicked up dirt inches from my face, the gritty particles stinging my eyes, but I kept moving. Behind me, I heard Grady's revolver barking defiance at the hidden killers. The sound echoed off the boulders, but it seemed to come from miles away. My entire world had narrowed to the woman lying broken in the dust ahead of me.

I reached her just as she stirred, her blue eyes fluttering open in the moon-bathed darkness. The relief that crashed over me was so intense I nearly vomited. She was alive. Shaken, maybe hurt, but alive.

"Stay down," I commanded, throwing my body over hers as another volley of shots rang out. My broad shoulders and back made a shield between her and the guns, and I felt the impact as something hot tore through the meat of my left arm. The pain was distant, unimportant. All that mattered was the warm, breathing woman beneath me.

"Deacon," she whispered, her voice shaky but strong. "You're bleeding."

"Doesn't matter," I growled, raising my gun to return fire toward the nearest muzzle flash. The Colt bucked in my hand, the familiar weight and balance grounding me despite the chaos. "Stay still."

The gunfight raged around us like a thunderstorm made of lead and fire. I lost track of time, lost track of everything except the rhythm of shooting and reloading while keeping Lilian covered with my body. Grady had found cover behind a fallen log and was laying down steady fire, his shots forcing the ambushers to keep their heads down.

A bullet caught me in the side, the lead burning a furrow before spinning off into the darkness. I grunted and kept shooting, ignoring the warm wetness spreading across my shirt. Another grazed my right thigh, the hot metal searing through fabric and flesh like a branding iron. I didn't care. They could shoot me full of holes as long as I kept the woman I loved safe.

The woman I loved.

The thought hit me harder than any bullet. Somewhere between her smile when I reorganized the brand wall and this moment when I would die for her, I'd fallen completely, hopelessly in love with Lilian Harper.

Bullets pinged off the granite around us, sending sharp fragments of stone flying. The whine of ricochets mixed with the thunder of gunshots, creating a symphony of violence. Behind us, Lilian's wounded horse let out another keening wail that cut through the gunfire like a blade. The sound made my jaw clench—no animal should suffer like that.

"There's too many of them!" Grady shouted over the thunder of gunshots. "We need to move!"

But moving meant exposing Lilian, and I wouldn't do that. Not if it meant watching her die while I stood helpless. I'd failed too many people in my life—sick animals I couldn't save, friends I couldn't help. I would not fail her.

"Deacon!" she hissed urgently. "Behind that boulder. Ten yards to your left. We can make it."

I looked where she pointed and saw the granite outcropping that would give us better cover. But it meant crossing open ground under fire, and if I was wrong about her injuries, if she couldn't run...

"Can you run?" I asked, not taking my eyes off the killers' positions. I could see at least four muzzle flashes, maybe more. Too many for us to fight from this position.

"I can run." She pulled her pistol from beneath her coat, checking the cylinder with practiced efficiency. "And I can shoot."

"On my signal, we run together. You lay down covering fire while we move. Stay low, and if I fall, you keep running. Don't look back."

"I'm not leaving you."

The steel in her voice reminded me why I'd fallen for her in the first place. This wasn't some fragile flower who needed protecting. This was a woman with the courage to ride alone through the night to warn us of danger, the strength to face down killers without flinching.

"Together then," I breathed, checking my remaining ammunition. Two shots left. Not enough, but it would have to do. "On three. One... two..."

"Now!" I roared, hauling her to her feet and propelling her toward the boulder.

We ran through the gauntlet together, Lilian's pistol barking as she sent shots toward the muzzle flashes, forcing the attackers to duck for cover. Bullets snapped past us like angry hornets, the sharp crack of rifles mixing with the deeper boom of pistols and the reports from Lilian's gun. The smell of cordite filled my nostrils as rock chips exploded from the boulder beside my head, stinging my cheek. I felt another bullet tug at my sleeve, heard Lilian gasp as stone fragments peppered her face, but we reached the cover intact. I slammed her against the boulder and pressed my back to the stone, my breath coming in ragged gasps that misted in the cool night air.

The gunfire was tapering off now as Grady worked his way closer to the ambushers' position. I heard shouts in the darkness, the sound of horses being mounted in haste. Boot heels scraped against rock as the attackers retreated. The cowards were running now that their easy targets had found cover and started shooting back.

"They're pulling out!" Grady called. "Stay down till

I'm sure they're gone!"

I nodded, though he couldn't see me in the darkness. My legs felt weak as the adrenaline began to fade, and I noticed the warm wetness soaking through my shirt in three different places. The metallic taste of blood filled my mouth, and my vision started to blur around the edges.

"Let me see," she breathed, reaching toward the worst of my wounds with gentle fingers.

"I'm fine," I lied, though black spots were dancing at the edges of my vision.

"You're not fine. You're bleeding from at least three places that I can see." Her fingers probed gently at the bullet graze across my ribs, and I hissed through my teeth at the contact. "This needs attention."

"Your horse," I said, remembering the animal's cries. The keening wails had stopped, which somehow made it worse. "Is she...?"

Lilian's face crumpled, and I had my answer. We made our way carefully back to where her mare lay on the trail, and the sight that greeted us made my chest tighten with familiar dread.

The horse was still alive, but barely. A bullet had shattered her front leg and torn a gash along her flank, and she was making sounds that no living thing should have to make. Pained snorts that came in agonizing gasps beyond endurance. Her dark eyes rolled in terror as she tried futilely to rise, her hooves scrabbling against the rocky ground, leaving dark streaks in the dirt.

"Oh, no," Lilian whispered, tears streaming down her face. "Can you... can you help her?"

I kneeled beside the suffering animal, my veterinarian's training taking over despite the circumstances. My hands moved automatically, checking pulse, breathing, the extent of the damage. One look told me everything I needed to know. The leg was destroyed beyond repair, multiple fractures visible through the torn flesh. Dark blood pooled beneath her, too much blood. Even if I had a fully equipped surgery, even if we could somehow get her to town, there was nothing to be done.

"I'm sorry," I whispered, my throat tight with emotion and professional duty. "She's in too much pain to save."

Lilian understood immediately. She nodded through her tears and stepped back, unable to watch, but knowing it had to be done. Her hands shook as she wrapped her arms around herself.

I drew my Colt with hands that trembled slightly, whether from blood loss or emotion, I couldn't say. This went against everything I'd sworn to uphold as a healer. My job was to save lives, to ease suffering through medicine and skill, not to end it with bullets.

But sometimes mercy required difficult choices. Sometimes love meant letting go.

"Easy, girl," I murmured, placing my free hand on the mare's neck. Her coat was slick with sweat and blood, but still warm with life. "Easy now. No more pain."

The shot echoed through the night like a benediction, and the suffering ended.

I stood slowly, holstering my gun with movements that felt ancient and weary. Three years of veterinary training, countless hours learning to heal and preserve life, and it all came down to this. Putting a bullet in a dying horse while the woman I loved wept in the darkness.

"Deacon." Lilian's voice was soft, understanding. "You did the right thing."

"Doesn't make it easier," I said, my voice rougher than I intended. I rubbed my index finger and thumb over my damp eyes.

She stepped closer, close enough that I could smell the lavender in her hair despite the smoke and blood that hung heavy in the air. "That's what makes you a good man. The fact that it's not easy."

I looked down at her in the starlight, this remarkable woman who'd risked everything to warn us, who'd faced down killers without flinching, who could see mercy in what felt like murder. My heart, already racing from the gunfight, began to pound for entirely different reasons.

"We need to get you home," I said, though what I really wanted was to pull her into my arms and never let her go.

"What about you? You're hurt."

"I'll live." I whistled for Sergeant, who came trotting over with the patient air of a horse accustomed to his rider's dangerous profession. "Can you ride double?"

"I grew up on a ranch," she said with a ghost of her usual spirit. "I can ride however I need to."

I swung carefully into the saddle, biting back a groan as the movement pulled at my wounds. The leather creaked under my weight, and I had to grip the saddle horn as dizziness washed over me. Then I reached down and helped her up behind me, her arms circling my waist as she settled against my back.

The contact sent electricity through my entire body despite the pain and exhaustion. I could feel her warmth through my shirt, feel her breath against my neck as she pressed close for balance. Every step Sergeant took sent new waves of sensation through me. Her hands were flat against my abdomen, her body moving in rhythm with mine, the trust implicit in the way she held on.

"You saved my life," she whispered as we rode through the darkness toward town, her voice barely audible over the rhythmic clip-clop of Sergeant's hooves on the rocky trail.

"You saved mine first," I replied, my voice steadier than I felt. "Coming to warn us took courage."

"I was terrified," she admitted, her arms tightening around me. "When I saw that man in black, when he talked about meeting you... I knew something terrible was going to happen. But Shane taught me to ride and shoot, told me that sometimes you have to take risks to protect the people you love."

"Why?" I asked, though I thought I knew the answer. "Why risk yourself for us?"

She was quiet for so long that I thought she wouldn't answer. When she finally spoke, her words were barely audible over the sound of hoofbeats and the whisper of wind through the pines.

"Because I care about you, Deacon. More than I probably should."

My heart stopped beating for the second time that night, but this time it wasn't from fear. This time it was from hope, from possibility, from the realization that the feelings growing in my chest might not be one-sided after all.

"Lilian," I said, and her name sounded different in my mouth now. Not just friendly, but intimate. Precious. "I care about you, too."

Her arms tightened around me, and I felt her smile against my shoulder blade. The simple gesture sent warmth spreading through my chest despite the cold night air and the pain from my wounds. We rode the rest of the way in comfortable silence, both of us processing what had just been said and what it might mean for our future.

By the time we reached the outskirts of Prescott, I was lightheaded from blood loss and dizzy from emotions I was only beginning to understand. Ahead, the town lights resembled fallen stars, yet I was only aware of the woman holding me.

The gunfight had changed everything. Not just because we'd survived, but because it had stripped away all pretense, all careful politeness, all the barriers that had kept us from acknowledging what was growing between us.

Whatever came next—whether it was hunting down the men who'd tried to kill us or building something real together—we'd face it as more than just colleagues. We'd face it as two people who'd found something worth fighting for in each other.

That was worth getting shot for any day of the week.

8 - Sweet Medicine

Grady

THE WARM GLOW of lamplight spilling from the Harper house windows felt like a beacon of safety after the chaos we'd just survived. My face stung where rock fragments had peppered my cheek during the gunfight, and my right arm throbbed from a bullet graze that had torn through my shirt sleeve. The bitter taste of fear still lingered in my mouth, mixing with the dust we'd kicked up during our desperate ride to town. But physical pain was nothing compared to the churning in my gut as I watched Deacon help Lilian down from his horse.

He moved carefully, favoring his right side where blood had soaked through his shirt, but his hands were gentle as he steadied her on her feet. The way she looked at him, with gratitude and something deeper, made my chest tighten. After years of watching my best friend care for everyone else, it was good to see someone caring for him in return.

"Justine! Hayley!" Lilian called as we approached the front porch, her voice carrying both relief and urgency. "I need help!"

The door burst open before we reached the steps,

and two women rushed out. The scent of herbs and cooking food drifted from the house behind them, mixing with the cool night air. The younger one, Hayley I assumed, looked to be about seventeen, with honey-blond hair and worried golden eyes that quickly assessed our battered condition.

But it was the other woman who stopped me dead in my tracks.

She was maybe nineteen, with honey-colored hair braided down her back and natural beauty that made a man forget his own name. But it wasn't just her looks that hit me like a sledgehammer to the chest. It was everything about her. The way she moved with quiet confidence, the concern that immediately filled her warm brown eyes when she saw our injuries, the gentle authority in her voice as she took charge of the situation.

"Bring them inside," she breathed, stepping back to hold the door wide. Her voice was soft but clear, carrying the calm competence that came from experience with emergencies. "Hayley, put water on to boil. Lilian, where's your medical kit?"

I stood there like a fool, staring at this angel who'd appeared out of nowhere, until Deacon's grunt of pain snapped me back to reality. I moved to his other side, helping support his weight as we climbed the porch steps. The wooden boards creaked under our combined weight, and I could smell the lingering aroma of wood smoke from their fireplace.

"I'm Justine," the brown-eyed woman said to me as we entered the small house. "Lilian's sister."

"Grady," I managed, though my voice came out rougher than intended. "Grady Thatcher."

Her smile was like sunshine breaking through storm clouds. "I know who you are. Lilian has mentioned you."

The way she said it, with a slight blush coloring her cheeks, made my heart race faster than it had during the gunfight. Had Lilian said good things? Bad things? Did it matter, as long as this remarkable woman knew my name?

The interior of the Harper house was cramped, but spotlessly clean and filled with homey touches that showed women who cared about making a house into a home. Dried herbs hung from the kitchen rafters, filling the air with the scent of lavender and sage. A quilt that had clearly been hand-stitched with love covered the back of the worn sofa. The lamplight cast warm shadows on the scrubbed wooden floors, and everything spoke of careful tending despite limited means.

"Set him here," Justine instructed, motioning to a chair at the small kitchen table. The space was barely large enough for four people, but somehow we all fit without bumping into each other.

I helped ease Deacon into the chair, noting how his face had gone pale beneath the tan. Blood loss was taking its toll, and the sooner we got him patched up, the better. He caught my eye and gave me the slightest nod—our signal that he was hurting but managing.

"Let me see," Justine murmured, kneeling beside his chair with practiced efficiency.

As she examined Deacon's wounds, I studied her profile in the lamplight. Her skin was smooth as cream, with a light dusting of freckles across her nose that made her look younger and more approachable. When she concentrated, she bit her lower lip in a way that made my mouth go dry. Her hands moved with sure competence, probing gently but thoroughly.

"This one needs stitching," she announced, touching the bullet graze across his side with gentle fingers. "The others we can clean and bandage."

"You know how to stitch wounds?" I asked, impressed despite my growing attraction.

"Life on a ranch," she said simply, though I caught the quick glance she shared with her sisters. "You learn to patch up all sorts of injuries when the nearest doctor is a day's ride away."

That made sense, though something about the easy competence with which all three sisters moved around medical supplies suggested more experience than most ranch women would have. They worked together like a well-oiled machine, Hayley producing clean cloths while Lilian gathered bottles and instruments.

But before I could think too hard about it, Justine was turning her attention to me.

"What about you?" she asked, and her proximity made my pulse stutter. The scent of roses clung to her hair, mixed with soap and clean cotton. "You're bleeding too."

I looked down at my torn sleeve, suddenly aware of the burning sensation along my right forearm where a bullet had creased the skin. Rock fragments had left a constellation of minor cuts across my left cheek, and my knuckles were scraped raw from diving for cover on the rocky trail.

"Nothing serious," I whispered, though the truth was I'd barely noticed my own injuries until she mentioned them.

"Sit," she commanded, pulling another chair close to mine. "Let me clean those cuts before they get infected."

The moment her fingers touched my face, I forgot how to breathe. Her touch was feather light as she dabbed at the cuts with a damp cloth, but each contact sent sparks through my entire body. This close, I could see the long, dark lashes that framed her beautiful eyes. The cloth was warm and soft against my skin, and her breath whispered across my cheek as she worked.

"This might sting," she warned softly, reaching for a bottle of whiskey.

"I can handle it," I said, though my voice came out huskier than intended.

She smiled at that, a real smile that lit up her entire face. "I'm sure you can. Lilian told us about your work with the Livestock Commission. Dangerous job."

"Someone has to do it." I winced as the alcohol hit

the cuts, the sharp burn making my eyes water, but the pain was worth it for the way she immediately murmured an apology and blew gently on my cheek to ease the burning.

"Sorry," she whispered, and I could see her own breathing had quickened. Her hand trembled slightly as she continued cleaning the wounds, and I realized she was feeling the same charged connection that was making my heart race.

Across the small kitchen, Lilian was tending to Deacon's more serious injuries, with the same gentle competence her sister was showing me. But I barely registered their quiet conversation, too focused on the woman whose careful ministrations were doing more than healing my cuts. They were healing something in my soul I hadn't even realized was wounded.

"There," Justine breathed, sitting back to examine her handiwork. "That should heal nicely."

"Thank you," I said, though the words felt inadequate for what she'd given me. It wasn't just medical care. It was the way she'd stayed by my side, the concern in her eyes that went beyond mere kindness.

"Now let me look at that arm."

She reached for my torn sleeve, her fingers working the fabric away from the bullet graze with infinite care. The wound wasn't deep. The bullet had barely parted the skin. But it stretched from my elbow to my wrist in an angry red line that was already beginning to throb.

"You're lucky," she said, cleaning the graze with the same gentle thoroughness she'd shown my face. The cloth was cool against the heated wound. "Another inch to the left and it would have shattered bone."

"Lucky," I agreed, though I was beginning to think my luck had less to do with dodging bullets and more to do with ending up in this kitchen with this woman tending my wounds.

"What happened out there?" she asked as she

worked, her voice carefully neutral. "Lilian said there were men shooting at you."

I glanced toward where her sister was stitching up Deacon's side with steady movements, noting how both women moved with practiced efficiency that spoke of long experience with gunshot wounds and violent injuries. Most ranch women could handle cuts and broken bones, but this level of skill suggested something more.

"Cattle rustlers," I said carefully. "They didn't appreciate us investigating their outfit."

"Are they the same men who killed your parents?"

The question caught me off guard, both because of its directness and because it meant Lilian had shared my personal history with her family. I looked into Justine's warm brown eyes and saw genuine compassion there, not just curiosity.

"I don't know," I admitted. "Maybe. It's been six years, and there are a lot of pieces that don't fit together yet."

Her hand stilled on my arm, and when I looked up, she was studying my face with an intensity that made my breath catch.

"I'm sorry," she whispered. "I can't imagine losing my parents that way. It must be terrible, carrying that weight for so long."

Something in her voice, in the way she seemed to understand the burden of secrets and pain, made me want to tell her everything. About the nightmares that still woke me in cold sweats. About the guilt that ate at me for hiding while my parents died. About the burning need for justice that had driven every decision I'd made for the past six years.

Instead, I just nodded and let her continue cleaning my wounds.

"It's just the three of us here now," Justine said quietly as she worked, worry flickering in her brown eyes. "Shane stayed back at the ranch with Flynn and Ike, our younger brothers. Someone has to watch over them, and Shane..." She paused, her hands stilling on the bandage she was wrapping. "He's always been the one to stand between us and danger. But Ike is only fourteen, and Flynn's sixteen. They're just boys, and I hate that they're still there while we're safe here."

The pain in her voice hit me harder than any bullet. I knew what it was like to worry about family, to feel responsible for people you couldn't protect. "Fourteen," I repeated softly. "That's just a child."

"Yes." Her voice was barely audible. "Shane taught us to patch up injuries when he was barely more than a boy himself. He said if we were going to survive in our father's world, we needed to be prepared for anything. Now he's still there, trying to protect Flynn and Ike while we get established here."

The weight of family responsibility, the fear of loss—I understood both intimately. "Your brother sounds like a good man."

"He is. He taught us that family protects family, no matter what." She resumed wrapping my arm, her touch gentle but sure. "Our father... He associates with rough men. Men who get into fights, who come home with injuries that needed tending. We learned by necessity."

There was something in her tone, a carefully controlled neutrality, that told me there was more to the story. But before I could pursue it, Lilian was calling for help to move Deacon to the sofa.

"He needs to rest," she explained as we carefully transferred him from the kitchen chair to the more comfortable couch. "Those stitches need time to set, and he's lost more blood than he wants to admit."

Deacon insisted he was fine, but he sagged against the cushions the moment he lay down, exhaustion written in every line of his body. His color somewhat better.

"You both should stay the night," Justine said, glancing between us with concern. "It's not safe to ride in the dark after what happened, and Deacon shouldn't be jostled around on horseback until those wounds have had time to start healing."

"We couldn't impose," I started, though the thought of spending more time in this warm, welcoming house, with this remarkable woman, was more appealing than I wanted to admit.

"It's not an imposition," Lilian said firmly. "It's practical. You can take the parlor. There are extra blankets in the chest."

The next few hours passed in a haze of quiet conversation and domestic comfort. I'd known family care before, but this felt different. Charged with feelings I was only beginning to understand. Justine produced a tin of cookies that she claimed were nothing special but tasted like heaven to a man accustomed to his own questionable cooking. Hayley made coffee that was strong enough to wake the dead, the rich aroma filling the small house.

As the evening wore on and Deacon dozed on the sofa, I found myself drawn into easy conversation with all three sisters. They were intelligent, funny, and refreshingly direct in a way that spoke of women who'd learned to rely on themselves. But it was Justine who held my attention, Justine whose laugh made my chest warm, Justine whose quick wit and gentle humor were weaving themselves around my heart with alarming speed.

"Do you miss it?" she asked during a lull in the conversation. "Ranch life, I mean. Lilian said you grew up on a farm."

"Sometimes," I admitted. "There's something to be said for working with your hands, for seeing the direct results of your labor. But the work I'm doing now... It feels important. Like maybe I can prevent other families from going through what mine did."

She nodded thoughtfully, her fingers tracing the rim of her coffee cup. "Justice is important. But so is healing. So is building something new instead of just tearing down what's broken."

Her words hit me like a physical blow, not because they were harsh, but because they were true. For years, I'd been focused on finding my parents' killers, bringing down their organization, making them pay for what they'd stolen from me. But when was the last time I'd thought about building something? About creating a life worth living instead of just surviving until I could claim my revenge?

"You're right," I breathed. "I've been so focused on the past that I've forgotten about the future."

"The future's not going anywhere," she said with a smile that made my heart skip. "It'll wait for you to catch up."

As the evening grew later and the conversation turned to lighter topics, I studied Justine with the same intensity I usually reserved for tracking cattle thieves. Every gesture, every expression, every laugh seemed to reveal new depths to her character. She was beautiful, yes, but more than that, she was kind without being weak, intelligent without being condescending, strong without losing her femininity.

When Lilian and Hayley finally retired to their rooms, leaving Justine to arrange our makeshift beds in the parlor, I realized I was in serious trouble. This wasn't just attraction or infatuation. This was something deeper, something that threatened to turn my world upside down. In an altogether welcomed way.

"The couch should be comfortable enough for Deacon," she said, shaking out blankets with brisk efficiency. "And I found extra pillows for you."

She handed me a pillow that smelled faintly of lavender, and our fingers brushed in the exchange. The contact sent that familiar jolt through me, and from the way her breath caught, I knew she felt it too.

"Justine," I said, then stopped, not sure how to put into words what was happening to me.

"Yes?" She looked up at me with those warm brown eyes, and I felt like I was drowning in their depths.

"Thank you. For everything. For taking care of us, for welcoming us into your home. For..." I gestured helplessly, unable to articulate the way she'd made me feel human again, made me remember there were things worth living for besides revenge.

"You're welcome," she whispered. "Both of you. I'm just glad we could help."

I should have said goodnight then. Should have let her retire to her room and tried to get some sleep on the hard parlor floor. Instead, I stepped closer, drawn by the gentle warmth in her eyes and the way the lamplight caught the golden highlights in her hair.

"Justine," I said again, my voice dropping to barely above a whisper. "I need you to know... Meeting you tonight, it's changed something for me. Something I didn't even know needed changing."

Her cheeks flushed pink, but she didn't step away. "Grady..."

"I know it's crazy. I know we just met. But I've spent six years feeling dead inside, and you've made me remember what it's like to be alive."

She was quiet for a long moment. Her gaze searched my face, as if looking for something she needed to find. Whatever she saw there must have satisfied her, because she smiled. A genuine smile that lit up her entire being.

"It's not crazy," she whispered. "Or if it is, then I'm crazy, too."

The admission hung in the air between us like a promise, and I felt something tight in my chest finally relax. She felt it too, this connection that had blindsided us both.

"I should let you get some rest," she said, though she made no move to leave.

"Probably," I agreed, though the last thing I wanted was for this moment to end.

She started to turn away, then seemed to think better of it. "Grady? What you said about building something for the future instead of just tearing down the past? Maybe... maybe we could talk about that sometime. When you're not recovering from being shot at."

My heart started beating so fast I was surprised it didn't wake Deacon. "I'd like that. I'd like that very much."

"Good," she said, and there was something almost shy in her smile now. "Goodnight, Grady."

"Goodnight, Justine."

I watched her disappear down the narrow hallway toward the bedrooms, then settled down on my makeshift bed with a grin I couldn't have wiped off my face if someone had paid me. Tomorrow, I'd have to think about the investigation, about the men who'd tried to kill us tonight, about the long road that still lay ahead in bringing my parents' murderers to justice.

But tonight, for the first time in six years, I fell asleep thinking about something other than death and revenge. Tonight, I dreamed about warm brown eyes and gentle hands and the possibility that maybe, just maybe, I could build a life worth living after all.

———

DAWN CAME TOO soon, creeping through the parlor windows with fingers of pale gold that made me reluctant to leave the warmth of my blankets. The house was quiet except for the soft sounds of me stirring. Nearby, Deacon stirred on the couch, wincing as the movement pulled at his stitches.

"How do you feel?"

"Like I got shot three times and spent the night on a couch," he said with a rueful smile. "But alive, which is better than I expected last night."

We gathered our things quietly, folding the blankets and straightening the parlor as best we could. The quilt smelled like lavender and home, and I found myself reluctant to let it go. It felt wrong to leave without thanking our hostesses properly, but we both knew that staying any longer would only fuel gossip about the Harper sisters' reputations.

We were almost to the door when Justine appeared, still in her nightgown with a wrapper pulled hastily around her shoulders. Her hair was loose around her face, flowing like honey in the morning light, and she looked so beautiful that I forgot how to breathe.

"You're leaving without saying goodbye?" she asked, and there was genuine hurt in her voice.

"We didn't want to wake you," I said, my heart racing at the sight of her. "We thought it would be better for your reputation if we were gone before the neighbors started stirring."

"I appreciate the thought," she said with a smile that made my chest warm. "But I would have regretted not seeing you off properly."

She stepped closer, close enough that I could smell the faint scent of roses in her hair and see the sleep-soft vulnerability in her brown eyes. This close, she looked even younger, more fragile, and the protective instincts that had been dormant for so long stirred to life in my chest.

"I'm glad I got to meet you," she whispered. "Even under the circumstances."

The opening was there, clear as daylight. As usual, I charged ahead. "Have dinner with me."

The words came out more like a command than a request, but instead of being offended, she smiled. "I'd like that."

"Good," I said, feeling like I'd just won the lottery. "I'll stop by soon to firm up the plans."

"I'll be here," she promised.

Without thinking about propriety or what Deacon might think, I reached for her hand and lifted it to my lips. Her skin was soft as silk and warm beneath my mouth, and the way her breath caught at the contact sent fire through my veins.

"Until then," I said, pressing a gentle kiss to her knuckles.

Her cheeks flushed pink, but her eyes sparkled with pleasure. "Until then."

As we rode away from the Harper house toward the rising sun, I whistled for the first time in years. The morning air was crisp and clean, filled with the scent of pine and possibility. Behind me, Deacon chuckled softly.

"You've got it bad," he observed.

"What's that supposed to mean?"

"It means you kissed her hand like you were some knight in a fairy tale. It means you're whistling. It means you've been grinning like a fool since we left her porch."

I tried to school my expression into something more serious, but it was no use. The grin kept breaking through like sunshine after a storm.

"Maybe I do have it bad," I admitted. "Is that such a terrible thing?"

"Not terrible at all," Deacon said with a warmth in his voice that made me look over at him. "Just unexpected. Yesterday you were focused on nothing but tracking down your parents' killers. Today you're planning dinner dates."

"Maybe that's not such a bad thing either," I said, thinking about Justine's words about building something for the future instead of just tearing down the past. "Maybe it's time I started living for something other than revenge."

"Your parents would be proud," Deacon said quietly. "They'd want you to find happiness, to build a life worth living. They wouldn't want you to spend forever chasing ghosts."

The words should have stung, but they felt like absolution instead. For six years, I'd carried the weight of survivor's guilt, the belief that I owed it to my parents' memory to dedicate my life to hunting their killers. But maybe the best way to honor them was to embrace the life they'd wanted for me. A life filled with love and purpose and hope for the future.

As we crested the hill overlooking Colter Ranch, I made a silent promise to the woman whose gentle hands had worked their own kind of healing magic on more than just my wounds. Whatever it took, however long it took, I was going to make myself worthy of her.

The hunt for justice would continue, but it would no longer be the only thing driving me forward. Now I had something else to fight for, something to protect and nurture instead of a past to avenge.

I had found my future, and her name was Justine Harper.

9 - Vengeance and Love

Grady

I CHECKED MY reflection in the small mirror above our washbasin for the third time, running my fingers through my sandy hair to make sure it lay flat. The scent of bay rum clung to my freshly shaved cheeks, and I'd polished my boots until they gleamed. My hands were actually trembling, which was ridiculous. I'd faced down rustlers, but the thought of taking Justine Harper to dinner had me nervous as a green colt.

"You look fine," Deacon said from the doorway, amusement clear in his voice. "Better than fine, actually. That's your good shirt."

"Is it too much?" I turned to face him, tugging at the collar of my white dress shirt. The starched cotton felt stiff against my neck, unfamiliar after weeks of work clothes. "I don't want her to think I'm putting on airs."

"Grady, you're taking the woman to dinner, not a barn dance. She'll appreciate the effort."

I nodded, though my stomach was still doing strange things. The anticipation felt worse than waiting for a gunfight. "What if I say something stupid? What if she gets bored? What if—"

"What if you stop overthinking and just go enjoy yourself?" Deacon clapped me on the shoulder, his grip steady and reassuring. "Justine likes you, or she wouldn't have said yes to dinner. Just be yourself."

"That's what worries me," I muttered, straightening my vest for the fourth time. The black wool felt foreign after months of simple work shirts. "What if myself isn't good enough?"

"You're a good man, Grady. An honest man with a steady job and honorable intentions." His expression grew serious, brown eyes reflecting the lamplight. "Any woman would be lucky to have your attention, and Justine Harper is smart enough to see that."

That helped, somewhat. I grabbed my hat from the peg by the door and settled it on my head, checking the angle in the mirror one last time. "Wish me luck."

"You won't need it."

The ride to town seemed to take forever and no time at all. Sunbeam's hooves kept steady rhythm on the packed earth, and the evening air carried the scent of pine and dust. Before I knew it, I was standing on the Harper sisters' front porch, my heart hammering against my ribs like it was trying to escape.

Hayley answered my knock with a knowing grin that made heat creep up my neck. "She's almost ready. Come in."

I stepped into the small parlor, hat in hand, and tried not to fidget. The house smelled wonderful—bread and cinnamon and something else I couldn't identify, maybe vanilla or honey. The familiar scents of home cooking reminded me of my mother's kitchen, bringing a bittersweet pang to my chest.

"Justine, your beau is here!" Hayley called, then winked at me. "She's been fussing over her dress for an hour."

"I have not!" came Justine's voice from the back room, followed by Lilian's knowing laughter.

"Yes, you have," Lilian said, appearing in the doorway with her strawberry hair neatly pinned and a warm smile on her face. "Good evening, Grady. Don't you look handsome."

Heat crept up my neck like a slow burn. "Thank you, Miss Lilian."

"Justine will be right out. She just wanted to—"

"I'm ready," Justine said, stepping into the room, and my breath caught in my throat.

She wore a dress of deep green that made her brown eyes look like warm honey in the lamplight. Her blond hair was pinned up in some complicated style that left little curls framing her face, and tiny pearl earrings caught the light when she moved. But it was her smile that really stopped my heart—soft and shy and just for me.

"You look..." I swallowed hard, searching for words that wouldn't sound foolish. The sight of her hit me like a physical blow, making my chest tight and my thoughts scatter. "Beautiful. You look beautiful."

Pink bloomed in her cheeks like roses in the morning light. "Thank you. You clean up pretty well yourself, Mr. Thatcher."

I offered her my arm, marveling at how natural it felt when she slipped her hand through the crook of my elbow. Her touch sent warmth spreading through my entire body, and I caught a hint of rose water in her hair. "Shall we?"

"Have fun!" Hayley called as we stepped out into the evening air.

"Take care of each other!" added Lilian.

"We will," Justine replied, her hand briefly touching mine.

I'd chosen the hotel restaurant for our dinner—the nicest place in Prescott, though that wasn't saying much. Still, they had white tablecloths and candles, and the food was better than saloon fare. The maître d' led us to a table by the window where we could watch the evening bustle of the town square.

"This is lovely," Justine breathed, her eyes taking in the crystal glasses and silverware with something like wonder. "I've never eaten here before."

"Really?"

"Too expensive on our wages," she said with a laugh that carried no bitterness. "We save our money for practical things like rent and food."

I felt a pang of guilt. I'd been so worried about impressing her I hadn't considered whether she might feel uncomfortable in such a fancy place. "We could go somewhere else," I offered. "Maybe just get some pie at the café?"

"Grady Thatcher, don't you dare." Her eyes sparkled with humor, and she reached across the table to touch my hand. "I've been looking forward to this all week. Besides, a girl likes to feel special sometimes."

The waiter brought us water in crystal glasses and took our order—roast beef for me, chicken for her. When he left, an awkward silence fell between us. I scrambled for something to say that wouldn't sound idiotic.

"How's the work at the dry goods store?" I finally managed.

"It's good. Mr. Patterson is very kind, and I'm learning about the business side of things. Managing inventory, dealing with suppliers." She paused, then added quietly, "It's nice to feel useful. To know I can take care of myself."

Something in her tone made me look at her more closely. The candlelight flickered across her face, highlighting the delicate curve of her cheek. "You sound like you didn't always feel that way."

Her smile faltered slightly. "Growing up on the ranch... Well, Papa didn't believe girls needed to know about business. Or much of anything beyond cooking and cleaning and doing what they were told."

The bitterness in her voice stirred something protective in my chest. "Your father sounds like a fool."

"Grady!" But she was smiling again. "You shouldn't say such things."

"Why not, if they're true?" I leaned forward, suddenly serious. "You're one of the smartest people I know, Justine. Anyone who can't see that isn't worth your consideration."

She looked down at her hands, but I caught the pleased flush in her cheeks. "You really think I'm smart?"

"I think you're brilliant. And brave. And kind." The words came easier now, because they were true. "I think any man would be lucky to have your attention."

"Even a Livestock Inspector who goes around getting himself beaten up by outlaws?"

I winced at the memory. "Especially him. Though he promises to be more careful in the future."

Our food arrived then, and the conversation turned to lighter topics. She told me about her sisters, about the books she liked to read, about her dreams of maybe opening her own shop someday. Her voice was musical when she got excited about something, and I studied the way her eyes lit up when she talked about the future.

I talked about things I'd never shared with anyone— my memories of my parents, my hopes for the future, my fears about whether justice would ever really be served.

"Six years is a long time to carry such pain," she whispered when I finished telling her about that terrible day. Her hand found mine across the table, warm and soft. "I can't imagine how you've borne it."

"Some days are better than others," I admitted. "But having Deacon, having the Colter family... They helped me remember that there's still good in the world. And lately..." I turned my hand palm up and intertwined our fingers. "Lately you've been helping me remember that, too."

Her fingers curled around mine, warm and strong. "I'm glad. You deserve happiness, Grady. You deserve peace."

"So do you." I brought her hand to my lips and pressed a gentle kiss to her knuckles, breathing in the faint scent of rose water on her skin. "What you went through with your father, with his associates... No one should have to endure that."

"It's behind me now. Behind all of us." Her voice grew stronger, more determined. "Shane's making sure of that, keeping Flynn and Ike safe while we get established here. We're building something new, something better."

"We are," I agreed, and realized I meant it. For the first time in years, I was thinking about a future that held more than just revenge. A future that might include the woman sitting across from me, looking at me like I was something precious.

After dinner, we strolled back toward her house, neither of us eager for the evening to end. The spring air was cool but not cold, and stars were appearing in the darkening sky. The scent of night-blooming jasmine drifted from someone's garden, mixing with the dusty smell of the street.

"Thank you for tonight," Justine said as we paused on her front porch. The porch light cast golden shadows across her face. "It was perfect."

"Even though I was nervous as a cat in a room full of rocking chairs?"

She laughed, that musical sound that never failed to make my heart skip. "Especially because of that. It's nice to know I'm not the only one who gets nervous."

"You were nervous?"

"Terrified," she admitted, her cheeks pink in the lamplight. "I kept worrying you'd realize you could do much better than a rancher's daughter who works in a shop."

I cupped her face in my hands, marveling at the softness of her skin beneath my palms. "Justine Harper, there is no one better than you. Not in this territory, not anywhere."

Her eyes fluttered closed as I leaned down, and when our lips met, it was everything I'd dreamed it would be. Soft and sweet and full of promise. She kissed me back with a tenderness that made my chest ache, her hands fisting in my shirt to pull me closer.

When we finally broke apart, we were both breathing hard.

"I should go," I whispered, though everything in me wanted to stay.

"I know." But she didn't step away, and neither did I.

"Justine... I have to leave town tomorrow. With Deacon. Commission business."

Her face fell slightly, disappointment flickering in her brown eyes. "How long?"

"I don't know. A few days, maybe a week." I brushed a strand of hair from her face, the silky texture sliding between my fingers. "I wish I didn't have to go."

"But you do. I understand." She managed a smile. "Just... be careful. Come back to me in one piece."

"I promise." I kissed her again, quick and fierce, trying to memorize the taste of her. "Wait for me?"

"As long as it takes."

I forced myself to step back, to tip my hat and say goodnight like a proper gentleman. But as I walked back to where I'd tied Sunbeam, I could feel her watching me from the porch, and it took every ounce of willpower I had not to turn around and run back to her.

The ride home passed in a blur of contentment and anticipation. Whatever dangers waited for us in Chino Valley, I now had something worth coming back for. Someone worth staying alive for.

For the first time since my parents' death, I had hope for a future that held more than just justice.

I had hope for love.

———

THE MORNING AIR was crisp as Deacon and I rode

the familiar trail toward Chino Valley, our horses' breath creating small clouds in the cool air. The scent of morning dew filled my nostrils. My stomach churned with a mixture of anticipation and dread that had been building since we'd decided to make this trip. After six years of dead ends and cold leads, we finally had solid evidence that my parents' killers were part of something bigger than random violence.

"You sure you're ready for this?" Deacon asked, his voice gentle with concern.

I adjusted my grip on Sunbeam's reins, feeling the familiar weight of responsibility settling on my shoulders. The leather was smooth and worn from years of use, comforting in its familiarity. "Been ready for six years. Just never had anywhere to look before."

The truth was more complicated than that. Yesterday's dinner with Justine had opened my eyes to possibilities I'd never dared imagine. For the first time since my parents' death, I could envision a future hopeful future. She'd talked about building something new, and her words had lodged themselves in my heart like seeds waiting to sprout.

But before I could build that future, I owed it to my parents to finish what those killers had started. They deserved justice, and I was the only one left who could give it to them.

"What if we find nothing new?" Deacon asked as we crested the hill overlooking the valley where I'd been born.

"Then we keep looking." I paused, watching the familiar landscape spread out below us. The rolling hills and scattered farmhouses looked smaller than I remembered, less imposing. "But I have a feeling this trip is going to change everything."

The sheriff's office in Chino Valley was smaller than I remembered. A narrow building squeezed between the bank and the general store. A young man who couldn't have been much older than me sat behind the desk, his badge still shiny enough to catch the morning light streaming through the windows.

"Help you gentlemen?" he asked, looking up from a stack of paperwork. Ink stained his fingers, and he had the pale complexion of a man who spent more time with books than outdoors.

"I'm Grady Thatcher," I said, removing my hat. "My parents were Lee and Amy Thatcher. They were murdered six years ago."

Recognition flickered across his face. "Right, the farming family. Rustlers, wasn't it? I'm Sheriff Dickerson. That case was before my time, but I know former Sheriff Rawlings handled it."

My heart sank. Another dead end, another official who knew nothing about the most important event of my life.

"Do you still have the files?" Deacon asked, his voice carefully neutral.

"Of course. File cabinet's right there if you want to look." Dickerson stood and walked to a battered wooden cabinet. "Not much in there, though. Just the basic incident report and witness statements."

He handed me a thin manila folder that felt impossibly light for something that contained my entire world. The paper was yellowed at the edges, and the ink had faded to brown. I opened it with hands that trembled slightly, revealing the same sparse documentation I'd seen years ago. But now I had the knowledge and experience to read between the lines.

"The witness descriptions," I said, studying the faded ink. "They mention four men. One in all black, two younger men who looked like brothers, and an older man with silver hair and ivory-handled guns."

"That's what it says," Dickerson agreed. "You think you know who they were?"

"We're investigating a rustling operation that matches the description," Deacon said carefully. "The Mason

Gang. Ever heard of them?"

Dickerson shook his head. "Can't say I have. But like I said, that was before my time. You might want to talk to Rawlings. He's retired now, lives about five miles north of town. Might remember more than what made it into the official report."

Twenty minutes later, we were riding up to a modest farmhouse where smoke curled lazily from a stone chimney. The smell of bacon and coffee drifted in the morning air, making my stomach rumble despite my nervousness. Former Sheriff Rawlings turned out to be a weathered man in his sixties with tired eyes and work-worn hands that spoke of a life spent dealing with other people's troubles.

"Grady Thatcher," he said, recognition immediate as he shook my hand. His grip was firm but gentle, and his eyes held genuine warmth. "Boy, you've grown up. Come in, come in. Coffee's fresh."

His kitchen was warm and welcoming, filled with the smell of bacon. Sunlight streamed through gingham curtains as he poured coffee into chipped ceramic mugs. I studied his face for any sign of the answers I'd been seeking.

"I always wondered if you'd come back," Rawlings said, settling into a chair across from us. "That case... It haunted me for years. Still does, if I'm being honest."

"Tell us what you remember," I said, leaning forward. "Everything, even if it didn't make it into the official report."

Rawlings sighed, his weathered fingers wrapped around his coffee mug. Steam rose from the dark liquid. "Truth is, I didn't do right by your parents. Had too much territory to cover, too many cases, not enough help. By the time I could really dig into what happened, the trail was cold."

"But you remember details about the killers?"

"Some. The witnesses were pretty shaken up, but they were consistent about what they saw." He paused, his eyes growing distant. "Four men, like the report says. But here's what I remember that didn't make it onto paper. The man in black, he wasn't the leader."

My pulse quickened. "What do you mean?"

"According to Mrs. Henderson, she watched the whole thing from her attic window. Said the man in black did the actual shooting, but he was taking orders from the older fellow with the fancy guns."

"The one with ivory handles?"

"That's right. She said he stayed back, giving directions like he was the boss. Well-dressed, she said. Not like the others. Had the bearing of a man used to being obeyed."

I exchanged glances with Deacon. This matched what we'd learned about the rustling operation, how it was too organized and well-funded to be the work of common outlaws.

"Did she say anything else about him?" Deacon asked.

"Said he talked about having a big spread somewhere south. Mentioned his children a few times, like he was proud of having a large family." Rawlings's expression darkened. "Mrs. Henderson got the impression he thought killing your parents was just business. No anger, no passion. Just something that needed doing."

The coffee turned bitter in my mouth. My parents had died not in a moment of rage or desperation, but as part of some cold calculation by a man who probably went home and had dinner with his children afterward.

"What about the other two?" I asked, fighting to keep my voice steady.

"Mrs. Henderson was pretty sure one of them was a Mason. Caleb Mason, she thought. Recognized him from town. Had that scar across his face even then."

The name hit me like a physical blow. Caleb Mason. The same man who'd beaten me senseless outside the Palace Saloon, who'd been recruiting for the rustling operation. He'd been there the night my parents died, had probably watched while the man in black put bullets in them.

"The fourth man?"

"Younger fellow, looked like he might be related to the Masons. Could have been another brother, or maybe a cousin." Rawlings shook his head. "I'm sorry I can't give you more. I should have done better by your family."

"You did what you could," I said, though the words felt hollow. Six years of wondering, six years of nightmares, and it came down to this simple truth: my parents had been killed by a gang of outlaws led by a man who was still out there somewhere, probably still destroying families.

We talked for another hour, Rawlings sharing every detail he could remember about the investigation and the witnesses. We left his farm midday; the sun blazing overhead, and my mind reeling from so much new information.

"You alright?" Deacon asked as we rode back toward the main road.

"Getting there," I said, though my hands shook slightly on the reins. "I've been hunting shadows. Now I know there's a real man behind all this. Someone with a name, a face, a family."

"We'll find him."

"I know we will." I paused, feeling the weight of what we'd learned settling into my bones. "But first, I need to make a stop."

The cemetery sat on a hill overlooking the valley, its weathered headstones standing like silent sentinels against the sky. The wrought-iron gate creaked as we opened it, and the scent of wildflowers mixed with the dusty smell of old stone. I'd only been here once since the funeral, and approaching my parents' graves felt like walking through quicksand.

"You want me to wait here?" Deacon asked as we dismounted.

"If you don't mind."

The graves were easy to find, two matching head-stones under an oak tree that had grown taller in the years since I'd last stood here. Someone, probably Mrs. Henderson, had been caring for them. The grass was neat, the stones clean, and fresh wildflowers lay at the base of each marker.

Lee Thatcher - Beloved Husband and Father

Amy Thatcher - Beloved Wife and Mother

I kneeled between the graves, pulling my hat off as the afternoon breeze stirred the oak leaves above me. The sound was peaceful, like gentle voices whispering secrets. For a moment, I just listened to the sound of wind and birdsong, trying to find the words for what I needed to say.

"Ma, Pa," I whispered finally. "I'm sorry it's taken me so long to come back. Sorry it's taken so long to find the truth."

The silence stretched around me, peaceful in a way I hadn't felt in years. Here, surrounded by the evidence of lives lived and lost, the burning anger that had driven me for six years seemed to quiet.

"I know who killed you now. Well, some of them anyway. There's still work to do, still justice to claim. But I wanted you to know... I wanted you to know I'm not just living for revenge anymore."

I thought about Justine's smile, about the way she'd made me remember what it felt like to hope for something beyond vengeance.

"I met someone, Ma. A woman who sees something in me worth caring about. Pa, you'd like her. She's got your practical sense and Ma's kind heart. Makes me want to be the man you raised me to be, not just the hunter I became."

A tear rolled down my cheek, and I didn't bother to wipe it away. "I'm still going to find them. The man with the ivory guns, Caleb Mason, all of them. They're going to pay for what they did to you. But when it's over, when justice is done, I'm going to build something good. Something you'd be proud of."

The wind picked up, rustling the leaves overhead in what sounded almost like a whisper of approval. I stayed there for a few more minutes, letting the peace of the place wash over me, before finally standing and settling my hat back on my head.

"I love you both," I breathed. "And I won't let you down."

Deacon was waiting by the horses, his expression carefully neutral. He didn't ask what I'd said or how I felt, just squeezed my shoulder as we mounted up and headed back toward the main road.

We'd ridden about halfway back to Prescott when I noticed the dust cloud on the horizon.

"Riders," I said, pointing toward the distant plume. "Moving fast, driving cattle."

Deacon pulled out his field glasses and studied the distant figures. "Looks like our friends the rustlers. Four men, maybe thirty head of cattle."

My blood heated, the familiar fire of the hunt stirring in my chest. "Think it's them? The Mason Gang?"

"Could be. Distance is too far to tell for sure, but the timing's right. They'd want to move stolen stock during daylight when they can see any pursuit coming."

I reached for my gun without thinking about it. After everything we'd learned today, the thought of the Mason Gang operating so brazenly in the same area where my parents had died felt like a personal insult.

"We need to follow them," I said. "See where they're taking those cattle."

"Agreed. But we also need backup. If that's really the Mason Gang, we're outnumbered and outgunned."

I studied the dust cloud, my mind racing through our options. The cattle were moving toward rough country, where it would be easy to lose them if we didn't act swiftly.

But Deacon was right about the odds.

"You follow them," I decided. "Stay at a distance, see where they hole up. I'll ride hard for Prescott, bring back Perry and the sheriff."

"Grady, I don't like the idea of splitting up. After what happened to you at the saloon—"

"This is our chance," I interrupted. "First solid lead we've had on their operation. If we let them disappear, we might never get another shot at them."

Deacon was quiet for a moment, his brown eyes thoughtful as he weighed the risks. Finally, he nodded.

"Alright. But you stay safe getting to town, and don't come back without enough men to handle whatever we find."

"Same goes for you. Don't be a hero. Just follow and observe."

We shook hands—the gesture carrying added weight. Then Deacon spurred his horse toward the distant dust cloud while I turned Sunbeam toward Prescott and rode like the devil himself was chasing me.

Behind me, my best friend disappeared into the wilderness, hunting the same men who'd murdered my parents. Ahead of me lay the promise of justice, finally within reach after so many years of searching.

And somewhere in between, in the space where past pain met future hope, I carried the memory of Justine's smile.

The hunt was finally coming to an end. One way or another.

10 - Left for Dead

Deacon

THE DUST CLOUD hung in the air like a promise of violence, growing larger as I pushed Sergeant harder across the broken terrain. Four riders driving stolen cattle through country that the Almighty himself seemed to have forgotten—all jagged rocks, thorny scrub, and arroyos deep enough to swallow a man whole.

My jaw clenched as I thought about the man with the ivory-handled guns that Rawlings had described. The man who'd ordered my best friend's parents murdered while he sat back like some king giving orders to his killers. Today, maybe we'd finally get close enough to start making him pay.

I reined Sergeant to a halt behind a cluster of boulders and pulled out my field glasses, sweeping them across the valley floor ahead. The late afternoon sun beat down mercilessly, already dropping toward the western mountains, but still hot enough to shimmer off the rocks. There—maybe two miles distant—I could make out the riders more clearly now. Four men, just like Rawlings had said. Just like the night they'd killed Lee and Amy Thatcher.

The cattle were moving at a steady pace toward a series of deep washes that cut through the landscape like scars. Smart place to take stolen stock. A hundred hiding spots, easy to defend, hard to assault. If they made it into that maze of rock and sand, we might never root them out.

I had to get closer.

Sergeant picked his way carefully down the rocky slope, his hooves finding purchase on stone that would have sent a lesser horse tumbling into the abyss. We'd been together for eight years, and he knew this work as well as I did. Patient. Methodical. Deadly serious. The familiar creak of leather and jingle of his bit provided a steady rhythm as we descended.

The afternoon heat was brutal, sweat soaking through my shirt despite it being spring. This was hard country, the terrain that killed careless men and buried their bones under shifting sand. But it was also the terrain where a man could disappear completely if he knew what he was doing.

And I knew exactly what I was doing.

I followed at a distance for over an hour, using every piece of cover the landscape offered. Rock formations that rose like ancient cathedrals. Dry creek beds were deep enough to hide a mounted man. Stands of juniper and oak that clung to life in this forsaken place with stubborn determination. The air smelled of dust and sage, with an underlying scent of minerals baked into the stone by countless years of desert sun.

The rustlers were good, I'd give them that. They moved with the confidence of men who knew this territory, who'd used these trails before. But they weren't looking back. Why would they? Who was crazy enough to track four armed killers through this rough terrain alone?

Apparently, I was.

As the sun began its descent toward the western mountains, painting the sky the color of fresh blood, the rustlers drove their stolen herd into a box canyon that dead-ended against a wall of red stone. Perfect. They'd trapped themselves, and all I had to do was mark the location and wait for Grady to return with help.

I dismounted and led Sergeant into a dry wash about a quarter mile from the canyon mouth, close enough to keep watch but far enough away to avoid detection. The arroyo was maybe eight feet deep, carved by flash floods that hadn't visited this country in years. The sandy bottom was soft under my boots, and the walls provided excellent cover from observation.

I hobbled Sergeant and loosened his saddle to let him breathe easier, then climbed carefully to the rim of the wash and stretched out on my belly behind a screen of sagebrush. Through my field glasses, I could see smoke rising from the canyon—they were making camp, probably figuring they were safe for the night.

Fools.

I settled in to wait, my Winchester beside me and my Colt loose in its holster. All I had to do was be patient. Grady would be back by morning with Perry Quinn, the sheriff, and enough men to bottle up this canyon like a cork in a whiskey jug. Then we'd see how tough these killers were when they faced someone ready to fight back.

The sun disappeared behind the mountains, and the desert began its nightly transformation from furnace to icebox. The temperature could drop forty degrees after dark in this country. I'd need to conserve body heat to avoid hypothermia. I pulled my coat tighter and kept watching, noting every detail I could make out in the fading light. Four men, confirmed. Approximately thirty head of cattle bearing brands I couldn't quite make out from this distance. Horses picketed near what looked like a natural spring.

This was it. The break we'd been waiting for.

I must have dozed, because the next thing I knew, something was pressing cold steel against the back of my neck.

"Well, well. If it ain't Deacon Colter, playing tracker."

The voice was like broken glass dragged across sandstone, and I recognized it immediately. Caleb Mason. The scar-faced man who'd beaten Grady senseless, who'd been there the night my best friend's parents died.

"Hands where I can see them, nice and slow."

I raised my hands, my mind racing through options. My Winchester was inches away, but I'd be dead before I could reach it. The Colt on my hip might as well have been on the moon. The click of his gun hammer being pulled back filled the night air.

"That's better. Now roll over, real gentle-like."

I did as he said, coming face to face with the man who'd haunted Grady's nightmares. The scar across his left cheek was even more pronounced in person, a twisted line of white tissue that pulled his mouth into a permanent sneer. His pale blue eyes held emptiness that comes from doing terrible things without feeling remorse.

"You know, Colter, you've been a real pain in the hindquarters. You and that friend of yours, stirring up trouble with your Livestock Inspector badges." He spat in the dirt beside my head. "Boss doesn't much like people poking around in his business."

"Your boss the man with the ivory guns?" I asked, figuring I had nothing to lose by pushing for information.

Caleb's sneer widened. "Smart man. Too smart for his own good, seems like."

Movement caught my eye, and I saw two more men sliding down into the wash. One was built like a bull, with arms the size of tree trunks and a face that looked like it had been rearranged with a sledgehammer. The other was younger, maybe early twenties, with the same sharp features as Caleb.

"My brother Bart," Caleb said, noticing my gaze. "And that's Snake Morrison. Snake, say hello to the man who's been causing us all this trouble."

Snake's fist crashed into my jaw with the force of a freight train, snapping my head back against the rocky ground hard enough to make stars explode behind my eyes. The taste of blood filled my mouth immediately, copper and salt mixing with grit from the sandy wash bottom. Before I could recover, Bart was hauling me to my feet while Snake drove his boot into my ribs.

The impact drove the air from my lungs in a whoosh, and I felt something crack in my chest—probably a rib. The pain was immediate and sharp, making each breath feel like swallowing glass.

"That's for getting in our business," Snake snarled, punctuating his words with another kick that sent fresh waves of agony through my torso.

With practiced efficiency, they relentlessly assaulted me. Fists and boots, targeting places that would hurt without killing. My ribs, my gut, my face. Each blow accompanied by curses and threats, by promises of what they'd do to me and everyone I cared about.

Despite my efforts to resist, the three experienced outlaws easily overpowered me. Every time I landed a punch, two more came back at me. My vision blurred, my legs went wobbly, and blood filled my mouth with the taste of copper pennies.

"Enough," Caleb finally breathed, hard from exertion. "Don't want to kill him too quick. Boss wants him to understand what happens to people who don't mind their own business."

They let me fall to my knees in the sandy bottom of the wash, my whole body screaming in agony. I could feel my left eye swelling shut, and something warm was trickling down my face—blood from a gash somewhere on my scalp. But it was what happened next that really drove the knife into my heart.

"Take his horse," Caleb ordered.

"No," I gasped, struggling to get back to my feet. "Leave him alone."

Snake's boot caught me in the chest, driving me back down and sending fresh agony through my damaged ribs.

"Shut up. You don't get a say in this anymore."

I watched in helpless rage as Bart untied Sergeant's hobbles and swung into my saddle. My horse, my companion for eight years, the animal I'd trusted with my life more times than I could count. They were stealing him like he was just another piece of property.

"Easy, boy," Bart said as Sergeant tossed his head nervously, sensing the wrongness of the situation. "You got yourself a new rider now."

"I'll kill you," I managed through swollen lips. "I'll hunt you down and put you in the ground."

Caleb laughed, a sound like nails on a coffin lid. "No, you won't. Know why? Because you ain't gonna live long enough."

He kicked sand into my face, then gestured to the others. "Leave him his gun. Man ought to have a choice about how he dies."

They climbed out of the wash, taking my horse, my rifle, my saddlebags with food and water. Everything I needed to survive in this wasteland. The sound of hoofbeats faded into the night, leaving me alone with my pain and the vast, uncaring desert.

I lay there for a long time, taking inventory of my injuries and trying to work up the strength to move. Cracked ribs, definitely—I could feel the grinding sensation when I breathed deeply. Possible concussion from when my head hit the rocks—my vision was still blurry around the edges, and I felt nauseous. Cuts and bruises too numerous to count. But I was alive, and as long as I was breathing, I had a chance.

The canteen on my gun belt was still there—they'd missed it in the darkness. Maybe two swallows of warm water. Not much, but in this climate, a man could survive maybe three days without water if he was careful. Less if he exerted himself or lost blood. I had to ration every drop.

My Colt was still in its holster, five rounds plus the

one in the chamber. Six bullets between me and whatever this desert might throw at me.

I forced myself to stand, using the wall of the arroyo for support. Every movement sent fresh waves of agony through my battered body, but I gritted my teeth and pushed through it. The Mason Gang thought they'd left me here to die. They were wrong.

Lord, I prayed silently, give me strength to get home. Help me survive this so I can see justice done.

The climb out of the wash nearly finished me. Twenty feet of loose rock and crumbling earth that fought me for every inch. My veterinary training had taught me about shock and blood loss—I was displaying classic symptoms. Weakness, dizziness, rapid pulse. I had to be careful not to push too hard too fast, or I'd collapse before I made it a mile.

By the time I hauled myself over the rim, my hands were raw and bleeding, my shirt was torn to rags, and I was gasping like a landed fish. But I was out.

The desert stretched around me in every direction, silver and black under the star-filled sky. No landmarks I could recognize, no roads or trails to follow. Just endless miles of rock and sand and death waiting for the careless or unlucky.

I pulled out my compass, grateful they hadn't thought to take it. Southeast toward Prescott. The needle pointed steadily in the right direction, but I'd need to sight on a landmark to maintain my bearing in the darkness. I chose a distinctive mesa silhouetted against the stars—it looked to be roughly southeast, and its flat top would be visible even in poor light.

Maybe fifteen miles through some of the most unforgiving country in the territory. In my condition, with no horse and almost no water, it might as well have been fifteen hundred. But I started walking anyway.

The first mile was pure agony. Every step jarred my broken ribs, sent lightning bolts of pain through my skull.

The rocky ground turned my boots into instruments of torture, and more than once, I stumbled and nearly fell. But I kept moving, one foot in front of the other, following my chosen landmark and checking the compass regularly.

Desert survival was about conserving energy and body heat while making steady progress. I set a pace I could maintain—slow but steady. No rushing, no wasted motion. Under Ray's tutelage, I'd learned that injured animals instinctively moved at sustainable speeds. The same principle applied to injured humans.

By the second mile, I'd established a rhythm. Not fast, but steady. I counted steps to measure distance—roughly two thousand steps per mile at my current pace. The rhythm helped focus my mind away from the pain and toward the mechanical process of putting one foot in front of the other.

Every step was fueled by rage, by the memory of Sergeant being led away by men who had no right to touch him. That horse had carried me through more dangerous situations than I could count. He'd trusted me to protect him, and I'd failed.

The third mile brought me to a steep-sided canyon that blocked my path like a stone wall. I could go around, adding maybe an hour to my journey, or I could try to climb down and back up the other side. My body voted for the detour, but my water supply voted for the direct route. Every extra mile meant more dehydration, more energy expended.

I chose the climb.

Going down wasn't too bad, despite the loose rock that tried to send me tumbling into the darkness below. I used basic mountaineering techniques—three points of contact at all times, testing each hold before trusting my weight to it. But coming up the other side was like climbing out of the abyss. Hand over hand, foot by bloody foot, using every crack and ledge I could find.

The key was pacing myself. Climb for thirty seconds, rest for thirty. Keep my breathing controlled to avoid hyperventilation, which would waste precious water through respiration. Twice I slipped and nearly fell, catching myself at the last second with fingertips that screamed in protest.

By the time I reached the top, I was done. Finished. My legs were shaking so badly I couldn't stand, and my vision kept tunneling down to a narrow point of light—classic signs of severe fatigue and shock. I crawled behind a boulder and allowed myself one precious sip of water, letting it trickle down my throat like liquid salvation.

The water was warm and tasted of metal from the canteen, but it was life itself. I swished it around my mouth before swallowing to get maximum benefit from every drop.

Then I forced myself back to my feet and kept walking.

The fourth mile brought coyotes. I heard them before I saw them, their yipping calls echoing off the canyon walls like the laughter of demons. They paced me for a while, staying just at the edge of vision, testing my resolve. Pack hunters, they were evaluating me as potential prey—looking for signs of weakness or injury that would make me an easy target.

One got bold enough to show himself, a lean shadow slinking between the rocks maybe thirty yards away. In the desert, coyotes could be dangerous to an injured, weakened man. They'd wait for me to collapse, then move in for the kill.

I drew my Colt and put a bullet into the ground at his feet, the gunshot cracking across the desert like thunder. The coyotes melted back into the darkness, but I knew they'd be back. They could smell the blood on me, could sense the weakness. If I went down, they'd be on me before I could draw another breath.

I kept the gun in my hand after that and projected strength, even though every step was misery. Predators could sense fear and weakness. I had to convince them I was still dangerous.

My mind latched on to the time-honored verses from Psalm 23, recalling valleys of the shadow of death. Then I asked the Lord not to let it be my time. I'd only just found the perfect woman. Just started dreaming of what could be. With her.

The half-thoughts, half-prayers gave me another burst of energy, so I trudged on.

Mile five brought me to a dry creek bed filled with smooth stones that rolled and shifted under my feet like ball bearings. Treacherous footing that could turn an ankle or send me sprawling. I fell twice, once hard enough to drive the air from my lungs and leave me gasping in the sand. The second time, I stayed down for several minutes, seriously considering whether it might not be easier to just give up.

My mouth was getting sticky now—an early sign of dehydration. My lips were starting to crack, and I could feel my tongue beginning to swell. In this dry air, I was losing moisture with every breath. I needed to be more careful about exertion.

Then I thought about Sergeant, about the way he'd looked at me as Bart rode him away. My horse was counting on me to come for him. Grady was counting on me to bring back information about the gang's hideout. Lilian was counting on me to come home alive.

I got back up.

Miles six and seven blurred together into a haze of pain and exhaustion. I was moving on pure stubbornness now, my body running on empty but my mind fixed on the single goal of putting one foot in front of the other. The stars wheeled overhead, marking my progress in tiny increments that felt like hours.

The temperature was dropping fast now. Desert nights could be brutal—I'd seen it go from ninety degrees at sunset to near freezing by dawn. Without proper shelter or a fire, hypothermia was a real danger. I had to keep moving to maintain body heat, but not so fast that I exhausted myself.

Somewhere around mile eight, I started talking to myself. Not crazy talk, just commentary on my situation to keep my mind focused. "Well, Deacon, this is about as stupid as you've ever been. Following armed killers into the wilderness without backup. What would your mama say?"

My mama would say I was an idiot. She'd also say I was her idiot, and she'd be proud of me for not giving up.

Talking helped combat the psychological effects of isolation and pain. It kept my mind engaged and prevented me from slipping into the despair that killed men in survival situations.

Mile nine brought me to a mesa that rose like a fortress wall against the stars. Going around would add miles I didn't have strength for, but trying to climb it in my condition would probably kill me. I stood at its base for maybe ten minutes, weighing my options, before I noticed the narrow game trail that switchbacked up its face.

Animal trails always led somewhere—usually to water or better grazing. If deer could make this climb, so could I. And the elevation would give me a better view of the surrounding country, help me navigate more effectively.

The ascent took over an hour and used up my last reserves of strength. I climbed in stages, resting frequently to keep my heart rate manageable. My damaged ribs made breathing difficult, and I had to be careful not to hyperventilate. By the time I reached the top, I was crawling on hands and knees, leaving a trail of blood on the rocky ledges.

But the view from the summit made it all worthwhile.

There, maybe five miles to the southeast, I could see the glow of lights from Prescott. Civilization. Safety. Help. The sight gave me a surge of hope that carried me through the next phase of the journey.

I'd made it.

The descent was almost worse than the climb, my legs so weak I had to lower myself from ledge to ledge like a man rappelling down a cliff face. But gravity was my friend now, pulling me inexorably toward home.

Miles ten and eleven passed in a walking dream. I was beyond pain now, beyond exhaustion, running on something deeper than physical strength. Call it determination. Call it stubbornness. Call it the refusal to let evil men win.

My tongue was severely swollen now, and my saliva had become thick and ropy. Classic signs of moderate dehydration. I allowed myself another small sip of water—just enough to wet my mouth and ease the swelling. I had to make the remaining water last until I reached help.

Mile twelve brought me to the old mining road that led to Prescott. Actual wheel ruts in the dirt, the first sign of human presence I'd seen since the wash. I fell to my knees and actually kissed the ground, tasting dust and salt and the promise of salvation.

Then I heard the creak of wagon wheels. *Thank you, Lord.*

An old prospector was making his way down the road, his mule pulling a wagon loaded with supplies and equipment. He looked like he'd stepped out of a storybook—long gray beard, floppy hat, clothes that had seen better decades.

"Whoa there, Bessie," he called to his mule as he caught sight of me. "Mister, you look like you been chewed up and spit out by something mean."

"Water," I croaked, my voice nothing but a whisper.

He was beside me in seconds, pressing a canteen to my lips and letting me drink my fill. The water was warm and tasted like heaven, washing the dust and blood from my throat. I had to force myself to drink slowly—too much, too fast, could cause vomiting, which would waste precious fluids.

"Name's Clancey Smith," he said as I finally stopped

drinking. "What in tarnation happened to you?"

"Rustlers," I managed. "Beat me. Stole horse. Left me for dead."

Clancey's weathered face hardened. "Well, you ain't dead yet, and that's what counts. Can you climb up in the wagon?"

With his help, I managed to crawl into the back of his wagon among the picks and shovels and sacks of supplies. He covered me with a musty blanket that smelled like horses and old sweat, but it was the most comfort I'd felt in hours.

"We'll have you in town before you know it," Clancey promised as he climbed back onto the driver's seat. "Doc Armstrong will fix you right up."

As the wagon lurched into motion, carrying me toward safety, I allowed myself a moment of satisfaction. I'd survived. Against all odds, with God's help and through sheer determination and proper survival technique, I'd made it out of that desert alive.

But the job wasn't finished. Not by a long shot.

The Mason Gang thought they'd broken me, thought they'd scared me off their trail. They were wrong. Dead wrong. And when I got my strength back, when I had men and guns behind me, I was going to show them just how wrong they were.

They'd taken my horse. They'd beaten me half to death. They'd left me in the desert to die.

But I was still breathing. And as long as I drew breath, I was coming for them.

All of them.

The wagon rolled on through the night, carrying me home to see justice done.

11 - Ivory-Handled Betrayal

_____

Grady

THE SUN WAS climbing toward noon when I finally reached Prescott. Sunbeam was lathered with sweat from the hard ride. The acrid smell of dust and horse sweat filled my nostrils as I dismounted, my legs shaking from the pounding pace I'd maintained for the last ten miles. My shirt clung to my back, soaked through with perspiration, and my throat felt like I'd been chewing sand. My heart hammered against my ribs as I tied him to the hitching post outside the livestock inspection office and burst through the door.

"Perry! We found them!" I shouted, then stopped short when I saw only Lilian behind her desk, her blue eyes wide with alarm.

"Grady, what's wrong? Where's Deacon?"

"Following the Mason Gang. We need men, now. Where's Perry?"

"Court hearing in Phoenix. He won't be back until tomorrow." Her face went pale as milk. "Deacon's alone with them?"

My stomach dropped like a stone. Tomorrow would be too late. By then, the gang could disappear into the canyons where we'd never find them again. The taste of failure was already bitter on my tongue.

"The sheriff," I said, already turning toward the door. "He'll have to do."

But Sheriff Wilkes was out serving warrants in the county, and his deputy was a green kid who looked ready to wet himself at the mention of armed rustlers. The mayor was in Flagstaff on business.

Every door I knocked on led to the same result: the men I needed were elsewhere, and the men available weren't enough to face down the Mason Gang. Each rejection felt like another nail in my parents' coffin. Another year added to their killers' freedom.

By the time I returned to the livestock office, the sun was past its peak and moving toward the western mountains. The afternoon heat shimmered off the dusty street, and my boots felt heavy as lead. Lilian looked up from her paperwork with hope in her eyes that died when she saw my expression.

"No luck?" she whispered.

I slumped into the chair across from her desk, feeling the weight of failure settling on my shoulders like a lead blanket. The leather creaked under my weight, and I noticed how my hands trembled slightly as I removed my hat. "Perry's our only proper authority, and he's not due back until tomorrow. By then..."

"They'll be gone."

I nodded, staring at my hands. Years of hunting my parents' killers, and when I finally had them in my sights, I couldn't do anything about it. Worse, I'd left my best friend alone to watch them, exposed. The thought made my chest tighten with guilt.

"He'll be alright," Lilian breathed. "Deacon's smart. He knows how to stay hidden."

But the worry in her voice betrayed her words. I could see it in the way she kept glancing toward the window, in the way her hands trembled slightly as she tried to focus on her work. She cared about him. Really cared about him. The realization should have pleased me—Deacon deserved someone who saw past his rough edges—but right now, it only added to my guilt.

The hours crawled by like wounded animals. I paced the small office until I wore a path in the floorboards, checking my pocket watch every few minutes. The tick of the clock on the wall seemed to mock me with each passing second. Three o'clock became four, then five, then six. The sun began its descent toward the mountains, painting the sky orange and red like spilled blood.

"He should have been back by now," I muttered, more to myself than to Lilian.

"Maybe he's still following them. Maybe he found their hideout and wants to be sure before he leaves."

I wanted to believe that. But Deacon was careful. He'd scout for an hour, maybe two, then fall back to report. He wouldn't stay out this long without sending word unless something had gone wrong. Unless they'd spotted him. Unless—

"I should have stayed with him," I said, the words tasting like ashes in my mouth. "Should not have split up."

"You did what you thought was best. You couldn't have known—"

"I could have known!" The words exploded from me with more force than I intended, and Lilian flinched. "I've been so focused on finding these men that I stopped thinking straight. Deacon's been my friend, my brother, for six years. He's the best man I know, and I left him alone to face down killers because I was impatient for revenge."

Lilian was quiet for a moment, her blue eyes studying my face with compassion that I didn't deserve. "You care about him."

"More than anyone knows." I sank back into my chair, the admission wrung from somewhere deep in my chest. "When my parents died, I was fifteen and angry and lost. The Colters took me in, but it was Deacon who saved me. Not just by giving me a place to sleep, but by seeing something in me worth saving."

The memories came flooding back like water through a broken dam. Those first terrible nights at Colter Ranch, when the nightmares woke me screaming, and I'd find Deacon sitting beside my bed, patient and calm, talking me through the terror until I could breathe again. Never once did he make me feel weak or broken.

"He never made me feel like a charity case or a burden," I continued, my voice rougher than intended. "Just accepted me as family, as a brother. When I decided to become a veterinarian, he encouraged me. When I wanted to take this livestock inspector job to hunt down rustlers, he came with me even though he had a good life at the stockyards."

"That's what family does," Lilian murmured.

"But I'm not really family. I'm just the orphan they took in. My sister married into the Colters. Deacon was born into them. But me... I'm the outsider they were kind enough to include."

"Do you think Deacon sees it that way?"

I considered that, thinking about all the times he'd stood by me, supported me, followed me into dangerous situations without question or complaint. How he'd rearranged his entire life to support my quest for justice. "No. To him, I'm just his brother. Period."

"Then maybe you should stop seeing yourself as anything less."

Her words hit me harder than I expected. For years, I'd carried the weight of being grateful, of feeling like I had to earn my place in the family through achievement and loyalty. But Deacon had never made me feel that way. He'd simply accepted me as I was, rough edges and all.

And now he was out there alone, possibly hurt or captured, because I'd been too focused on my personal vendetta to think clearly about tactics. Because I'd let my hunger for revenge override my duty to him.

The sound of slow hoofbeats and creaking wheels outside made us both look up sharply. I rushed to the window, hope and dread warring in my chest like battling armies. An old prospector's wagon was approaching, pulled by a tired-looking mule, its wheels kicking up small clouds of dust. But it was the figure sitting beside the bearded driver that made my heart stop.

"Oh, no," Lilian breathed from beside me.

The passenger was slumped against the wagon seat, his clothes torn to rags, his face battered and bloody. Even from a distance, even in his beaten condition, I recognized the set of his shoulders, the way he held his head.

Deacon.

I was out the door before Lilian could speak, running toward the wagon as it pulled up to the hitching post. My boots pounded against the hard dirt, and the late afternoon heat hit me like a physical blow. The driver, an old prospector by the look of him, was helping a familiar figure down from the wagon bed.

"Deacon!"

My best friend looked like he'd been dragged behind a wild horse for twenty miles. His shirt was torn to rags, exposing bruised ribs and angry red skin. His face was a map of cuts and bruises, his lips split and swollen, one eye nearly swollen shut. Blood had dried in dark streaks down his neck, and he moved like every step caused him pain. But his brown eyes were alert, focused, alive.

"Sorry I'm late," he said with a weak attempt at his usual humor, his voice hoarse and cracked. "Had some transportation difficulties."

I caught him as his legs buckled, feeling how much weight he'd lost in just one day, how the muscle trembled with exhaustion and pain. His skin was hot to the touch— fever setting in from his injuries. But he was breathing, he was talking, he was here.

"What happened to you?" I asked, though I could

guess from the nature of his wounds.

"Got too close. They found me watching their camp." He winced as I helped him toward the office, each step tentative and careful. "Caleb Mason and two others. Roughed me up pretty good before they figured I wasn't worth the effort to kill."

Lilian met us at the door, her face white with shock at seeing Deacon's condition. Without a word, she guided us to a chair and immediately began examining his injuries with the competent efficiency of someone who'd tended wounded men before. Her hands were gentle but sure as she assessed the damage.

"We need to get you to a doctor," she said, her voice tight with controlled emotion. I could see the way her hands shook slightly as she worked, the worry etched in the lines around her eyes.

"Later," Deacon said, catching her hand with surprising gentleness. "First, Grady needs to know what I learned."

"The doctor can wait ten minutes," I said firmly, though every instinct screamed at me to hear his report. "What did you see?"

As Lilian cleaned his wounds with water and antiseptic from the office supplies, and I listened to his report, the full scope of what we were facing became clear. This wasn't just a rustling operation. It was a criminal enterprise with tentacles reaching across the territory.

"Box canyon about twenty miles northeast of here," Deacon continued, wincing as Lilian dabbed antiseptic on a deep cut across his cheekbone. "Natural spring, good grass, perfect place to hold stolen cattle until they can be moved. Defensible position—only one way in or out."

"How many men?"

"Saw four at the camp. Could be more." His eyes met mine, and I saw the exhaustion there, the pain he was trying to hide for my sake. "They took Sergeant."

The simple statement hit me like a physical blow to

the chest. Sergeant wasn't just Deacon's horse. He was his companion for eight years. That horse had been as much a part of him as his own right arm. Losing him would be like losing a piece of his soul.

"We'll get him back," I said, meaning it with every fiber of my being. "I promise you that."

"They're planning to move the cattle soon," Deacon continued, his voice growing stronger as he focused on the mission. "Heard them talking about a buyer coming from California. Railroad shipment scheduled for next week."

Next week. That gave us time to plan, to gather men, to do this right instead of rushing in half-cocked like I'd wanted to do today. But it also meant the Mason Gang would be on high alert, expecting pursuit. They'd be ready for us.

"There's something else," Deacon said, his voice dropping to barely above a whisper. "The man giving orders to Caleb. He called him 'boss.' Description matches what Rawlings told us about the man with ivory guns."

My blood turned to ice water in my veins. The man who'd ordered my parents' death was out there, twenty miles away, close enough that I could ride to him before midnight if I pushed hard enough. Close enough to touch. Close enough to kill.

"Grady," Lilian's voice cut through my building rage like a knife through fog. "There's something you need to know. Something that might help."

I turned to her, noting the way she was worrying her lower lip between her teeth. She looked nervous, almost guilty, as if she were about to confess to some terrible crime.

"What is it?"

"I received a letter from my brother Shane yesterday. He... He mentioned seeing strangers at our father's ranch. Men who matched the description of the Mason brothers."

The words hung in the air like gunpowder smoke. I felt Deacon stiffen beside me as the implications hit us both simultaneously. The Harper ranch. Near Congress. Where we'd been planning to search for the gang's base of operations.

"Your father's ranch," I said slowly, pieces of a terrible puzzle beginning to fall into place.

She nodded, her blue eyes filled with something that might have been shame. "Shane said they'd been there for weeks. Father was treating them like honored guests, giving them the run of the place."

"Lilian," Deacon said gently, his voice careful despite his obvious pain, "does your father carry guns?"

"Yes." Her voice was barely above a whisper.

"What type?" I asked, though something cold was already settling in my stomach like a lead weight.

"A pair of six-shooters. Colt .45s with ivory handles. He's very proud of them, wears them like they make him important."

The words hit me like a physical blow to the chest. My vision tunneled, the room spinning around me as bile rose in my throat. I gripped the edge of Lilian's desk so hard my knuckles went white, fighting the urge to vomit right there on her clean paperwork.

Galen Harper. The man with ivory guns who'd ordered my parents' murder. The boss of the Mason Gang.

Justine's father.

"No," I whispered, the word torn from somewhere deep in my chest. "No, no, no..."

The beautiful woman whose gentle hands had tended my wounds, whose smile had made me think about building a future, whose brown eyes had shown me what love could look like—she was the daughter of the monster who'd destroyed my world.

"Grady?" Deacon's voice seemed to come from miles away.

I stumbled backward, my legs hitting the chair behind me. The betrayal cut deeper than any physical wound. I'd hunted this man for years, and when I finally found love, finally found hope, it led me straight into the arms of his blood.

How could God let this happen? How could He be so cruel?

I stared at the woman who'd been caring for my best friend's wounds, who'd worried herself sick while he was missing, who'd welcomed us into her life with kindness and trust. And her father was the monster I'd been hunting.

"I'm sorry," Lilian whispered, tears starting to roll down her cheeks. "I should have told you sooner. Should have said something when you first mentioned the ivory guns. But I hoped... I hoped I was wrong."

"How long have you known?" I asked, my voice coming out rougher than intended.

"Suspected since you described the man from Rawlings's report. Knew for certain when Shane's letter mentioned the Mason brothers." She looked up at me with eyes full of pain and regret. "I left my father's ranch because of men like them. Because of what they did to people, to families. To me."

The pieces were falling into place now, creating a picture I didn't want to see. Why she'd been so competent in treating gunshot wounds. Why she'd known to carry a pistol. Why she'd seemed familiar with violence and its aftermath.

"Your brothers," Deacon said quietly, his tactical mind still working despite his injuries. "Shane mentioned them in his letter. Are they..."

"Innocent," Lilian said firmly, her voice gaining strength. "Shane protects them as much as he can, but Father... Father associates with dangerous men. Men who don't respect boundaries."

I thought about my own family, about the Colters who'd taken me in and made me part of something good and decent. Then I thought about children growing up in a house where killers were welcomed as guests, where violence was a way of life.

"We have to get them out of there," I said, the words coming out before I'd fully formed the thought.

"What?" Lilian looked up sharply.

"Your brothers. If Galen Harper is harboring the Mason Gang, if they're using his ranch as a base of operations, then your brothers are in danger. Either from the gang or from the law when we bring them down."

"Shane's twenty-six," she said, worry etching lines around her eyes. "Old enough to make his own choices. But Flynn and Ike..." Her voice trailed off.

"How old are they?"

"Sixteen and fourteen. Still boys, really. Shane tries to protect them, but if something happens, if there's a fight..."

She didn't need to finish the sentence. When we moved against Galen Harper and his gang, anyone at that ranch would be in the line of fire. Including two boys who'd had the misfortune to be born to the wrong father.

"Then we get them out first," I said, my mind already working through the logistics. "Before we make our move against the gang."

"How?" Deacon asked, though I could see in his eyes that he was already thinking along the same lines, even through his pain and exhaustion.

"Shane," Lilian said suddenly, hope creeping into her voice. "If I could get word to Shane, tell him what's coming, he could get the boys away from the ranch before you move against Father."

It was a good plan, but it would require trust. Trust that Shane Harper could be counted on to protect his younger brothers. Trust that he wouldn't warn his father about our approach. Trust that Lilian was telling the truth about her family's innocence.

Looking at her tear-stained face, at the genuine anguish in her blue eyes, I made my choice.

"Write the letter," I said. "We'll find a way to get it to

him."

"Thank you," she whispered, fresh tears spilling down her cheeks. "I know this complicates everything. I know you have every right to hate me for who my father is."

"I don't hate you," I said, and realized I meant it. "You're not responsible for your father's crimes. But I need you to understand something. When we go after Galen Harper, when we bring him to justice for what he did to my parents, I won't show mercy just because he's your father."

She nodded, wiping tears from her cheeks with the back of her hand. "I wouldn't ask you to. What he did to your family, to other families... Justice needs to be served."

"Good." I turned to Deacon, who was looking marginally better now that Lilian had cleaned and bandaged his worst injuries. "How long before you can ride?"

He tried to sit up straighter and immediately winced. "Give me a day to rest up, and I'll be ready for whatever you have in mind."

"You need more than a day," Lilian said firmly, her voice taking on an authoritative tone. "Those ribs might be cracked, and you've lost blood. A week of rest, minimum."

"We don't have a week," I said. "But we can give you three days. That should be enough time to get word to Shane and plan our approach."

"Then we plan," Deacon said, his jaw set with determination despite his obvious pain. "We gather men. We get those boys to safety, and then we end this thing once and for all."

As I looked around the small office—at my battered best friend, at the woman whose father had destroyed my childhood, at the evidence of crimes that stretched across the territory—I felt something shift inside me. This wasn't just about revenge anymore. It was about justice. About protecting the innocent. About making sure no other family suffered what mine had.

But even as I told myself that, I could feel the rage burning in my chest like a banked fire. Galen Harper had taken everything from me once. Now he'd taken Justine too, in a way. The knowledge that her father was the monster I'd been hunting would poison every moment of happiness I might have found with her.

The hunt was finally coming to an end. And this time, we'd do it right.

Even if it destroyed everything I'd hoped to build.

12 - Sins of the Father

Deacon

THE MORNING AIR carried a chill that had nothing to do with the weather as Grady and I rode toward Harper Ranch. Every step my mount took sent a fresh wave of pain through my ribs, and I had to grip the saddle horn tighter than I'd like to admit. The scent of sagebrush and dry earth filled my nostrils, mixed with the familiar smell of leather and horse sweat, but even breathing deep enough to appreciate it made my chest ache.

My new horse, a sturdy bay gelding named Bear I'd borrowed from Uncle Adam, moved beneath me with unfamiliar rhythms—his gait shorter and choppier than what I was used to. Nothing like Sergeant's smooth stride, and right now every jarring step reminded me of Caleb Mason's fists and boots. The bruises along my back protested with each movement, and I had to consciously keep from favoring my left side where the worst of the damage was.

"You sure about this?" I asked for the third time as we crested the hill overlooking the valley where Galen Harper's spread lay sprawling across the flat grassland. My voice came out rougher than intended, my throat still tender from the aftereffects of dehydration.

"We can't leave them there," Grady said, his jaw set with determination that had become as familiar as his breathing over the past few days. "Not knowing what we know about their father."

I checked my Winchester one more time, the metal cold under my fingers as I made sure a round was chambered. The clicking sound of the bolt seemed unnaturally loud in the morning stillness. We'd planned this carefully—ride in fast, get the Harper boys out, gather what evidence we could, and retreat before any of the Mason Gang could respond. Simple. Clean. But I'd learned that operations rarely went according to plan once you encountered real people with their own agendas.

"Remember," I said as we started down the slope toward the open range, our horses' hooves kicking up small clouds of dust, "we're not here to fight the whole gang. Just get Shane, Flynn, and Ike, then get out."

"I know." But I could hear the tension in Grady's voice, see it in the way his hand rested on his gun butt. We were riding straight into the leader's stronghold—of the man who ordered his parents' murder. The irony wasn't lost on either of us.

"Grady," I said, pulling my horse to a stop. "I need to know you're thinking straight. If we run into trouble, if there's a choice between getting evidence and getting those boys out safely..."

His green eyes met mine, and for a moment I saw the conflict warring inside him. The need for justice battling against his hunger for revenge. "The boys come first," he said finally. "But Deacon, if we pass up this chance to gather evidence against Harper..."

"Then we find another way. But we don't risk innocent lives for it."

He nodded, though I could see the frustration in the set of his jaw. This was the closest we'd ever come to the men who'd destroyed his family, and I was asking him to prioritize someone else's family over his own justice.

The Harper Ranch looked exactly like what it was—a hardscrabble operation run by a man who cared more about hosting outlaws than raising cattle. Broken fences sagged between rotting posts, their barbed wire hanging loose like broken promises. The barn doors hung askew on rusted hinges, and the house looked ready to collapse in the next strong wind. Paint peeled from every surface, and weeds grew tall around the foundation. The buildings sat exposed on the flat grassland with nowhere to hide, which made our approach feel like riding across a target range.

But it was the silence that made my skin crawl. No dogs barking. No chickens pecking in the yard. No sounds of life beyond the whisper of wind through dry grass.

"Too quiet," Grady muttered, echoing my thoughts.

We approached cautiously, guns drawn, expecting at any moment to face down Caleb Mason or one of his brothers. My heart hammered against my ribs as we drew closer, every shadow seeming to hide a potential threat. Instead, we found nothing. No horses in the corral except a couple of worn-out nags that looked like they hadn't been fed in days. No men lounging in the shade. No sign of the thieving outlaws that had terrorized the territory.

"Hello the house!" I called out, my voice echoing off the ramshackle buildings and disappearing into the vast emptiness.

A door creaked open on hinges that needed oiling, and a young man stepped onto the porch. Even from fifty yards away, I could see he was too thin, his clothes hanging loose on his frame like hand-me-downs from a bigger brother. His pants were held up with rope instead of a proper belt, and his shirt had been patched so many times it was more patches than original fabric. But he moved with the careful alertness of someone who'd learned to be wary of strangers.

"You the law?" he called back, his voice carrying the hoarse quality of someone who didn't talk much.

"Livestock Inspectors," Grady replied. "We're looking for the Harper boys."

The young man's posture changed, hope flickering across his gaunt features like sunlight through clouds. "That's me. Shane Harper." He paused, studying our faces with eyes that seemed too old for his age. "You know my sisters?"

"Lilian sent us," I said, holstering my gun as it became clear we weren't walking into a firefight. The relief in his face was immediate and overwhelming. "She's worried about you and your brothers."

Shane's knees nearly buckled at the mention of his sister's name. He gripped the porch railing to steady himself, his knuckles going white. "Lilian? She's... Is she alright?"

"She's fine. Working in Prescott." I dismounted and walked toward him, noting the dark circles under his eyes, the hollow look of someone who'd been going hungry for a long time. "When's the last time you had a decent meal?"

Shane looked away, embarrassed color creeping up his neck. "Been a while. Father took most of the provisions when he left with his... associates."

"How long ago?"

"Three days. Maybe four." Shane ran a hand through his unwashed hair, leaving it standing at odd angles. "Flynn and Ike are inside. They're... they're not doing too good."

The house was worse inside than out. Bare cupboards hung open, revealing empty shelves coated with dust. The pantry was nothing but cobwebs and mouse droppings. Three bedrolls lay on the floor of what had once been a parlor, the thin blankets threadbare and stained. The air smelled of unwashed bodies and desperation. And huddled together on those thin blankets were two boys who looked more like scarecrows than human beings.

"Heaven have mercy," I breathed, the words torn from somewhere deep in my chest.

The younger one, who couldn't have been more than fourteen, looked up at us with huge eyes in a gaunt face.

His cheekbones stood out sharp as knife blades, and his wrists were so thin I could have circled them with my thumb and forefinger. "Shane? Who are these men?"

"Friends of Lilian's," Shane said gently, his voice taking on a protective tone I recognized from my own interactions with Sam when we were young. "They've come to take us to her."

The older boy, Flynn, struggled to sit up, the effort clearly taxing what little strength he had left. He was maybe sixteen, but so thin I could have counted his ribs through his shirt. His eyes held the same wariness as Shane's, but underneath it was something that might have been hope. "Take us where?"

"Prescott," Grady said, his voice tight with barely controlled rage. I could see his hands clenching into fists as he took in the boys' condition. "Your sisters are there. They've got food, warm beds, safety."

"All of us?" Flynn asked, and I heard the disbelief in his voice. Like he'd stopped believing in rescue long ago, like this might be another cruel joke life was playing on them.

"All of you," I confirmed, kneeling down to his level. "But first, we need to gather some evidence. Shane, is there anywhere your father kept papers? Business records?"

Shane's face darkened, fear replacing hope in his expression. "The barn. There's a room he kept locked. Said he'd tan our hides if we ever went in there."

Twenty minutes later, I understood why Galen Harper had been so protective of that room. It was a criminal's war room, complete with maps marked with ranch locations across three counties, stacks of forged documents arranged in neat piles, and, most incriminating, a collection of branding irons designed to alter legitimate brands into something else entirely.

The maps showed a web of operations that stretched from the Mexican border to as far north as Flagstaff. Red

X marks indicated ranches that had been hit, while circles marked potential future targets. Notes in Harper's spidery handwriting detailed guard schedules, herd sizes, and market prices.

"B. Irving," I said, reading the signature on a stack of bills of sale. The forgery was of high quality. Someone had taken the time to perfect that signature. "That's your father's alias."

Shane nodded miserably, his shoulders slumping under the weight of confirmation. "I figured it was something like that. The men who came through here... They weren't ranchers or legitimate cattle buyers. They had the look of men who lived by violence."

I gathered up the most incriminating documents while Grady examined the branding irons. Each one was a masterpiece of criminal craftsmanship, designed to transform honest brands into forgeries that would fool casual inspection. The metalwork was precise, showing skill that took years to develop.

"Lazy N becomes Lazy M," Grady observed, holding up one of the irons and tracing the altered lines with his finger. "Flying P becomes Flying R. Professional work."

"Look at this," I said, studying a map that showed potential targets across three counties. Red lines connected ranches to railroad shipping points, with notes about timing and guard rotations. "He's been planning this for years. This isn't just rustling. It's systematic theft on a territorial scale."

The scope of the operation was staggering. Harper had identified vulnerabilities in ranching operations across hundreds of miles, mapped out supply chains, and created a network of corrupt buyers who would take stolen cattle with minimal questions asked.

By the time we finished cataloging the evidence, Shane had helped his brothers gather their few possessions—a pitiful collection that fit into two small canvas sacks. Watching Flynn and Ike move, seeing how they had to stop and rest after any exertion, made my chest tight with anger. What breed of man abandoned his own children to starve while he lived well on stolen money?

"Can you boys ride?" I asked gently, trying to keep the fury out of my voice.

"We can try," Flynn said, though I could see the doubt in his eyes. His legs shook when he stood, and he had to grip the wall for support.

"Ike can ride with me," Grady offered, his voice softer than I'd heard it in days. "Flynn, you think you can manage Shane's horse if he rides with Deacon?"

The next few hours tested every bit of patience I possessed. We had to stop frequently to let the boys rest, their bodies too weakened by malnutrition to handle even the gentle pace we set. Twice I thought Ike might pass out entirely, his small body swaying dangerously in the saddle in front of Grady. But slowly, carefully, we made our way back toward Prescott.

Shane proved to be a font of information about his father's operation. The Mason Gang had been using the ranch as a base for months, coming and going as they pleased with the casual arrogance of men who believed themselves untouchable. Galen Harper was definitely the man in charge, the one who planned operations and gave orders to men like Caleb Mason.

"He never let us in on the details," Shane explained as we paused to water the horses at a small creek. The sound of running water seemed unnaturally loud after the silence of the ranch. "But we saw enough. Men coming in with fresh brands on cattle that were still bleeding. Money changing hands. Planning sessions that went late into the night."

"Were you ever part of it?" I asked carefully, watching his face for any sign of deception.

Shane's face flushed with shame, the color stark against his pale skin. "I helped move cattle a few times. Didn't ask questions about where they came from. I knew it was wrong, but..." He gestured toward his younger brothers. "He said if I didn't help, Flynn and Ike would go hungry."

"You were protecting them," I said, meaning it. "That's what brothers do."

"I should have found another way. Should have gotten them out of there sooner." His voice broke slightly. "When Lilian left, I thought about following her. But Father made it clear what would happen if I tried."

As the sun began to sink toward the western mountains, painting the sky in shades of orange and red, we finally crested the hill overlooking Prescott. The lights of the town twinkled below us like earthbound stars, promising safety and warmth and family reunions too long delayed.

"Is that it?" Ike whispered weakly from where he sat in front of Grady's saddle.

"That's it," Grady confirmed, his voice gentle in a way that reminded me why I'd followed him on this dangerous path. "That's where your sisters live."

I watched Flynn's face as he stared down at the town. Hope warred with disbelief, as if he couldn't quite accept that rescue was real. His hands trembled on the reins, and I saw him swallow hard against emotion.

"They really want us there?" he breathed.

"Son," I said, "they've been worried sick about you. Lilian's been planning for weeks how to get you away from your father's ranch."

The Harper house was blazing with light when we arrived, every window glowing like a beacon in the gathering darkness. I could see figures moving around inside, and the warm yellow light spilling onto the porch promised everything these boys had been denied for too long. Before we'd even dismounted, the front door burst open and three women came rushing out.

"Shane! Flynn! Ike!" Lilian's voice cracked with emotion as she saw her brothers, the sound carrying all the worry and love and relief of months of separation.

What happened next was chaos of the best kind. Tears, embraces, questions flying so fast nobody could answer them. I helped Ike down from Grady's horse, steadying the boy when his legs nearly gave out. His small frame felt fragile as bird bones in my hands. Justine caught Flynn in a hug that lifted him off his feet despite his size, her tears soaking his shirt as she held him like she'd never let go. Hayley was crying and laughing at the same time as she held onto Shane like he was a dream that might disappear if she loosened her grip.

But it was Lilian who took my breath away. When she finally looked up from examining her brothers, checking them for injuries with hands that shook with emotion, her blue eyes met mine across the chaos of reunion. The gratitude and relief in her expression hit me like a physical force, making my chest tight with emotions I couldn't name.

She walked toward me slowly, as if she couldn't quite believe this was real. "You brought them home," she whispered, her voice thick with tears.

"They're safe now," I said, my own voice rougher than intended. "All of them."

And then she was in my arms, her lips finding mine with a desperation full of weeks of worry and fear finally released. The kiss was soft and fierce and full of promise, tasting of salt tears and hope. When she finally pulled away, I saw tears streaming down her cheeks, but her smile was radiant.

"Thank you," she breathed against my lips. "Thank you for bringing them back to me."

Looking around at the Harper family reunited, at the joy on faces that had known too much sorrow, I felt something settle in my chest that had been twisted tight for weeks. This was why we did the work. Not just for justice or law and order, but for moments like this. For families torn apart by evil men, finally made whole again.

But when I looked for Grady to share the moment,

he was already mounting Sunbeam. He touched his hat brim briefly toward the Harper sisters, mumbled something about checking on his horse, and rode off into the darkness without another word.

I understood his need to leave. Watching this reunion, seeing what an actual family looked like when they were allowed to love each other without fear, had to be both a blessing and a torment for him. These were the children of the man who'd murdered his parents, and yet they were innocent of their father's crimes. The complexity of that reality would take time to process.

The hunt for Galen Harper and his gang would continue. There would be more danger, more violence, more hard choices ahead. We had evidence now, enough to build a solid case when we finally brought them to justice. But tonight, three boys who'd been abandoned and left to starve were safe in their sisters' arms.

Tonight, that was enough.

13 - Hearts Divided

Grady

THE SOUND OF feminine laughter drifting through the livestock inspection office made my gut clench with a familiar mixture of longing and guilt. I looked up from the stack of brand registration forms I'd been pretending to read for the past hour to see Justine Harper standing beside her sister's desk, a wicker basket in her hands and a smile that could light up the darkest corners of a man's soul.

Three days. Three days since we'd brought her brothers to safety, and I'd been doing everything in my power to avoid being alone with her. The irony wasn't lost on me—I'd rescued her family from her father's criminal empire, yet every time I looked at those warm brown eyes, I saw ivory-handled guns gleaming in the sunlight. Every time she smiled, I heard the echo of my mother's final scream.

"I brought lunch for Lilian," Justine was saying, unpacking sandwiches wrapped in clean cloth and fresh fruit from her basket. The domestic normalcy of it made my chest ache. "And cookies for the hardworking livestock inspectors."

The smell of fresh-baked sugar cookies filled the office, rich with butter and vanilla, and despite everything churning in my chest, my mouth watered. I hadn't eaten much in the past few days, too twisted up inside to have much appetite. The evidence we'd gathered from the Harper ranch sat locked in Perry's desk drawer—maps, forged documents, modified branding irons—all proving that the woman I loved was the daughter of the monster who'd destroyed my world.

"Grady," Lilian called, her voice carrying the forced cheer of someone trying to smooth over an awkward situation, "come get some of these before Deacon eats them all."

I stood reluctantly, my boots feeling like they were made of lead against the worn wooden floor. Justine turned toward me with that radiant smile, and I had to grip the edge of Perry's desk to keep myself steady. The afternoon sunlight streaming through the window caught the highlights in her hair, and for a moment she looked like an angel descended from heaven.

"I made extra," she murmured, holding out a cookie wrapped in a clean cloth napkin. "I know how much you like them."

Our fingers brushed as I took the offering, and the familiar spark shot through me like lightning through a summer storm. For just a moment, I forgot about ivory guns and murdered parents and the weight of nightmares. For just a moment, she was simply the woman who'd made me believe in love again, who'd shown me what it meant to hope for something beyond darkness.

Then reality crashed back down like a falling tree.

"Much obliged," I mumbled, taking a bite of the cookie to avoid having to meet her eyes. The sugar dissolved on my tongue, sweet as her smile, but it might as well have been sawdust for all I could taste it. "But I need to get going. Perry wants me to check on some reports in the county clerk's office."

It was a lie. Perry was in Phoenix again, testifying in

another rustling case, and the only reports I needed to check were sitting right there on my desk. But I couldn't stay in that room with her scent of roses and soap filling my nostrils and her smile warming places in my heart that I'd thought were frozen solid.

"Oh," Justine said, and I caught the hurt in her voice before she covered it with forced brightness. The change was subtle—a slight tightening around her eyes, a barely perceptible straightening of her shoulders—but I knew her well enough to recognize the wound I'd just inflicted. "Of course. Important work."

I grabbed my hat and headed for the door, pausing only long enough to nod goodbye to Lilian and Deacon. As I stepped onto the boardwalk, the afternoon heat hit me like a physical blow, but it was nothing compared to the words I heard behind me.

"Did I do something wrong?" Justine's voice was quieter now, tinged with confusion and pain that cut through me like a knife.

I didn't hear Lilian's response, but I could imagine it. What could she say? That her sister's only crime was being born to the wrong father? That the man she was falling in love with was twisted up inside with guilt and rage and a thirst for justice that might never be satisfied?

I spent the rest of the afternoon riding aimlessly through the countryside, letting Sunbeam pick his own path through the pine-scented hills while I tried to sort through the tangle in my head. The sun beat down mercilessly, and sweat gathered under my hatband, but I barely noticed. Every rational part of me knew Justine wasn't responsible for her father's crimes. She'd been as much a victim of Galen Harper's evil as anyone else, forced to flee her own home to escape the violence and corruption he'd brought into their lives.

But knowing something and feeling it were two different things entirely.

The evidence we'd collected painted a picture of a

massive criminal enterprise that stretched across the territory. Galen Harper wasn't just a rustler—he was the architect of the thefts that had destroyed dozens of families like mine. And Justine was his blood, his daughter, raised in the same house where he'd planned those crimes.

How could loving her be anything but a betrayal of my parents' memory?

By the time I returned to Colter Ranch, the sun was setting behind the mountains in a blaze of orange and red, and my stomach was growling loud enough to wake the dead. I unsaddled Sunbeam and gave him a thorough rubdown, taking my time with the familiar ritual. The barn smelled of hay and leather and honest work, a comforting contrast to the chaos in my mind.

As I headed toward the main house where I could smell Ellie Mae's cooking drifting on the evening breeze— roast beef and fresh bread that reminded me painfully of my mother's kitchen—the sound of hoofbeats behind me made me turn.

Instead of Deacon returning from town, I found myself looking at Justine Harper riding sidesaddle on a pretty little mare, her blond hair pinned up under a blue bonnet that matched her riding dress. The sight of her there, silhouetted against the sunset like something from a painting, made my heart start beating so fast I was surprised it didn't burst right out of my chest.

"Miss Harper," I said formally, touching the brim of my hat while fighting to keep my voice steady. "What brings you out to the ranch?"

She dismounted with fluid grace, not waiting for my help, and tied her horse to the hitching post with the competent movements of a woman who'd grown up around livestock. When she turned to face me, I saw steel in her brown eyes that I'd never noticed before—a determination that reminded me she was tougher than her gentle demeanor suggested.

"I think you know exactly what brings me here,

Grady Thatcher." Her voice was calm, controlled, but I could hear the determination underneath, like iron beneath silk. "We need to talk."

"I don't think that's a good idea."

"I don't much care what you think right now." She stepped closer, close enough that I could smell the faint scent of roses in her hair, could see the tiny freckles across the bridge of her nose. "Three days ago, you looked at me like I was the most important thing in your world. Yesterday, you could barely stand to be in the same room with me. Today, you ran away rather than spend five minutes in my company. So yes, we definitely need to talk."

I looked around desperately, hoping for some escape, some excuse to avoid the conversation I'd been dreading. But the ranch was quiet, most of the family already inside for supper, and Justine showed no signs of backing down. If anything, she looked like she was prepared to plant herself right there until I gave her answers.

"There's a path around the lake," I said finally, my voice coming out rougher than intended. "We can walk and talk."

She nodded and fell into step beside me as we headed toward the water. The evening air was cooler now, carrying the scent of pine and wild roses. For several minutes, we walked in silence, the only sounds the gentle lapping of waves against the shore and the evening calls of birds settling in for the night. Our footsteps crunched softly on the rocky path, and I was acutely aware of her presence beside me—the rustle of her skirts, the rhythm of her breathing, the way the fading light caught in her hair.

It was peaceful, beautiful even, but I felt like I was walking to my own execution.

"I know what this is about," Justine said finally, her voice cutting through the evening quiet.

I stopped walking and turned to face her, my boots scraping against the small stones. "Do you?"

"My father." The words came out flat, matter-of-fact,

like she was discussing the weather. "Learning that he's connected to the men who killed your parents. That he ordered their deaths. That's what's changed, isn't it?"

"Justine—"

"Let me finish." She held up a hand, and I saw it trembled slightly despite her controlled voice. "I've been thinking about this for days, trying to understand why you've been avoiding me. At first, I thought maybe I'd misread your feelings, that maybe you'd decided you didn't care for me after all. But then I remembered the way you looked at me that night we tended your wounds. The way you kissed my hand when you left the next morning."

She took a shaky breath, her chest rising and falling beneath the blue fabric of her dress. "You do care for me. You're just trying not to because of who my father is."

The words hit me like a punch to the gut, partly because they were true and partly because they made me sound like the worst variety of coward.

"It's not that simple," I said, my voice barely above a whisper.

"Then explain it to me." She stepped closer, those brown eyes searching my face with an intensity that made me feel exposed. "Tell me what's really going on in your head, because right now I feel like I'm drowning and I don't understand why."

Looking at her standing there in the fading light, vulnerable and determined and more beautiful than any woman had a right to be, I felt something crack open inside my chest. The walls I'd built up over the past three days, the careful distance I'd tried to maintain, all of it crumbled like a house of cards in a strong wind.

"Sit with me," I said, gesturing toward a fallen log near the water's edge where wildflowers grew in gentle profusion.

She settled beside me, close enough that our knees almost touched, and waited. The scent of her hair, roses and something uniquely her, surrounded me. In the growing darkness, I could hear my own heartbeat, loud as thunder in my ears, and the gentle sound of water lapping against the muddy shore.

"I was fifteen when it happened," I began, my voice barely above a whisper. "My parents and I were having lunch, just a normal day on our farm. Ma had made beef stew and fresh bread, and Pa was telling me about a horse he was training. Everything was perfect—sunshine streaming through the kitchen window, the smell of Ma's cooking, the sound of Pa's laughter. I thought life would always be that way, that my parents would live forever."

Justine's hand found mine in the darkness, her fingers intertwining with mine. Her skin was warm, soft, and the contact gave me strength to continue.

"Then we heard hoofbeats. Four riders coming fast down our lane, dust clouds trailing behind them. Pa told me to hide in the barn loft, and I wanted to argue, wanted to stay and help fight. But he used that tone that meant business, the voice that had trained countless horses and raised a stubborn son. So I ran."

The words came easier now, years of bottled-up pain finally finding release like water through a broken dam. I told her about watching from the loft as the men surrounded our house, how my hands had shaken as I'd peered through the gaps in the boards. About the leader in black who shot my father without warning, without mercy, as casually as a man might swat a fly. About my mother's scream when she saw Pa fall—a sound that still woke me in the middle of the night.

"The man with ivory guns," I said, and felt Justine flinch beside me, her fingers tightening on mine. "He didn't pull the trigger himself, but he gave the orders. Watched the whole thing like it was entertainment, like my parents' lives meant nothing more than pieces on a chessboard. When the man in black put his gun to Ma's head, your father just stood there and let it happen."

"Oh, Grady." Her voice was thick with unshed tears,

rough with emotion. "I'm so sorry. I'm so very sorry."

"I hid like a coward while they murdered my parents," I continued, the old guilt rising like bile in my throat. "Fifteen years old and too afraid to do anything but watch. By the time I came down from the loft, they were burning everything. Our house, our dreams, our future. All of it gone because of men like your father."

Justine was crying openly now, tears streaming down her face in the moonlight, silver tracks that caught the pale light. "I didn't know. I swear to you, I didn't know he'd done something so terrible."

"I know you didn't." I turned to face her fully, seeing my own pain reflected in her eyes. "That's what's been tearing me apart these past few days. You're not responsible for his crimes. You're as much a victim as anyone else. But every time I look at you, I see those ivory guns, and I remember what they represent. Every time you smile, I hear that gunshot echoing across our yard."

"So where does that leave us?" she breathed.

It was the question I'd been avoiding for three days, the one that had kept me awake at night staring at the ceiling while the rest of the ranch slept peacefully. Because the truth was, despite everything, despite knowing who her father was and what he'd done, I still loved her. Maybe even more than before, if that was possible.

"I don't know," I admitted, the words feeling like they were torn from my chest. "I wish I could turn off my feelings like blowing out a lamp, but I can't. Every instinct I have says I should stay away from you, that loving you is some betrayal of my parents' memory. But my heart..."

"What does your heart say?"

I looked at her sitting there in the moonlight, this brave, beautiful woman who'd ridden out to confront me when I was too much of a coward to face the truth myself. Who'd listened to the story of her father's crimes without making excuses or trying to defend him. Who'd wept for my pain as if it were her own.

"My heart says you're the best thing that's happened to me. That you make me want to build something great. Something lasting. That maybe... maybe my parents would want me to find happiness instead of carrying their deaths like a stone around my neck forever."

"They would," she said with a quiet certainty that somehow reached through all my doubt. "Any parent who loved their child would want that."

"But your father—"

"Will face justice for what he's done," she interrupted firmly, her voice taking on that steel edge I'd heard earlier. "When you catch him, when you bring him to trial, I won't stand in your way. I won't ask you to show mercy or go easy on him because he's family. What he did to your parents, to other families, is unforgivable."

The strength in her voice, the absolute conviction, surprised me. "You mean that."

"I do." She turned toward me, her brown eyes fierce with determination that reminded me she'd survived years in Galen Harper's house and emerged with her soul intact. "My father stopped being a father to us years ago, when he chose his criminal associates over his own children. When he let dangerous men into our home and put us all at risk. When he abandoned Flynn and Ike to starve while he played outlaw king."

She paused, collecting herself with visible effort. "Do you want to know what my childhood was really like, Grady? What it was like growing up in that house?"

I nodded, though part of me wasn't sure I wanted to hear it.

"We lived in fear," she said simply, her voice steady but quiet. "Never knowing when one of Father's associates might decide they wanted something that wasn't theirs to take. Never knowing when violence might erupt around our dinner table. Lilian bore the worst of it, because she was the oldest girl, the prettiest. But we all learned to make ourselves small, invisible, hoping we wouldn't attract the wrong attention."

My hands clenched into fists at the thought of these women, these children, living in terror in their own home while their father counted stolen money and planned his next crime.

"I've seen men shot over card games," Justine continued, her voice growing stronger with each revelation. "I've helped bandage wounds that came from disagreements over stolen cattle. I've watched my father count money that I knew was taken from honest people at gunpoint. By the time I was sixteen, I knew exactly what he was, and I started planning my escape."

"Is that why you came to Prescott?"

"Lilian came first, to establish herself and find work. She was so brave, leaving everything she knew to build a new life. Then she sent for me and Hayley. We wanted to bring the boys too, but Shane said they weren't ready to leave, that he could protect them better by staying." Her voice broke slightly. "I've regretted listening to him every day since."

"You couldn't have known how bad it would get."

"Couldn't I?" She looked at me with eyes that held too much knowledge for someone her age. "I knew what he was. I knew the men he associated with. Maybe if I'd insisted, if I'd found a way to bring Flynn and Ike with us..."

"You'd all be dead," I said bluntly, the truth harsh but necessary. "Your father would never have let his sons go willingly. If you'd tried to take them, he would have stopped you. Violently."

She nodded, accepting the truth of it even though it clearly hurt. "I know. But that doesn't make the guilt any easier to bear."

"Guilt over things beyond your control," I said, recognizing something of my own struggle in her words. "I've been carrying that weight, blaming myself for not being brave enough to help my parents. Maybe it's time we both learned to let go of guilt that isn't rightfully ours."

"Maybe it is." She turned to face me fully, her hand still holding mine, warm and solid. "But I need you to know something, Grady. I understand if you can't get past who my father is. I understand if every time you look at me, you see his crimes instead of me. But I need you to make a choice."

"What choice?"

"Either you trust that I'm not him, that I'm my own person who chose a different path, or you don't. Either you believe that love can exist separate from the sins of our families, or you don't. But I won't spend the rest of my life wondering if you're going to pull away every time something reminds you of my father."

The challenge in her voice, the quiet strength, made me love her even more. She wasn't asking me to forget or forgive Galen Harper's crimes. She was asking me to see her as herself, not as an extension of her father's evil.

"I'm scared," I admitted, the words feeling like pulling thorns from my throat. "Scared that loving you somehow diminishes what my parents meant to me. Scared that I'm betraying their memory by finding happiness with the daughter of their killer."

"What if it's the opposite?" she whispered, her voice gentle but sure. "What if loving me, choosing to build something good, is the best way to honor their memory? They loved each other, didn't they? They built a life together, a home, a family. Isn't that what they would want for you?"

Her words hit me like lightning, illuminating truths I'd been too blind to see. My parents had been happy together. They'd found joy in their simple life, in their love for each other and for me. The afternoon they died, Pa had been laughing at his own story, and Ma had been humming while she worked. They wouldn't want me to spend my life consumed by hatred and the thirst for vengeance.

They'd want me to live. To love. To build something good and lasting and true.

"You're right," I said, the words feeling like a weight lifting from my chest. "You're absolutely right."

"So what does that mean for us?"

I stood up and pulled her to her feet, my hands framing her face in the moonlight. Her skin was soft as silk under my palms, and I could feel the warmth of her breath against my wrists.

"It means I've been a fool. It means I'm sorry for putting you through three days of wondering if you'd done something wrong. It means..."

I paused, searching for the right words to express everything churning in my heart.

"It means I love you, Justine Harper. Not despite who your father is, but because of who you are. Because you're brave enough to face hard truths, strong enough to choose your own path, and generous enough to forgive a stubborn man for taking too long to come to his senses."

Her smile was like the sunrise after the longest night of winter, transforming her entire face with its radiance. "I love you too, Grady Thatcher. All of you, including the parts that are still healing from old wounds."

When I kissed her there beside the lake, with the moon reflecting off the water like scattered diamonds and the night birds calling from the reeds, it felt like coming home. Like finding the missing piece of my soul that I hadn't even known was lost. Her lips were soft and warm and tasted of hope, and when she sighed against my mouth, I felt something settle in my chest that had been twisted and broken for years.

The hunt for Galen Harper would continue. Justice would be served, one way or another. The evidence we'd gathered would help build the case that would finally bring him to trial. But for the first time since that terrible day six years ago, I was looking toward the future instead of dwelling in the past.

And that future was bright with possibility. With her.

14 - Hard Evidence

Grady

THE EVIDENCE SPREAD across Perry Quinn's desk told a story of betrayal that made my stomach roil like churning butter. Falsified bills of sale with ink still sharp enough to cut glass. Altered branding irons that showed the careful craftsmanship of years spent perfecting criminal artistry. Maps to hidden properties marked in Galen Harper's spidery handwriting. All the proof we needed that Harper had built a criminal empire on the backs of honest ranchers like my parents, their blood money funding his reign of terror.

The afternoon heat made the small office stifling, and sweat gathered under my collar as I studied the evidence. The smell of dust and old paper mixed with the scent of the branding irons, creating an atmosphere heavy with the weight of impending justice.

"This is more than we hoped for," Perry said, picking up one of the modified branding irons and turning it in the lamplight. The metal gleamed dully, each alteration a testament to calculated theft. "With Shane's testimony and this physical evidence, we can finally move against the entire operation."

I glanced at Shane Harper, who sat straighter in his chair than when we'd first brought him to town. Three days of Justine's cooking had put color back in his gaunt cheeks and strength in his shoulders. The hollow-eyed scarecrow we'd rescued from that ramshackle ranch was slowly transforming into a man who looked like he might survive whatever was coming. Hard to believe this was the same person who'd been slowly starving while his father counted stolen money.

"The hideout is here," Shane said, pointing to a blank piece of paper. He picked up Perry's pencil and began sketching with steady strokes. "About twenty miles northeast of our ranch. Papa calls it the B. Irving property, but it's really just a front for moving stolen cattle. The buildings are positioned to give excellent sight lines in all directions."

Sheriff Wilkes leaned forward, his chair creaking under his weight. "How many men does he typically keep there?"

"Depends on the operation. Could be anywhere from four to a dozen." Shane's jaw tightened, the muscle jumping beneath his skin. "Victor Mason is usually there. He's the one who..." His eyes flicked to me, and I saw sympathy mixed with shame. "He's the enforcer."

The man who murdered my parents. My hands clenched into fists so tight my knuckles went white before I forced them to relax. The leather of my gun belt creaked as I shifted in my chair. Justine's words from our reconciliation by the lake echoed in my mind like a prayer: *Don't let vengeance consume the good man you are.*

"What about the layout?" Deacon asked, ever the strategist. His voice was calm, but I caught the slight tension in his shoulders that meant he was reading my mood and preparing to intervene if necessary. "Buildings, approaches, escape routes?"

Shane continued sketching additions to his map, his strokes quick and sure. "Main house here, barn there. Corral for the stolen cattle behind the barn. There's a wash that runs along the south side—suitable cover for an approach, but it gets muddy after rain. The ground's hard-packed near the buildings, so you can't approach quietly on foot."

"Guard positions?" Deputy Jakes inquired, mopping sweat from his forehead with a damp handkerchief.

"Papa's paranoid. Always has been." Shane's voice held traces of bitter experience. "Usually keeps one man watching the road with a rifle, another by the corral with clear sight lines to the approach. During big operations, more scattered around the property. They use a whistle system to communicate—one short blast means all clear, two means trouble."

I studied the emerging map, my mind working through possibilities like pieces on a chessboard. Every line, every marking represented a chance to finally face the men who'd destroyed my world. "When's their next big operation?"

Shane hesitated, his pencil hovering over the paper. "I was never part of the planning, but... Papa mentioned something about a large shipment coming through this week. Cattle from up north heading to the railroad. Said it would be the biggest score yet."

Perry and the sheriff exchanged glances, heavy with meaning. "If we can catch them with stolen cattle and evidence..." Perry began.

"We'll have them dead to rights," Sheriff Wilkes finished, his voice carrying the satisfaction of a man who'd spent years chasing shadows. "But we need to move fast. If word gets out that Shane is helping us..."

"They'll scatter like roaches when you light a lamp," I said, the urgency burning in my chest like swallowed fire. We were so close now I could taste it.

"I could handle reconnaissance," I said quickly, too quickly judging by the sharp look Deacon gave me.

"Grady," he murmured, his voice carrying the patient

tone he used when he thought I was about to do something reckless. "We need to be smart about this, not reckless."

He was right, but the fire in my blood didn't want to hear reason. Victor Mason was within reach—the man who put a gun to my mother's head and pulled the trigger without a moment's hesitation. Who shot my father like he was nothing more than a rabid dog that needed putting down.

"I'm fine," I said, though my voice came out rougher than intended, like gravel in my throat.

Shane cleared his throat, the sound cutting through the tension like a knife. "Papa's been talking about leaving the territory. Says it's getting too hot around here, too many people asking questions."

The words hit like a punch to the gut, driving the air from my lungs. "When?"

"Soon. Maybe within the week. He's been moving money, making arrangements."

Perry slammed his hand on the desk with enough force to make the evidence jump. "Then we move in a few days. Can't risk losing them now."

"That soon?" Deputy Jakes looked uncertain, his youth showing in the way his voice climbed slightly.

"Has to be," Sheriff Wilkes said, his tone brooking no argument. "We'll coordinate with Xavier and the other livestock inspectors. Make this a territorial operation with enough manpower to bottle them up tight."

I felt Deacon's eyes on me as the planning continued, his gaze steady and knowing. He knew me well enough to read the war going on inside my head—could probably see it in the set of my shoulders, the way my hands kept clenching and unclenching. Justice was finally within reach, but at what cost? Would capturing my parents' killers bring me peace, or would it just feed the darkness that had been growing in my heart?

The room fell silent except for the ticking of the

clock on the wall and the distant sound of horses in the street. Rage roared through my veins like wildfire, consuming everything in its path, and for a moment, all I could see was red.

"I need some air."

I was at the door before anyone could respond, my hands shaking with the effort to maintain control. The afternoon sun hit my face as I stepped onto the boardwalk, but it did nothing to cool the fury burning inside me like a forge fire.

Six years of wondering why. Six years of trying to understand how someone could murder two innocent people in cold blood. And now we were finally going to face them.

"Grady."

I turned to find Deacon beside me, his expression full of concern that cut through my rage like cool water. His presence was steady, grounding, the way it had been since that first terrible night when he'd sat beside my bed and talked me through the nightmares.

"You alright?"

"No." The word came out like a growl from somewhere deep in my chest. "I want to kill him, Deacon. I want to put a bullet in Victor Mason's head and watch him die. I want him to know fear the way my mother knew fear."

Deacon was quiet for a long moment, studying my face with those steady brown eyes. When he finally spoke, his voice was gentle but firm as steel. "That's not justice, Grady. That's vengeance."

"Maybe they're the same thing."

"No, they're not. Justice is about making things right, about protecting others from what happened to you. Vengeance is about making yourself feel better." He placed a hand on my shoulder, the weight of it familiar and calming. "Which one do you think your parents would want?"

The question cut through my rage like a knife through silk. Mama and Papa had raised me to believe in right and wrong, in law and order, in doing things the proper way. They'd never wanted me to become a killer, no matter what had been done to them. They'd wanted me to be better than the men who'd destroyed them.

But the fire still burned in my chest, demanding satisfaction, demanding blood for blood.

"I don't know if I can face him and not pull the trigger," I admitted, the words feeling like they were torn from my throat.

"Then we'll make sure you don't have to. That's what partners are for."

I looked at my best friend—my brother in everything but blood—and felt some of the rage ebb away like a tide retreating from the shore. Deacon had stood by me through everything. He'd taken this job to help me find justice, had followed me into danger without question or complaint. The least I could do was trust him to help me see it through the right way.

"Alright," I said finally, my voice steadier now. "Let's go catch some outlaws."

We headed back inside, where Perry was studying Shane's completed map with tactical intensity. Every building, every approach route, every potential hiding spot carefully marked.

As I listened to the final details being discussed, one thought kept echoing in my mind: Soon, I would finally face my parents' killer. And somehow, I had to find a way to choose justice over vengeance.

Even if it killed me to do it.

15 - The Plan

Grady

MY SHOULDERS FELT like twisted wire, every muscle pulled tight enough to snap. Three days of waiting since we'd seen all that evidence had brought me to this moment—sitting in this cramped office while Perry Quinn marked tactical positions on Shane's map, planning to finally corner the bastards who murdered my parents.

I forced myself to breathe steady, to keep my hands from shaking where they rested on my knees. But the rage was there, burning just beneath my skin like banked coals. It took everything I had not to reach for my gun, not to demand we ride out right now and settle this the way it should have been settled six years ago.

"The plan is solid," Perry was saying, his voice distant through the roar in my ears. He marked positions with precise strokes on the detailed map Shane had drawn for us—every building, every approach route carefully outlined. "Sheriff Wilkes and Deputy Jakes approach from the east along the main road. Xavier and I take the north road and block that escape route. Deacon and Grady circle around through the wash on the south side."

I watched him mark the positions, each X on the map

bringing us closer to Victor Mason. The man in black who haunted my dreams. The killer who'd looked down at me with those dead eyes and promised to find me when he was ready.

Well, I was ready now.

"What about me?" Shane asked, his voice carrying the same need I felt gnawing at my gut—the desperate hunger to be part of bringing down his father's empire.

"You stay with the horses," Sheriff Wilkes said firmly. "This is going to be dangerous enough without worrying about civilians getting caught in crossfire."

Shane's jaw went tight, the muscle jumping under his skin. I knew that look—knew the frustration of wanting to act while others made you wait. "That's my father out there. My responsibility. I know his habits, his tricks."

"Which is exactly why you need to stay back," Perry replied. "No telling how you'll react when the shooting starts. Family makes everything complicated."

Family. The word hit me like a fist to the gut. My family was six feet under because of Victor Mason's greed. Nothing complicated about that—just cold, simple murder that demanded payment in kind.

"How do we coordinate the timing?" Deacon asked, and I could hear the concern in his voice. He was studying me from across the room, probably noting the way my hands kept clenching into fists. "If one group moves too early, we lose the element of surprise and they scatter."

"Signal flares," Sheriff Wilkes said, pulling a small cylinder from his coat. "We all get in position, then I fire a flare to start the operation. Should give us coordinated movement and the element of surprise."

I leaned forward, my attention sharpening like a hunting blade. Every detail mattered. Every second could mean the difference between justice and letting these murderers slip away again. "What if they try to run?"

"That's why we're surrounding them," Perry said, tapping various points on Shane's map. "Block all the escape routes, force them to surrender or face overwhelming odds."

"And if they don't surrender?"

The words came out harder than I'd intended, carrying an edge that made everyone in the room look at me. I didn't care. I'd been thinking about this moment for six years—what I'd do when I finally faced Victor Mason again. What I'd say to the man who'd destroyed my world for a few head of stolen cattle.

Perry met my eyes steadily. "Then we do what we have to do. But we try to take them alive if possible. Dead men can't stand trial, and we want this to be legal."

Legal. The word tasted like ash in my mouth. There'd been nothing legal about what happened to my parents. Nothing legal about a fifteen-year-old boy hiding in root cellar while his mother screamed for mercy she'd never receive.

My hands clenched again, knuckles going white. I wanted Victor Mason to pay, but I wanted to look him in the eyes when it happened. Wanted him to know who was pulling the trigger and why. A bullet in the dark during a raid wouldn't satisfy the hunger that had been eating at me—it would just feed the darkness that grew a little stronger every day.

"There's something else," Shane said, reluctance heavy in his voice. "Papa's been acting even more paranoid lately. He might have gotten word that we're closing in."

"All the more reason to move fast," Sheriff Wilkes said grimly. "We strike tomorrow night or risk losing them entirely."

Tomorrow night. After six years of waiting, it came down to hours. My hand drifted toward my gun without conscious thought, fingers brushing the worn grip. The same gun I'd cleaned and loaded every night for six years, waiting for this chance.

"And there's something you should know about Victor Mason," Shane continued, his voice dropping to barely above a whisper. "He's not just Papa's enforcer. He enjoys what he does. The violence, the fear. When he killed your parents, it wasn't just business for him. It was pleasure."

The room went silent except for the ticking of the clock on the wall and the distant sound of horses in the street.

The words hit me like a sledgehammer to the chest. Six years I'd carried the image of my parents' deaths, but I'd always told myself it was just business—wrong, evil, but business. Outlaws killing for money or cattle or whatever they thought they could gain.

But this... this was something else entirely. Something darker.

I couldn't breathe. The walls felt like they were closing in, the air too thick to fill my lungs. Without a word, I rushed for the door, my legs unsteady beneath me.

Outside on the boardwalk, I gripped the railing with white knuckles, gulping the cool evening air. But it didn't help. Nothing could wash away the sickening chill that had settled deep in my bones.

"Grady."

I turned to find Deacon beside me, his face etched with concern.

"He's not just the man in black," I said, my voice barely recognizable. "Victor Mason... his soul is darkness itself. Pure evil. I can't believe he enjoyed—enjoyed killing my parents. Their deaths meant nothing to him. Nothing."

Deacon was quiet for a moment, then placed a steady hand on my shoulder. "We can't undo what Mason did. But we can see justice done. We can bring him in, take him to trial. Make him answer for his crimes."

"And if he doesn't make it to trial?"

"Then he'll answer to the ultimate authority." Deacon's voice was firm. "Either way, Grady, he'll be held accountable. But we do this the right way."

I stood there for a long moment, letting Deacon's words sink in. He was right. Mason would face judgment, one way or another. I took a shuddering breath and nodded.

"Let's go catch some outlaws."

We headed back inside, where Perry was finalizing the details of tomorrow night's raid. Maps, assignments, contingency plans. Everything we needed to bring down the Mason Gang once and for all.

As the meeting broke up and assignments doled out, Deacon approached me. I could see the worry in his brown eyes, the way he noted how my hand kept gravitating toward my weapon.

"You sure you're ready for this?"

I stared at Shane's map, memorizing every line and marking. The wash where Deacon and I would approach. The barn where we'd corner them. The place where six years of nightmares would finally end. "I've been ready for six years."

"That's not what I mean, and you know it."

I met his eyes, and I knew he could see it—the war raging inside me between the man my parents had raised and the killer their murder had created. Justice versus revenge. The badge on my chest versus the fury in my heart.

Pa's voice echoed in my memory: The truth has a way of making itself known, son. Sometimes it hurts, but it always sets things right in the end.

I wondered if Pa had known how much the truth would hurt, or how long I'd have to wait for things to be set right. If he'd known that his son would become a man who dreamed of murder in the dark hours before dawn.

"I'll do what needs to be done," I said finally, the words carrying the weight of six years' worth of rage.

Deacon's face went pale. "That's what I'm afraid of."

We walked outside together, the afternoon sun casting long shadows across the dusty street. A freight wagon rumbled past, wheels kicking up small clouds of dust that caught the light like gold. Normal life continuing while I prepared for something that would either bring justice or condemn my soul.

I sent up a silent prayer. Not for vengeance this time, but for the strength to do what was right instead of what felt satisfying. Pa had always said God would provide a way when the time came. Tomorrow night, I'd find out if that was true.

Either way, Deacon would be right beside me when it happened.

That's what brothers do.

16 - Blood and Betrayal

Deacon

THE WASH PROVIDED perfect cover as Grady and I belly-crawled through the darkness toward the B. Irving property, our clothes soaking up the muddy dampness from the creek bed. The smell of dank earth filled my nostrils as we inched forward. Twenty yards ahead, the outline of the barn rose against the star-filled sky like a black monument to criminal enterprise. Everything was going according to plan.

Too well, maybe.

"Guard position," Grady breathed, his voice barely audible as he pointed toward a shadow near the corral.

I squinted through the darkness and made out the silhouette of a man leaning against a fence post, rifle cradled casually in his arms. The red ember of a cigarette glowed like a tiny beacon in the night air. Just like Shane had said—one guard by the corral, relaxed and unsuspecting.

We waited for Sheriff Wilkes' signal flare, our hearts hammering against our ribs in the silence. The plan was simple—surround the property, coordinate the attack, take them alive if possible. Clean and expedient. Everything we'd trained for.

The flare burst overhead like a falling star, bathing the landscape in eerie red light that threw harsh shadows across the ground.

"Go," I hissed.

We sprinted from the wash toward the barn, keeping low and moving fast across the open ground. Behind us, I could hear horses thundering as Perry and Xavier approached from the north road, their hoofbeats like distant thunder. Sheriff Wilkes and his deputy would be coming from the east, closing the trap.

The guard by the corral shouted and reached for his rifle, the cigarette falling from his lips in a shower of sparks. Grady was on him before he could raise the weapon, tackling him to the ground with the solid impact of a charging bull. They rolled in the dirt, fighting for control of the gun, grunts and curses filling the air.

I made it to the barn door and pressed my back against the rough wooden planks, pistol drawn and ready. Through a gap in the boards, I could see movement inside—dark shapes scrambling for weapons and cover with practiced efficiency.

"This is the law!" Sheriff Wilkes' voice echoed across the property from somewhere in the darkness. "Come out with your hands up!"

The answer came as rifle fire from multiple positions. Muzzle flashes lit up the night like deadly fireflies, and the sharp crack of gunshots shattered the desert quiet. Wood splintered near my head as a bullet chewed into the barn wall.

Something was wrong. They were too ready for us, too organized. This wasn't the panicked response of men caught by surprise. This was a coordinated defense by people who'd been expecting us.

"Deacon!" Grady's warning came just as I felt the cold steel of a gun barrel press against the base of my skull, the metal so cold it seemed to burn.

"Drop your weapon, Livestock Inspector."

I recognized the voice from Shane's description—gravelly, with the cruel amusement of a man who enjoyed inflicting pain. Victor Mason. The man who murdered Grady's parents was standing right behind me, and there wasn't a thing I could do about it.

I let my pistol fall to the dirt with a dull thud.

"Smart man. Now call off your friend before I paint this barn with your brains."

Grady had the guard pinned, but looked up at Victor's words. Even in the dim light, I could see the rage that transformed his face when he saw my captor—a transformation from friend to avenging fury.

"Let him go!" Grady snarled, rising to his feet with his fists clenched.

"I don't think so. See, we've been expecting you boys. Had ourselves a nice little talk with someone who knows your plans real well."

My stomach dropped like a stone down a well. Someone had betrayed us. But who? Who had access to our plans and a reason to sell us out?

"Grady, run!" I shouted, desperation making my voice crack.

The butt of Victor's rifle crashed into my skull with the sound of splitting wood. Pain exploded behind my eyes like fireworks, and I dropped to my knees as the world tilted sideways. Through the ringing in my ears, I heard Grady roar my name with anguish that cut through me like a knife.

Then gunfire erupted from every direction, muzzle flashes strobing through the darkness.

I tried to stand, to help Grady, but my legs wouldn't cooperate. The world spun like a child's top, and I could taste blood in my mouth—bitter and warm. My vision swam in and out of focus.

More boots pounded around us, kicking up dust that mixed with the acrid smell of gunpowder. Rough hands grabbed my arms and hauled me upright. Through my blurred vision, I saw Grady fighting like a wildcat against three men, his fists connecting with solid thuds. He managed to break free and dove for his pistol.

"Behind you!" I tried to warn him, but the words came out slurred and thick.

A fourth man appeared from the shadows like a specter and brought a rifle stock down on Grady's head with sickening force. My best friend crumpled like a marionette with cut strings, his body going limp as he hit the ground.

"No!" The word exploded from my throat.

Victor's laughter was like breaking glass, sharp and cutting. "Don't worry, Inspector. We ain't gonna kill you. Not yet, anyway. Got ourselves a message to send first."

They dragged us toward the main house as gunfire continued to echo across the property like a war zone. I caught glimpses of Perry and Xavier pinned down behind an overturned wagon, their return fire sporadic and desperate. Sheriff Wilkes and his deputy had taken cover behind a water trough, returning fire as best they could.

But we were outnumbered and outgunned. The gang had been ready for us, and we'd walked straight into their trap like lambs to slaughter.

Inside the house, they threw us into a back room that smelled of dust and mouse droppings, then slammed the door. I heard the scrape of something heavy being dragged against it—a dresser or table barricading us in like prisoners in a tomb.

Grady lay motionless on the floor beside me. Blood matted his sandy hair where the rifle had connected, dark stains spreading across his scalp. For a terrifying moment, I thought they'd killed him.

"Grady. Grady, wake up." I shook his shoulder with trembling hands, feeling for a pulse at his neck. Strong and steady—*thank you, God*.

He groaned and his eyes fluttered open, unfocused and confused. "Deacon? What... where are we?"

"They got us. The whole plan went to pieces." The

words tasted like ashes in my mouth.

He struggled to sit up, wincing as he touched the gash on his head. His fingers came away bloody. "How? How did they know?"

"Someone talked. Had to be. Someone with access to our plans sold us out."

The gunfire outside was tapering off, growing sporadic and distant. Either our boys were winning, or they were dead. The silence that followed was more ominous than the shooting had been.

"Listen," Grady breathed.

Voices carried through the thin walls like whispers from demons. Victor Mason's among them, that cruel laugh unmistakable.

"Let 'em go. They got the message. Tell that sheriff if he wants his Livestock Inspectors back, he can find 'em at the old mine shaft come morning."

"What about the horses?" another voice asked—younger, nervous.

"Kill 'em. Most of 'em anyway. But make it slow for that blood bay. I want him to suffer."

My blood turned to ice water in my veins. Our horses were tied up in the wash where we'd left them, trusting us to return. Sergeant was out there, too, waiting for me to rescue him.

Victor's voice continued, thick with malicious pleasure that made my skin crawl. "Use your knife on the bay's throat. Let him bleed out slow. That'll teach these Livestock Inspectors what happens when they stick their noses where they don't belong."

"No," I whispered, the word barely a breath. "No, no, no."

The sound of rifle shots echoed from the direction of the wash. Two quick reports that cracked through the night air like breaking bones. Then silence.

But no third shot. Which meant...

I pressed my face against the wall and squeezed my

eyes shut, but I couldn't block out what was happening. Victor Mason was making Sergeant suffer, just like he'd made Grady's parents suffer. The horse who'd carried me faithfully for eight years was dying alone and afraid because of my failure.

"Deacon." Grady's voice seemed to come from very far away. "Deacon, we gotta get out of here."

I couldn't answer. Couldn't move. In my mind, I could see Sergeant alone and terrified, his life bleeding away into the dust while his killer watched with satisfaction.

"They're torturing him," I choked out, my voice breaking. "They're making him suffer."

Grady's hand gripped my shoulder with bruising force. "I know. But we can't help him now, and we can't help anybody else if we don't get out of here."

He was right, but I didn't care anymore. Let them come back and finish us. What was the point? We'd failed completely. The gang was still free, our mission was compromised, and my horse was dying because of my mistakes.

"This is my fault," I said, the guilt crushing me like a physical weight. "I should have seen it coming. Should have known it was too easy."

"It's not your fault."

"It is! I'm supposed to be the one who notices things, who sees the details others miss. And I led us straight into a trap." The words came out harsh and broken. "Sergeant trusted me, and I got him killed."

Grady grabbed my shoulders and forced me to look at him. Blood still trickled from his head wound, but his eyes were clear and determined.

"Listen to me. This isn't over. They think they've won, but they just made it personal. We're gonna get out of here, we're gonna regroup, and we're gonna make them pay for every life they've taken."

"How? They knew every detail of our plan. Someone

on our side is working with them."

"Then we figure out who. And we make them pay, too."

The sound of retreating horses reached us through the walls—hoofbeats fading into the distance like the last hope of justice. The gang was pulling out, probably heading for another hideout. By the time we got free and brought help, they'd be long gone.

We spent the next hour working at the boards covering the room's single window. The nails were old and rusty, and we managed to work three of them loose enough to pry the board away. My fingers were raw and bleeding by the time we finished, but the pain felt appropriate.

The window was small, but we squeezed through one at a time into the cool night air. The property was eerily quiet now. No sign of Perry, Xavier, or the sheriff's men—just empty darkness and the smell of gunpowder lingering like a dense fog.

We made our way toward the wash, though every step felt like walking to my own execution. I knew what I'd find there, but I had to see for myself. Had to face what my failure had cost.

The moonlight revealed the carnage in stark detail. Two horses lay scattered across the dried creek bed, their blood dark against the silt like spilled ink. Perry's sorrel. Xavier's paint. Both shot cleanly through the head—merciful deaths compared to what they'd done to Sergeant.

And there he was.

My blood bay gelding lay on his side, a deep gash across his throat where they'd sliced him open with deliberate cruelty. Blood had pooled beneath his neck, soaking into the dirt in a dark stain that seemed to stretch forever. His eyes were open and glassy, staring at nothing. The white blaze on his face that I'd stroked a thousand times was splattered with his own blood.

This wasn't how I had hoped to be reunited with my

old friend.

I dropped to my knees beside him and placed a trembling hand on his neck. Cold now. No pulse. No breath. No life. Just the empty shell of the animal who'd been my faithful partner for eight years.

"I'm sorry," I whispered, my voice breaking as I stroked his blaze one last time. "I'm so sorry, boy. You didn't deserve this. You trusted me, and I failed you."

Grady appeared beside me, leading Sunbeam and Bear by the reins. Both had somehow escaped the slaughter, though they bore scrapes and cuts from fleeing through the brush. Their eyes were wide with fear, and Grady's palomino shied away from the smell of blood.

"At least these two of them made it," Grady murmured, but I could hear the pain in his voice. He understood what Sergeant meant to me—more than just a horse, but a partner and friend.

I couldn't leave Sergeant like this. Couldn't just walk away and let the buzzards have him.

"Help me move him," I said.

"Deacon—"

"Help me!" The words came out sharper than I intended, but I didn't care.

Together, we dragged Sergeant's body to a small grove of mesquite trees, the effort leaving us both exhausted and covered in his blood. It wasn't much of a grave, but it was better than leaving him exposed to scavengers. I pulled off my jacket and laid it over his head, covering the terrible wound.

"He was a good horse," Grady murmured.

"The best. Never once failed me. And when I needed to protect him..." My voice broke entirely.

We gathered rocks to cover the body, working in silence as the moon tracked across the sky. We finished as the first light of dawn mocked us on the eastern horizon.

The ride back to Prescott took us most of the day. Grady and I avoided the main roads, cutting across country and staying hidden in case the gang had left scouts. My head still pounded from the rifle blow, and Grady wasn't much better off.

But the physical pain was nothing compared to the weight of our failure. The Mason Gang was still free. Our carefully planned raid had been a complete disaster. And three magnificent horses were dead because of our mistakes.

When we finally stumbled into town, we found Perry and Xavier at the Livestock Commission office, both nursing wounds of their own. Perry had a bandaged arm where a bullet had grazed him, the white cloth stained with dried blood. Xavier sported a black eye and a split lip that made him look like he'd been trampled.

"Thank God," Perry breathed when he saw us. "We thought you were dead."

"Might as well be," I muttered, slumping into a chair that creaked under my weight. The words tasted like ash in my mouth. Every time I closed my eyes, I saw Sergeant's trusting brown eyes as they led him away. Heard the echo of his hoofbeats fading into the distance.

Sheriff Wilkes joined us a few minutes later, his deputy trailing behind with his arm in a sling. Both men looked haggard, defeated.

"What happened out there?" the sheriff demanded, his voice tight with frustration. "It was like they knew we were coming."

"Because they did," Grady said grimly, touching the bandage on his head. "Someone tipped them off."

The silence that followed was heavy with suspicion and accusation. Someone in this room, or someone close to our operation, had betrayed us. Had gotten our horses killed and nearly gotten us all murdered. My throat tightened until I could barely breathe. Sergeant was dead because someone had sold us out for silver.

"I'm posting guards on all of you," Sheriff Wilkes said finally. "Until we figure out who the leak is, nobody's safe."

I barely heard him. All I could think about was Sergeant's final whinny as they dragged him away—a sound that would haunt me until my dying day. The horse who'd carried me through danger without hesitation, who'd trusted me to bring him home safe. And I'd failed him. Just like I'd failed everything else that mattered.

The grief sat in my chest like a physical weight, crushing the air from my lungs. I'd lost more than a horse—I'd lost my oldest friend, my most loyal companion. The one being who'd never judged my compulsions, never questioned my need for order, never made me feel broken.

Grady was saying something about regrouping and planning our next move, but his voice sounded like it was coming from underwater. The guilt was eating me alive from the inside out, and I wondered if this was how it felt to drown on dry land.

We'd lost this battle completely. The only question now was whether we'd live long enough to fight another one.

A knock on the office door interrupted Sheriff Wilkes mid-sentence. A young boy with dirt-streaked cheeks peered inside, clutching a folded paper.

"Got a message for Grady Thatcher," he said, his voice high and nervous.

I watched Grady take the note, and immediately knew something was wrong. The color drained from his face like water from a broken pitcher. His hands started shaking as he read, and when he looked up, his eyes held a wildness I'd seen only once before—when he found out who murdered his parents.

"What is it?" I asked, though part of me didn't want to know. We'd already lost so much today.

He couldn't seem to form words. Just held out the paper with hands that trembled like fall leaves. The crude block letters made my blood run cold: "Grady for Justine. V.M."

Victor Mason had her. And from the look on Grady's face, I knew he was about to do something that would get him killed.

And somehow, I had to save my best friend from himself.

17 - Unfair Trade

Grady

THREE DAYS AFTER the failed raid, I was still seeing red every time I closed my eyes. Not just from the blow to my head, but from the rage that burned hotter with each passing hour like coals in a forge. Victor Mason had Justine. My Justine.

The note had been simple enough, written in crude block letters: "Grady for Justine. V.M."

But the message was clear as mountain spring water. They wanted me dead, and they were willing to use an innocent woman—Galen Harper's own daughter—as bait to make it happen.

I crumpled the paper in my fist for the hundredth time, pacing the length of the Livestock Commission office like a caged wolf. The floorboards creaked under my boots with each turn, and the afternoon heat made the small room stifling. Perry Quinn sat behind his desk, studying maps of the Harper Ranch that Shane had drawn for us with painstaking detail. Sheriff Wilkes and Deputy Jakes flanked him, their faces grim as tombstones.

Deacon sat slumped in a chair by the window, staring at nothing through the dusty glass. He'd barely spoken since we'd returned from burying the horses, and the guilt was eating him alive like acid. Frankly, I was getting tired of his self-pity when Justine needed rescuing.

"We need to move now," I said, stopping my pacing to glare at the assembled men. "Every minute we wait is another minute that Justine is in danger."

"And rushing in blind is exactly what they expect," Perry replied without looking up from the maps, his pencil tracing possible approach routes. "We need a plan."

"I have a plan. I go in, make the trade, you follow behind and clean up the mess."

"That's not a plan, Grady. That's suicide."

I slammed my fist on Perry's desk with enough force to make the inkwell jump, sending papers scattering. Everyone startled except Deacon, who continued staring out the window like a mourning statue.

"Then what do you suggest? Send another telegram asking them nicely to let her go?"

"I suggest we use our heads instead of our hearts," Sheriff Wilkes said, his weathered face stern. "This Victor Mason has already proven he's one step ahead of us. Walking into his trap won't save Miss Justine."

"At least it's something!" I whirled to face Deacon, my patience finally snapping. "Are you going to sit there all day feeling sorry for yourself, or are you going to help me save the woman I love?"

Deacon's eyes finally focused on me, and I saw a flash of the old fire there—the spark that told me my best friend was still alive under all that grief. "Don't."

"Don't what? Don't ask you to do your job? Don't expect you to think about someone other than your dead horse for five minutes?"

He was on his feet faster than I'd seen him move since the raid, his chair scraping against the floor as he stood. His face flushed with anger, and his hands clenched into fists. "You think I don't care what happens to Justine? You think I'm not ready to ride out there right now and put a bullet in Victor Mason's brain?"

"Then why are we still here talking?"

"Because last time I rushed in without thinking, Sergeant died!" The words exploded out of him like a gunshot. "Because my mistakes got magnificent animals killed and nearly got us murdered, too!"

The office fell silent except for the ticking of the clock on the wall and the distant sound of horses in the street. Deacon's chest heaved as he stared at me, pain and fury warring in his brown eyes like battling storms.

"I won't make that mistake again," he hissed, his voice dropping to barely above a whisper. "Not with Justine's life at stake."

The fight went out of me as quickly as it had come, leaving me feeling hollow and ashamed. Deacon wasn't being selfish—he was being careful. Smart. Everything I wasn't being right now.

"I'm sorry," I said, the words feeling like gravel in my throat. "I just... I can't lose her, Deacon. Not like this."

"You won't. We'll get her back." His voice carried absolute conviction that somehow reached through my panic.

Shane had been quiet through our entire exchange, but now he cleared his throat. "There's something you need to know about my father."

All eyes turned to him. He looked healthier than when we'd first brought him to town—Justine's cooking had put meat on his bones and color in his cheeks—but there was a haunted quality to his expression that spoke of old wounds and older fears.

"He doesn't care about Justine. Never did. None of the girls meant anything to him except as tools to be used." Shane's voice was steady, but his hands trembled slightly where they rested on his knees. "If he's willing to trade her for Grady, it's because he figures she's expendable either way."

The words hit me like a physical blow to the chest,

driving the air from my lungs. "What are you saying?"

"I'm saying even if you make the trade, there's no guarantee he'll let her live. Papa doesn't leave loose ends, and Justine's seen too much, knows too much about his operation."

Sheriff Wilkes leaned forward, his chair creaking. "Then what do you recommend?"

Shane studied the map for a long moment, his finger tracing the buildings and terrain with practiced familiarity. "Let me go in first. Scout the situation, confirm where they're holding her. I can get close to the ranch without raising suspicion—it's still my home, after all."

"Absolutely not," Perry said firmly. "Too dangerous."

"More dangerous than sending Grady in blind? At least this way, we'll know what we're dealing with." Shane's jaw set with a determination that reminded me of his sisters. "I know every building, every hiding spot, every escape route on that property."

I wanted to object, to insist that I should be the one taking the risks. But Shane was right. He could get closer than any of us without being shot on sight.

"If you do this," I said, meeting his eyes, "and something happens to you, Justine will never forgive me."

Shane's smile was grim but determined. "If I don't do this, and something happens to her, I'll never forgive myself. She's the best of all of us, Grady. She deserves a chance at happiness."

An hour later, we were positioned in the hills overlooking the Harper Ranch, the afternoon sun beating down on our backs like a hammer. Shane had ridden down alone, playing the part of the prodigal son returning home. Through field glasses, I watched him dismount near the barn and walk casually toward the house, his movements relaxed and natural.

My heart hammered against my ribs as I lost sight of him around the corner of the building. Beside me, Deacon checked his rifle for the third time in as many minutes, the metallic clicking of the bolt unnaturally loud in the desert quiet.

"Easy," I murmured, though I wasn't sure if I was talking to him or myself.

"I should be down there with him."

"No, you should be right here, ready to cover our escape when this goes sideways."

Twenty minutes passed like twenty hours before Shane reappeared, walking back toward his horse with the same casual gait. But I could see the tension in his shoulders through the field glasses, the way his eyes kept darting toward the barn like a man who'd seen something that frightened him.

He mounted up and rode away from the ranch at an unhurried pace. Only when he was well out of sight of the buildings did he kick his horse into a gallop toward our position, dust clouds trailing behind him.

"She's there," he said without preamble when he reached us, sweat beading on his forehead despite the dry heat. "In the barn, tied up in the back room where Papa used to plan his operations. Victor Mason and two other men are guarding her. Papa's in the house."

"How did she look?" The question tore from my throat like a physical thing.

"Scared but unharmed. They haven't hurt her, at least not yet." Shane's expression darkened like storm clouds gathering. "But Victor was talking about what he planned to do to her after they killed you. We don't have much time."

The rage that had been simmering in my chest exploded into an inferno that threatened to consume everything in its path. Victor Mason wasn't just holding Justine hostage—he was threatening to...

I couldn't even finish the thought without seeing red.

"Change of plans," I growled, checking my pistol with hands that shook with fury. "I'm going in now."

"Grady, wait—" Deacon started, reaching for my

arm.

But I was already moving, sliding down the hillside toward the ranch with loose rocks scattering under my boots. Behind me, I heard cursing and the sound of boots scrambling over rocks as the others followed, their carefully laid plans forgotten in the face of my desperation.

The plan had been simple: I would approach openly, hands visible, and try to negotiate the exchange while Deacon and the others got into position. But hearing that Victor Mason intended to hurt Justine had burned away any pretense of strategy or patience.

I wanted blood. His blood.

The barn loomed ahead of me, its weathered wood gray in the afternoon sun. I could see movement through gaps in the boards—shadows moving back and forth like predators in a cage. Men with guns, waiting for their prey to walk into the trap.

Well, here I was.

"Victor Mason!" I called out, stopping about fifty yards from the barn where the cracked earth showed scuff marks from countless horses. "I'm here for the trade!"

A figure appeared in the doorway, like something emerging from the abyss itself. Tall, dressed in black, with a face like carved granite and eyes cold as winter stars. Yellowed teeth with one gold tooth in the front. This was the man who had murdered my parents. Who had slit Sergeant's throat and watched him bleed to death. Who was threatening the woman I loved.

"Well, well. Grady Thatcher. Right on time." Victor's voice carried clearly across the distance between us, smooth as silk and twice as dangerous. "You come alone?"

"Just me. Now let her go."

Victor laughed, the sound like breaking glass in the desert stillness. "Not so fast, boy. First, I want to hear you beg. Get on your knees and beg me to spare your sweetheart's life."

The words hit me like a slap across the face. Every instinct screamed at me to draw my gun and start shooting, to paint the ground with his blood and hang the consequences. But Justine was in there, helpless and afraid. One wrong move and she'd pay the price for my pride.

I started to kneel, my knees bending despite every fiber of my being screaming in protest.

"Grady, don't!"

Justine's voice rang out from inside the barn, clear and strong despite the fear threading through it. "Don't give them what they want! Just get out of here!"

The sound of her voice—alive, defiant, still fighting, even in captivity—cut through my rage like a cold mountain stream. In that moment, I realized something that should have been obvious all along.

This wasn't about vengeance anymore. It wasn't about justice for my parents or payback for Sergeant's death. This was about love. About saving the woman who meant more to me than my own life, who'd shown me what it meant to hope for the future instead of just hunting ghosts from the past.

Everything else could wait.

I straightened up, my hand moving to my gun with deliberate purpose. "I said let her go."

Victor's smile was cold as winter moonlight. "I don't think you're in a position to make demands, boy."

The crack of a rifle shot split the afternoon air like thunder. Victor spun and stumbled, clutching his shoulder as blood seeped through his fingers and stained his black shirt. Behind me, I heard Deacon's voice. "Now, Grady! Move!"

I sprinted toward the barn as chaos erupted around me like a war zone. More gunshots rang out from the hills where Perry and Sheriff Wilkes had taken position. Men shouted and cursed as they scrambled for cover, their voices mixing with the sharp crack of rifle fire.

I hit the barn door at a full run, my shoulder splintering the weathered wood as it burst open with a crash that echoed throughout the building. Inside, two men wheeled toward me, rifles half-raised and eyes wide with surprise. I put a bullet in the first one before he could bring his weapon to bear, the gunshot deafeningly loud in the confined space. The second man got off a shot that buzzed past my ear like an angry wasp, the bullet burying itself in the wall behind me.

Deacon appeared behind me like an avenging angel, his rifle barking as he dropped the second guard with precision that would have made his father proud. We moved deeper into the barn, our boots loud on the wooden floor, the smell of gunpowder thick in the air.

"Justine!" I called out, my voice echoing off the rafters.

"Here! In the back!"

I found her tied to a chair in the small room where we'd discovered Galen Harper's criminal records weeks ago. Her hands were bound behind her back with rough rope, her ankles tied to the chair legs. There was a bruise on her left cheek that made my vision turn red, but her brown eyes blazed with fury rather than fear.

I cut her bonds with my knife, the blade slicing through the rope like butter.

"I was wondering when you'd show up," she said, rubbing circulation back into her wrists. "Started making my own escape plans around hour two."

Despite everything—the danger, the gunfire still echoing outside, the blood on my hands—I laughed. Only Justine could make jokes while being held hostage by murderers.

"Are you hurt?" I asked, helping her to her feet and checking her over with hands that shook with relief.

"Nothing that won't heal. But Grady, my father—"

A new voice cut through the air behind us like a knife through silk. "Touching reunion."

I spun around to find Galen Harper standing in the doorway, a shotgun leveled at my chest. Up close, he looked older than I'd expected, with gray threading through his dark hair and lines carved deep around his eyes by years of cruelty. But those eyes were cold as January, without a trace of warmth or humanity.

"Papa, don't," Justine said, stepping protectively in front of me with courage that took my breath away. "This has gone far enough."

Galen's laugh was even colder than Victor's had been, like ice cracking on a frozen pond. "Far enough? Girl, this is just getting started. This boy has cost me everything. My operation, my men, my livelihood. Now he's going to pay the price."

"I'm your daughter!"

"You're nothing to me. Never were. Just another mouth to feed and a tool to be used when necessary." His finger tightened on the trigger, and I could see the murder in his eyes. "Stand aside, or you can die with him."

The casual way he spoke about killing his own child sent ice through my veins. This wasn't just a criminal—this was a monster who'd spawned children, only to discard them when they became inconvenient.

I started to push Justine aside, to shield her with my body. But before I could move, the sharp crack of a rifle split the air.

Galen Harper jerked backward, clutching his shoulder as blood seeped through his fingers. He staggered but remained on his feet, his face twisted with pain and rage that made him look like a wounded animal.

Behind him, Deacon stood in the doorway, smoke still curling from the barrel of his rifle like incense.

"Drop the shotgun," Deacon ordered, his voice steady as granite. "It's over, Harper."

Galen's eyes darted between us, calculating his chances like a gambler counting cards. For a moment, I thought he might try to bring the shotgun up anyway, might choose to die fighting rather than face justice. Then his wounded arm gave out, and the weapon clattered to the floor with a sound like breaking bones.

"You think this changes anything?" he snarled, pressing his good hand against the bleeding wound. "You think putting me in chains will make you a hero?"

"I think it'll make you pay for what you've done," I replied, my voice carrying six years of accumulated pain.

For the first time in years, I felt something like peace settle in my chest. Not the satisfaction of revenge, but the quiet certainty that comes from knowing what's right. Pa had always said God would provide a way when the time came—not necessarily the way we expected, but the right way.

Outside, the gunfire was dying down like a storm passing. I could hear Perry Quinn shouting orders, the sound of men surrendering. The Mason Gang's reign of terror was finally coming to an end.

Justine stepped forward, her face a mask of conflicted emotions as she looked at her wounded father. "Why, Papa? Why did it have to be this way?"

Galen's laugh was bitter as wormwood. "Because some of us take what we want instead of begging for scraps. You'll understand someday, girl. When that boy gets tired of playing house and moves on to someone else."

"That's enough," Deacon said, keeping his rifle trained on the wounded man.

But even as he spoke, I heard boots pounding across the barn floor like drumbeats. Victor Mason burst into the room, his black clothes torn and bloody, his face twisted with rage and pain from the bullet wound in his shoulder.

"You shot Harper!" he snarled, his gun swinging wildly between Deacon and me. "This was supposed to be clean!"

I moved without thinking, my body acting on something deeper than instinct. Something beyond my own thoughts moved me—the same voice that had whispered to my parents about mercy and forgiveness, the same presence Pa had always trusted. Without hesitation, I threw myself between Victor's gun and my best friend, the man who'd saved my life more times than I could count.

The pistol roared like thunder in the confined space.

Fire exploded in my chest as the bullet punched through my body with the force of a sledgehammer. I felt myself falling, the world spinning around me as I hit the wooden floor hard enough to drive the air from my lungs.

Through the ringing in my ears, I heard Justine screaming my name with anguish that cut through me worse than the bullet. Heard Deacon's rifle crack again, and Victor Mason crying out as the bullet took him in the leg, dropping him to the ground like a felled tree.

Sheriff Wilkes and Deputy Jakes poured into the room, weapons drawn and ready. They quickly secured both wounded men while Deacon dropped to his knees beside me, his hands pressing against the wound in my chest.

"Stay with me, Grady," he said, his voice thick with emotion I'd rarely heard from him. "You're going to be fine."

I could feel the life ebbing out of me with each heartbeat, warm blood pooling beneath me on the barn floor. But there was only one thing that mattered now. I grabbed Deacon's shirt with a trembling hand and pulled him closer.

"Is... Justine... safe?" I whispered, each word a struggle against the darkness closing in.

"She's safe," he said, his voice breaking. "She's right here, and she's safe."

I tried to turn my head toward the sound of her voice, but the darkness was closing in fast, like a tide I couldn't fight. The last thing I heard was Justine calling my name, begging me to stay with her.

Then everything went black.

18 - Brothers in Blood

Deacon

"Grady!"

His name tore from my throat as I dropped to my knees beside my best friend's still body. Blood spread across his shirt in a dark crimson stain that seemed to grow larger with each heartbeat. His face was ashen, gray like winter clouds, his breathing shallow and labored.

The metallic scent of blood mixed with the acrid smell of gunpowder that still hung in the air. My hands found the wound in his chest, fingers pressing against the torn fabric and flesh beneath. Warm blood seeped between my fingers like water through a broken dam. Too much blood. Too fast.

"No, no, no," I whispered, my hands trembling as I fought to maintain pressure on the wound. "Don't you die on me, Grady Thatcher. Don't you dare."

Around us, Sheriff Wilkes and Deputy Jakes were securing the prisoners. Victor Mason groaned and cursed as they bound his wounded leg, the sound of his complaints mixing with the clink of shackles. Galen Harper sat slumped against the wall, clutching his shoulder, his face gray with pain and defeat. But all of that felt distant and unimportant compared to the life ebbing away beneath my trembling hands.

"Is he...?" Justine's voice was barely a whisper as she kneeled beside me, her skirts rustling against the dusty ground.

"He's alive. But he's losing too much blood." I looked up at her, seeing my own fear reflected in her wide eyes. "I need to stop the bleeding, but I don't have proper medical supplies."

"Tell me what to do."

Her voice was steady despite the tears streaming down her face. This was the woman Grady loved—brave, determined, ready to fight for what mattered most. In this moment, I understood why my best friend had fallen so hard for her.

"Hold pressure here," I said, guiding her hands to the wound. "Press hard with both palms. Don't let up, no matter what happens."

I fumbled for my ammunition belt with trembling fingers. My veterinary training told me what needed to be done, but my hands wouldn't stop shaking. Six years of friendship. Six years of brotherhood. Six years of standing by each other through everything life threw at us—rustlers, loss, heartbreak, danger.

I couldn't lose him now. Not when he'd finally found something worth living for.

Breathe, I told myself. Calm down and do what needs to be done.

I closed my eyes for a moment, forcing the panic down, breathed a wordless prayer, before letting my training take over. When I opened them again, my hands were steady. This was just another injured animal. Assess the damage. Stop the bleeding. Keep the patient alive.

"What are you doing?" Justine asked as I pulled bullets from my belt and began prying them open with my knife, the brass casings clicking against each other.

"Cauterizing the wound. It's the only way to stop the

bleeding out here." I poured the black gunpowder from three bullets into my palm, the coarse grains rough against my skin. "It's going to hurt him, but it might save his life."

"Do it."

I looked at her, this brave woman who would help me hurt the man she loved in order to save him. But I also saw something else in her eyes—a flash of doubt, quickly suppressed.

"Justine, are you certain? When I light this, his body is going to react violently. He might thrash around even though he's unconscious. Can you hold him still?"

She shifted her position, bracing her knees against his shoulders. "Yes. I won't let him move."

I positioned the gunpowder over the worst of the bleeding and struck a match. The sulfur flared, and then the powder ignited with a sharp hiss and a flash of brilliant light. The acrid smell of burned gunpowder filled my nostrils.

Grady's body jerked violently as the flame seared his flesh, cauterizing the torn blood vessels. A low, agonized moan escaped his lips despite his unconscious state. The smell of burned flesh joined the gunpowder, making my stomach lurch.

Justine held him down with a strength I didn't know she possessed, her face set in determination even as tears continued to flow. Her jaw was clenched so tight I could see the muscles working beneath her skin.

"Again," I breathed, preparing another charge. "The exit wound."

We rolled him carefully onto his side, Justine supporting his head while I examined the back of his shoulder. The bullet had gone clean through, which was good—no fragments to dig out. But it also meant two wounds to seal.

"The exit wound is larger," I said, more to myself than to her. "It always is. The bullet tumbles as it exits."

The second cauterization was no easier than the first. Grady's body convulsed, and this time a strangled cry tore from his throat. But when the smoke cleared, and the sizzling stopped, the bleeding had ceased.

"Is that it?" Justine asked, her voice hoarse from the smoke and strain.

I checked his pulse at his wrist, then at his neck. Weak but steady. His breathing was still shallow, but some color was slowly returning to his face.

"For now. But he needs an actual doctor. Soon." I looked up at her. "You did good, Justine. Real good. He's lucky to have you."

Perry Quinn appeared at my shoulder, his face grim. "Congress has a doctor. About twenty minutes' ride if we push hard."

"Can we move him safely?"

"We'll have to. He won't make it if we don't."

Between the four of us—Perry, Sheriff Wilkes, Justine, and me—we carefully lifted Grady into the wagon. I spread my coat in the wagon bed first, trying to cushion the ride. Justine climbed in beside him without hesitation, cradling his head in her lap as I took the reins.

The ride to Congress felt like the longest twenty minutes of my life. Every bump in the road made Grady groan. Every jolt of the wagon made my heart skip a beat, wondering if it would be the one that finished what Victor Mason's bullet had started. The wagon wheels creaked and groaned over the rough terrain, and I apologized to Grady with every harsh jolt.

But Justine never stopped talking to him. Soft words of encouragement. Promises about their future together. Threats about what she'd do to him if he dared to die on her.

"You hear me, Grady Thatcher?" she murmured as we pulled up in front of the doctor's office. "You promised me forever, and I'm holding you to it. We haven't even had our first proper kiss yet."

The doctor—a thin, gray-haired man named Phillips—took one look at Grady and immediately went to work. He examined the cauterized wounds with professional efficiency, his weathered hands gentle but thorough.

"Good work with the gunpowder," he said without looking up. "Crude, but effective. You probably saved his life. The cauterization stopped the bleeding and likely prevented shock from setting in."

"Will he be alright?" Justine asked, still holding Grady's hand.

"Too early to say for certain. The bullet missed his heart and lungs, which is fortunate. Went through the muscle just below the clavicle." Dr. Phillips began cleaning the wounds more thoroughly with carbolic acid. "But he's lost a lot of blood, and there's always the risk of infection. The next few days will tell us everything we need to know."

Those next few days blurred together in a haze of worry and exhaustion. Justine refused to leave Grady's side, sleeping in a chair beside his bed, holding his hand through the long nights when fever wracked his body.

I stayed close too, sleeping on the floor of the doctor's office, ready to help however I could. My aunt and uncle Cahill lived nearby and offered us their spare room, but none of us wanted to be that far from Grady. Besides, someone needed to keep an eye on Justine—she barely ate or slept.

On the second night, when Grady's fever spiked, we nearly lost him. Dr. Phillips worked through the night, applying cool cloths and forcing laudanum between his lips. Justine never let go of his hand, whispering prayers and promises into the darkness.

"Don't you leave me," she breathed. "Not when I just found you."

That's when it hit me—watching her fight for him—that maybe I'd been holding too tight to our friendship. Grady needed someone to love him the way Justine did, with everything she had. And maybe I needed to step back and let him build a life that wasn't centered on our brotherhood.

It was a hard realization, but not a bitter one.

On the third day, his eyes finally opened.

"Justine?" His voice was barely a whisper, rough and dry.

"I'm here." She leaned forward, squeezing his hand. "I'm right here."

His gaze found mine across the room. "Deacon?"

"Right here too, partner."

A weak smile crossed his face. "Did we get them?"

"We got them. Victor Mason, Galen Harper, the whole gang. It's over, Grady. It's finally over."

He closed his eyes and was quiet for so long I thought he'd fallen asleep again. Then he spoke, his voice stronger this time.

"I don't want vengeance anymore." He looked at Justine, then at me. "I just want to live. To love. To build something good."

Justine leaned down and kissed his forehead gently. "Then that's what we'll do."

Something eased in my chest—a tension I'd been carrying for months without even realizing it. The darkness that had been eating at Grady's soul since his parents' death was finally gone. In its place was something better: hope and love.

"When can we go home?" he asked.

Dr. Phillips appeared in the doorway, wiping his hands on a clean towel. "Another week, at least. Maybe two. You're not going anywhere until I'm satisfied you won't tear those wounds open again."

Grady squeezed Justine's hand. "Will you marry me? As soon as I'm well enough to stand?"

"I thought you'd never ask," she said, laughing through her tears.

I watched my best friend—my brother in everything but blood—smile for the first time in six years without any shadow of pain behind it. We'd been through purgatory together, but we'd made it out the other side.

And for the first time since this entire ordeal began, I believed we were finally free.

19 - Justice Served

Grady

FOUR WEEKS AFTER taking Victor Mason's bullet, I stood at the front of the small church in Prescott, waiting for my bride. My chest still ached where the wound was healing, but Dr. Phillips had finally cleared me to travel and be on my feet for more than a few minutes at a time.

The church was simple—wooden pews worn smooth by countless Sunday services, a plain altar adorned with wildflowers, sunlight streaming through clear glass windows and casting golden rectangles on the plank floor. The air smelled of beeswax candles and the lingering scent of pine from the freshly scrubbed pews. Nothing fancy, but it didn't matter. All that mattered was the woman about to walk down that aisle to become my wife.

The sound of hushed conversations and rustling fabric filled the small sanctuary. Mrs. Peterson played the old pump organ, her weathered fingers coaxing sweet melodies from the keys. Children fidgeted in the back pews while their mothers whispered gentle corrections.

Deacon stood beside me as my best man, looking almost as nervous as I felt. His hands kept adjusting his tie, a sure sign of his anxiety. "You ready for this?" he whispered.

"Been ready since the day I met her," I replied, my voice barely audible over the organ music.

The church doors opened with a soft creak. Lilian walked down the aisle first. I heard Deacon's sharp intake of air and figured it wouldn't be too long before I stood next to him on his big day.

Then there she was. Justine wore a simple white dress that her sister Hayley had helped her sew during my recovery. The fabric was cotton, not silk, but it caught the afternoon light like it was spun from sunbeams. Her golden hair was pinned up with small white flowers we'd picked together yesterday from the meadow behind our new home, and she carried a bouquet of wildflowers—Indian paintbrush, lupines, and desert marigolds.

But it was her smile that took my breath away. Pure joy, untainted by the shadows that had haunted us for so long. Her brown eyes found mine across the sanctuary, and everything else faded away.

Shane walked her down the aisle, his face proud and emotional. The man who'd once been part of our nightmare was now family, dressed in his best suit with tears threatening to spill. Flynn and Ike sat in the front pew with Hayley, all of them beaming. Four weeks ago, they'd been scattered and broken by their father's crimes. Today, they were a family choosing to celebrate love instead of dwelling on the past.

When Justine reached me, Shane placed her hand in mine and whispered, "Take care of her."

"Always," I promised, my voice thick with emotion.

The ceremony was brief but heartfelt. Pastor Williams spoke about love conquering darkness, about redemption and new beginnings. We spoke our vows simply and from the heart, our voices carrying clearly through the small sanctuary. I promised to love her, protect her, and build a life with her free from the darkness of vengeance. She promised to stand by me, to be my partner in all things, and to help me remember what truly mattered in life.

"For better or worse, in sickness and in health, for richer or poorer," she breathed, her eyes never leaving mine.

"Till death do us part," I finished, meaning every word.

When the preacher pronounced us husband and wife, I kissed my bride with all the love and hope I'd been storing up during those lonely years. This was what my parents would have wanted for me—not revenge, but redemption. Not hatred, but healing.

The small reception was held at our new home—a modest four-room house on the edge of town that we'd purchased with money from the sale of my family farmland. Flynn and Ike had helped us move our few belongings while I was still recovering, and Hayley had filled the place with wildflowers and ribbon streamers. Lilian stood next to Deacon, whose face lit up when she placed her hand in his.

The afternoon air was crisp with the promise of fall, and the smell of Ellie Mae's apple pie mingled with the scent of roasting chicken that Hannah Colter had prepared. Laughter echoed from our small backyard as children played while their parents gathered around makeshift tables.

As the sun began to set, painting the sky in shades of orange and pink, I pulled my new wife aside.

"Any regrets?" I asked, taking her hands in mine. Her wedding ring caught the fading light, a simple gold band that had belonged to my mother.

"Only that it took us so long to get here," she replied, standing on her tiptoes to kiss me softly. "And that your parents couldn't see this day."

"They can see it," I murmured against her forehead. "I'm sure of it."

"Mrs. Thatcher," I said, testing out the sound of her new name.

"I like the sound of that more than I can say."

———

TWO WEEKS LATER, we sat in the courthouse for Victor Mason's trial. The building smelled of dust and old wood, with tall windows that let in harsh fall light. The man who had murdered my parents looked smaller somehow, sitting in shackles between two deputies. Without his black clothes and his gang around him, he was just another bitter outlaw facing justice.

The trial was swift and methodical. District Attorney Morrison presented the evidence with clinical precision—witness testimony, recovered stolen cattle, the murder weapon, Shane's detailed confession about the gang's operations. Too many witnesses, too much evidence. The jury of twelve local men deliberated for less than an hour before returning a verdict of guilty on all charges, including the first-degree murder of Lee and Amy Thatcher.

When Judge Stanton sentenced Victor Mason to hang by the neck until dead, I felt... empty. Not satisfied, not vindicated. Just empty. Years of burning rage had built up to this moment, and now that it was here, all I could think about was going home to my wife.

Justine squeezed my hand as we watched the bailiffs lead him away in chains. "How do you feel?" she whispered.

"Peaceful," I said, and meant it. "Finally peaceful."

Galen Harper's trial followed a week later. With Shane's testimony and the evidence we'd found in his secret room, the proceedings moved even faster. The jury convicted him of cattle rustling, conspiracy, and accessory to murder. Judge Stanton sentenced him to fifteen years of hard labor in Yuma Territorial Prison.

As they led him away in chains, Galen looked directly at his children sitting in the gallery. There was no remorse in his eyes, no regret for what he'd put them through. Just cold calculation, as if he was already planning his next move. The man would never change.

Shane stood and walked out without a word, his jaw set in hard lines. Flynn and Ike followed, their young faces grim. Hayley helped Justine to her feet. Lilian and Deacon followed behind as we all left the courthouse together, stepping into the clean October air.

"It's over," Justine said as we stood on the courthouse steps, watching wagons roll past on the dusty street.

"Yes," Shane said quietly, his voice rough with emotion. "Finally over."

Later that evening, Deacon stopped by our house. He looked better than he had since the night Sergeant died—more at peace with himself, less haunted by the weight of responsibility he'd carried.

"I've made a decision," he said as we sat on our front porch, watching stars appear in the darkening sky. "I'm quitting the Livestock Inspection job."

I wasn't surprised. The job had cost him too much—his horse, his peace of mind, nearly his life.

"Going back to the stockyards?"

"Derek Gardner offered me my old position back. Better pay, too, since I've got more experience now." He looked out toward the mountains, their peaks outlined against the purple sky. "I miss working with the animals, miss the quiet routine of it all. This job was about helping you find justice for your parents. Now that we have it, I want to go back to doing what I love."

I nodded, understanding completely. "What about Perry? He'll need a replacement."

"I was hoping you might have an idea about that."

I turned to look at Shane, who'd been sitting quietly on the porch swing with Justine. "What do you say, Shane? Want to be my partner?"

His eyes widened, hope and uncertainty warring in his expression. "You'd trust me to do that job? After everything I've done?"

"You know this territory better than anyone. You understand the criminal mind because you lived with it your entire life. And you want to make things right." I stood and extended my hand to him. "I can't think of anyone I'd rather have watching my back."

Shane stood and shook my hand firmly, his grip strong and sure. "I'd be honored, Grady. More honored than you know."

"Good. Report to Perry Quinn Monday morning. He'll get you started on the training. Fair warning—he's a stickler for proper procedures and paperwork."

As Deacon prepared to leave, I walked him to his horse. Bear stood patiently at our hitching post, much calmer than Sergeant had ever been.

"Thank you," I said, gripping his shoulder. "For everything. For taking this job, for saving my life, for being the brother I never had."

"Same to you." He mounted up, then paused, a grin spreading across his face. "You know, I have a feeling there might be another wedding around here soon."

I grinned back. "About time you made an honest woman out of Lilian Harper."

"She's part of your family now, too. And don't think I haven't noticed how she looks at you during Sunday dinner—like she's proud to have you as a brother-in-law."

I watched him ride away, then returned to the porch where my wife waited. She curled up beside me on the swing, her head resting on my shoulder. The night air carried the scent of wood smoke from chimneys and the distant sound of a harmonica from somewhere in town.

"What are you thinking about?" she asked, her voice soft in the darkness.

"My parents. How proud they'd be to see me now. Married to an amazing woman, doing honest work." I pressed a kiss to the top of her head. "They'd see that their deaths weren't meaningless—that something beautiful came from all that pain."

"They'd be proud," she agreed, snuggling closer. "And they'd love me, I'm sure of it."

"Without question. Ma would've been fussing over wedding plans for months. Pa would've been teaching you everything he knew about farming."

We sat in comfortable silence, watching the stars appear one by one in the darkening sky. A coyote called from somewhere in the distance, answered by another from across the valley. The swing creaked gently as we rocked back and forth.

Several years ago, I'd been a broken young man, consumed by rage and grief. Tonight, I was a husband with a future full of possibilities—maybe children someday, a bigger house, a thriving partnership with Shane, growing old beside the woman I loved.

The quest for justice was over. The quest for happiness was just beginning.

And for the first time since I was fifteen years old, I knew exactly who I was: Grady Thatcher, husband, Livestock Inspector, and a man finally at peace with himself and the world.

The darkness was behind us now. Ahead lay only light.

Epilogue

Grady

October 14, 1894

"COME ON, SHANE! We need to get this rustler to the sheriff and get home!" I called over my shoulder as we rode hard toward Prescott, our prisoner's horse tied to mine with a lead rope. The leather creaked with each stride, and dust clouds billowed behind us in the crisp fall air.

Shane spurred his mount to catch up, his horse's hooves drumming against the ground. "Grady, slow down before you kill our horses. The baby will wait for you."

"You don't know that!" I shouted back, my voice carrying across the desert landscape. "Justine said any day now, and that was three days ago!"

We'd been tracking cattle thieves up near Flagstaff when the telegram reached us at the remote line shack where we'd made camp. The message had been brief but urgent: *Come home soon. Baby coming. Love, Justine.*

That was yesterday morning. We'd caught our man by noon—found him trying to rebrand stolen Larson cattle in a hidden canyon—and ridden through the night to get back. The outlaw slouched in his saddle behind us, hands bound with rope, looking miserable after a night sleeping on the hard ground with nothing but a thin blanket.

"Should have thought twice before stealing Larson cattle," I muttered, glancing back at our prisoner. "Fifteen head, all with fresh brands burned over the original marks."

As the town came into view, I could see smoke rising from chimneys in the crisp October air, creating gray ribbons against the blue sky. The scent of burning wood mixed with the dust of the trail. Our house sat on the edge of town, and I breathed a sigh of relief when I saw Hayley's mare tied out front alongside Dr. Armstrong's buggy. She was there to help with the birth, and the doctor's presence meant...

My heart hammered against my ribs. It could mean everything was fine, or it could mean complications.

"Sheriff's office first," Shane reminded me as we clattered down Cortez Street, our horses' hooves echoing off the wooden storefronts.

"Right, right." I was so eager to get home I could barely think straight. My hands trembled as I held the reins.

We delivered our prisoner to Sheriff Wilkes in record time, barely taking time to fill out the paperwork properly. I was already turning to leave when the sheriff called after me.

"Grady! Congratulations on the new boy!"

I spun around, my heart stopping mid-beat. "My boy?"

Sheriff Wilkes grinned broadly, his weathered face creasing with laugh lines. "Heard you got yourself a healthy baby boy about an hour ago. Doc Armstrong said everything went smooth as silk."

My knees nearly buckled. A son. I had a son.

"Gotta go," I said, already running for the door.

Shane's laughter followed me into the street. "Tell

Justine congratulations from me! And Shane Harper wants to meet his nephew!"

I ran the six blocks to our house, my boots pounding against the wooden sidewalks and dirt streets. My heart was pounding harder than it had during any chase or gunfight. The sound of a baby's cry reached my ears as I bounded up the front steps, and I had to grab the porch railing to steady myself.

I burst through the front door to find Hayley coming down the stairs with a basin of steaming water and clean towels draped over her arm. Her face was flushed but happy, her sleeves rolled up to her elbows.

"Grady!" she said, her face lighting up with pure joy. "Perfect timing. They're both doing wonderfully."

"Both?" The word came out as barely a whisper.

"Your wife and your son." She pointed toward the stairs, her eyes bright with tears. "Go on up. She's been asking for you every few minutes. 'Where's his papa?' she keeps saying."

I took the stairs two at a time, my legs shaking with a combination of exhaustion and overwhelming emotion. I paused at our bedroom door, suddenly nervous. Through the crack, I could hear Justine's voice, soft and tired but filled with wonder.

"...and your papa will be home soon, little one. He's been so excited to meet you. He's going to teach you everything—about horses and cattle and being a good man."

I knocked gently and pushed the door open. "Justine?"

My wife looked up from the bundle in her arms, her face glowing despite the exhaustion evident in every line of her body. Her hair was damp with perspiration, but she'd never looked more beautiful. "There you are. I was thinking you were going to miss everything."

"I would never miss this." I crossed to the bed and sat carefully on the edge, the mattress dipping under my weight. The room smelled of lavender water and something else—something sweet and clean that I'd never experienced before. "How are you? Really?"

"Tired. Sore. Completely in love." She looked down at the baby, then back at me, her brown eyes shining. "Want to hold your son?"

My hands trembled as she placed the tiny bundle in my arms. He was so small, so perfect, wrapped in the soft blue blanket that Ellie Mae had knitted months ago. Dark hair like mine crowned his tiny head, but I could already see Justine's delicate features in his face—her nose, the shape of her lips.

"Hello there, little man," I whispered, my voice catching in my throat. "I'm your papa."

The baby opened his eyes—brown like his mama's, dark and alert—and looked directly at me. In that moment, everything else in the world faded away. All the anger I'd carried for so many years, all the darkness that had consumed me, all the hunger for revenge—none of it mattered. Hadn't for some time.

This was what mattered. This tiny life, this precious gift, this chance to build something good and lasting. This was the future my parents had died for without even knowing it.

"What should we call him?" Justine asked softly, reaching out to touch the baby's tiny hand.

I thought of my own father, the man who'd taught me about horses and hard work and doing what was right. The man who'd shown me how to gentle a wild colt and how to read the weather in the clouds. The man whose murder had set me on such a dark path, but whose memory now filled me with nothing but light and love.

"Lee," I said, my voice thick with emotion. "Lee Thatcher, after my pa."

"Lee Thatcher," Justine repeated, testing the sound on her lips. "I like it. Your father would be so proud."

"I hope so." I looked down at my son, imagining all the things I wanted to teach him. "I'll teach you about horses, little Lee. About the land and how to work it. About justice and mercy and choosing love over hatred. About being the kind of man your grandfather was."

Pa's words from so long ago echoed in my memory, as clear as if he were standing in the room with us: *Fear's a teacher, son, but it shouldn't be a master. Trust yourself. Trust God.*

I'd forgotten that lesson for too many years, lost in my quest for vengeance. But holding my newborn son, I finally understood what Pa had been trying to tell me. He'd known that someday I'd need to choose to let my fears go. Let go of the fear that his and Ma's death would be unavenged. Let go of the fear of moving forward. To trust God with my future, like I was doing now.

"You missed all the hard work," Justine teased, though her eyes were bright with happiness and exhaustion. "Showed up just in time for the good part."

"I'm sorry I wasn't here sooner. If I'd known—"

"You're here now. That's all that matters." She reached out and touched my cheek. "Besides, Hayley was wonderful. She knew exactly what to do."

Little Lee made a small sound and wrapped his tiny fingers around mine. The grip was surprisingly strong for someone so small, his skin impossibly soft and warm.

"He's going to be a horseman," I said, marveling at those perfect little fingers. "Look at those hands. Strong grip already."

"Just like his papa and grandpa." Justine settled back against her pillows, watching us with contented eyes.

I thought about the man I'd been when I first met Justine—angry, consumed with the need for retribution, more interested in destroying my enemies than building a future. That man felt like a stranger now, someone I'd once known but had grown beyond.

"You know," I said quietly, "I used to pray every night for Heaven to give me vengeance against my parents' killers. Now I'm so grateful those prayers weren't answered the way I wanted."

"What do you mean?"

"If I'd gotten my revenge right away, I never would have met you. Never would have learned what really matters." I looked down at our son, then back at her. "I would have missed all of this—this love, this family, this chance to be better than my anger."

"The Almighty's timing is perfect, even when we can't see it," she murmured, her voice growing drowsy.

"Especially when we can't see it."

Little Lee yawned and settled deeper into my arms, already falling asleep despite being barely an hour old. His face was peaceful, trusting, innocent of all the darkness that had once consumed his father's heart.

I thought about my parents, wishing they could be here to meet their grandson. But in a way, they were here. In the values they'd taught me, in the love they'd shown me, in the man they'd raised me to be before grief and anger led me astray. In this tiny boy who carried their family name forward into a brighter future.

Pa had been right all along. A man's true strength came from trusting God. And looking at my son, my wife, the life we were creating together, I knew I'd finally learned they were the something worth having.

The quest for retribution was over. The journey of love and family was just beginning.

And I couldn't wait to see what we'd build together— this little boy and the brothers and sisters who might follow, the ranch we'd expand, the legacy of love we'd leave behind.

"Welcome to the world, Lee Thatcher," I whispered. "Your story starts now."

Author's Note

THIS STORY BEGAN with inspiration from Karen Baney's *The Resourceful Stockman* from her Colter Sons Series. After reading about the Harper siblings and Grady Thatcher in her work, I knew I wanted to explore their story further. I'm deeply grateful to Karen for allowing me to collaborate with her and use characters she developed, while giving them my own interpretation. *Blood Justice* serves as both a prequel and a reimagining of her novel, exploring the darker chapters that shaped these characters before they found their way to hope and healing.

The historical framework for this story came from extensive research into Arizona Territory's early law enforcement. *Arizona Territory 1863-1912: A Political History* by Jay J. Wagoner proved invaluable in understanding the territorial period and provided the original inspiration for featuring Livestock Inspectors in this story. *Calling the Brands* by Monty McCord offered essential insights into the practical aspects of cattle ranching and brand identification that were crucial to the plot.

The Arizona Territorial Livestock Sanitary Commission was established in the late 1880s, with the first Livestock Inspectors—later called Livestock Detectives—appointed in March 1891. The timing was perfect for Grady and Deacon's story. Many of these early inspectors were indeed cattlemen or veterinarians, making their background authentic to the period. While the position of Veterinary Surgeon General existed in the territory during this era, Ray Sawyer and his role are fictional.

All the towns mentioned—Prescott, Chino Valley, and Congress—are real places in Arizona. Colter Ranch, created by Karen Baney for her Prescott Pioneers and Colter Sons series, is fictional but loosely based on historical ranching operations near Watson Lake.

This collaboration has been a joy, and I hope readers will explore Karen's wonderful series to see how the Colter Sons' stories continue. My personal favorite from her Colter Sons Series was the gritty prodigal son story in *The Restless Wrangler*, though the whole series appeals to both men and women. She has graciously allowed me to shape and develop the remaining Harper siblings: Shane, Hayley, Flynn, and Ike. Continue the journey with Hayley Harper and the famous rustler hunter, J.J. Westin in my novel *The Rustler Hunter*.

R.J. Sloane

About the Author

R.J. SLOANE CAPTURES the raw spirit of the American frontier in action-packed westerns that don't shy away from the harsh realities of territorial justice. Drawing inspiration from modern classics like *Longmire*, *Yellowstone*, and *Murdoch Mysteries*, R.J.'s stories blend historical authenticity with the timeless struggle between law and lawlessness.

A passionate student of Southwest history, R.J. spends countless hours researching the legendary lawmen of the region—from the Arizona Rangers to the territorial marshals who tamed pivotal frontier towns like Phoenix, Tombstone, Prescott, and beyond. Growing up watching John Wayne, James Garner, and Clint Eastwood westerns with dad on lazy Sunday afternoons instilled a deep appreciation for authentic frontier storytelling. This combination of classic western influence and dedicated historical research brings depth and authenticity to every story.

The Harper Justice series follows a family of territorial lawmen as they navigate the dangerous transition from frontier chaos to civilized order, where doing what's right often means defying what's legal.

Website:
https://www.rjsloanewesterns.com

Facebook:
https://www.facebook.com/rjsloane.westerns/

X (twitter):
@RJSloaneWest

The Rustler Hunter

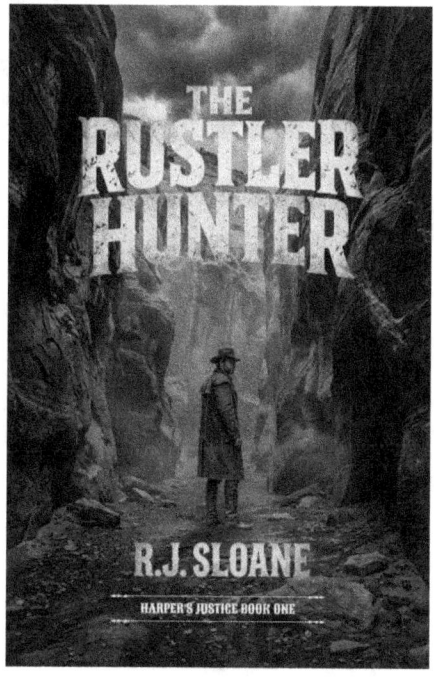

When forty-one successful manhunts make you a legend, there's only one way left to go—down.

J.J. Westin, the infamous Rustler Hunter, goes undercover at Arizona Territory's largest cattle ranch to expose the rustlers bleeding it dry. The thieves aren't just stealing cattle. They're trusted cowboys operating from inside the bunkhouse.

What he doesn't expect is Hayley Harper, the tough-as-nails cook with secrets of her own. She's a Pinkerton agent working the same case and the daughter of notorious outlaw Galen Harper.

When their covers are blown, they uncover something far deadlier than rustling. A corruption network spanning three territories. With enemies closing in and bullets flying, the legendary manhunter and the outlaw's daughter must survive the badlands of 1898 Arizona, where trust is deadly and justice comes at gunpoint.

In the shadow of Canyon Diablo, where the historic Aztec Land & Cattle Company's Hashknife outfit controlled over a million acres of the Arizona Territory's most lawless land.

Buy Now:
https://books.rjsloanewesterns.com/the-rustler-hunter

Desert Life Media Presents

DISCOVER THE COLTER SONS SERIES

The Colter Sons Series
by Karen Baney

Before the Harper brothers sought justice, the Colter sons fought to define their legacy.

Set in the rugged Arizona Territory of the 1880s and 1890s, the Colter Sons Series follows five brothers and their sister as they come of age in a land where grit, loyalty, and love are tested at every turn. From a shotgun wedding that upends a surveyor's plans to the rise of a railroad empire, each story explores the trials that shape a family—and the fierce devotion that binds them.

With themes of coming of age, redemption, prodigal sons, and the cost of ambition, these emotionally rich tales delve into the heart of frontier life. Whether it's a cattleman torn between duty and desire or a sister fighting for her own future, the Colters must each decide what kind of legacy they'll leave behind.

If you crave frontier grit, slow-burning romance, and characters who fight for their place in a changing world, the Colter Sons Series delivers.

The Colter Sons Series:

Available on Amazon, Barnes & Noble, Kobo, and more!

Visit: https://www.karenbaney.com/colter-sons-series